ALL CHANGE AT HARBOUR HOUSE

FENELLA J. MILLER

Boldwood

First published in Great Britain in 2025 by Boldwood Books Ltd.

Copyright © Fenella J. Miller, 2025

Cover Design by Colin Thomas

Cover Images: Colin Thomas and Alamy

The moral right of Fenella J. Miller to be identified as the author of this work has been asserted in accordance with the Copyright, Designs and Patents Act 1988.

All rights reserved. No part of this book may be reproduced in any form or by any electronic or mechanical means, including information storage and retrieval systems, without written permission from the author, except for the use of brief quotations in a book review. This book is a work of fiction and, except in the case of historical fact, any resemblance to actual persons, living or dead, is purely coincidental.

Every effort has been made to obtain the necessary permissions with reference to copyright material, both illustrative and quoted. We apologise for any omissions in this respect and will be pleased to make the appropriate acknowledgements in any future edition.

A CIP catalogue record for this book is available from the British Library.

Paperback ISBN 978-1-80549-312-9

Large Print ISBN 978-1-80549-310-5

Hardback ISBN 978-1-80549-309-9

Ebook ISBN 978-1-80549-311-2

Kindle ISBN 978-1-80549-313-6

Audio CD ISBN 978-1-80549-304-4

MP3 CD ISBN 978-1-80549-305-1

Digital audio download ISBN 978-1-80549-308-2

This book is printed on certified sustainable paper. Boldwood Books is dedicated to putting sustainability at the heart of our business. For more information please visit https://www.boldwoodbooks.com/about-us/sustainability/

Boldwood Books Ltd, 23 Bowerdean Street, London, SW6 3TN

www.boldwoodbooks.com

I'm known at Boldwood as one of the three Saga Sisters. Here's to us!
Sheila Riley, Lizzie Lane and Fenella J. Miller

1

WIVENHOE, MAY 1940

Emily Roby was staring at the classroom clock, convinced the minute hand hadn't moved at all. Today, after school, she'd be meeting her brother George and their foster brother Sammy for tea with their old housemaid, Nancy, at her new home in Head Street, Colchester.

Harbour House wasn't the same without Nancy, even though Mrs Annie Thomas, her replacement, was just as nice, although quite a bit older. Annie was a widow and Emily didn't know how her husband had died, but he'd been dead for a year so probably not anything to do with the war.

Her mind was drifting; religious education was her least favourite subject. She heard quite enough about God at Sunday school and church every week.

'Emily, it's your turn to be board-monitor this week. Have you forgotten?' Miss Bairstow, the elderly teacher, called out from the front of the room.

'I'm just coming, I'm sorry, I had forgotten.'

This was the least favourite of the jobs that were allocated – the teachers seemed to think that being any sort of monitor was something to be pleased about – however, of all the things they were asked to do, cleaning the big chalkboard with a duster was the worst.

While Emily rubbed away industriously, the clouds of chalk went up her nose and she had to keep her mouth shut to avoid swallowing it. At least it filled in the remaining few minutes of the day and she'd just finished when the bell was rung outside by whoever was bell-monitor that day.

'Put your chairs up, girls, and do it quietly,' Miss Bairstow said.

They all knew that if they failed to follow this instruction they'd be putting the chairs up and down for ages until the teacher was satisfied.

'Well done, that was exemplary. Good afternoon, girls.'

'Good afternoon, Miss Bairstow,' they chorused and were dismissed.

Emily flew through the door, dodged around the other girls heading for the cloakroom, and had changed into her outdoor shoes, put on her blazer and hat, slung her satchel over one shoulder and her gas mask over the other and was through the front door, almost the first to escape.

George and Sammy no longer caught a bus to the grammar school in Lexden Road, they were considered sensible enough to walk. They could cut through St Mary's churchyard which backed onto Balkerne Lane and be at Mortimer's Haberdashery as quickly as she could get there from the top of East Hill.

Running was strictly forbidden when in uniform but Emily hurry-walked past the grand houses on the same side of the road as Greyfriars, dashed past the castle with barely a glance and then on up the High Street, relieved that at four o'clock the various pubs and hotels weren't full of eager drinkers.

She crossed the road at the top of North Hill and risked

running the remaining hundred yards. Of course, she wanted to see Nancy, but it was Boyd, the huge hairy dog that Nancy had rescued a few weeks ago, who made Emily so eager to get there.

The back gate into the yard wasn't locked and as she pushed it open she was almost knocked from her feet by the dog, who was waiting behind it, a large smelly bone clutched in his jaws, as delighted to see her as she was to see him.

'Hello, silly Boyd, I really don't want that. You keep it for later. I'm just going to get your lead and then we have to wait for the boys and then we can go.'

Talking to an animal made no sense but everybody did it. Even her mummy chatted to Ginger, their huge cat at Harbour House, as if he was a real person. Emily frowned. For some reason, Ginger hadn't taken to Mr Stoneleigh, even though he was pleasant enough. He worked for Daddy at the shipyard and was lodging with them. He was a bit too sure of himself, thought he was God's gift, but she had to admit he was nice-looking. She rather liked his russet hair.

She shuddered. The cat hadn't liked Sammy's older brother and he'd been a good judge of character as Pete had turned out to be *a bad lot* as their housekeeper at home, Mrs Bates – Nancy's mother – said.

It was always a race on Wednesday night between herself and the boys to see who could get here first as whoever this was then had charge of the dog.

Emily clipped on the lead and immediately the dog stopped bouncing about and stood politely beside her, his long tail bumping the back of her knee. The gate flew open and the boys ran in.

'You got here first, I really thought we'd do it this time,' George said as he dropped his satchel on the concrete and pulled off his distinctive purple blazer. His tie and cap joined the pile. Sammy did the same.

'Come on then, let's go, I've been looking forward to this all afternoon. It was boring history and we almost fell asleep.'

'You did, George,' Sammy said, grinning. 'If I hadn't nudged you, sir would have rapped your knuckles with his ruler.'

There was no need to disturb Nancy, who would be busy serving in the shop that she ran for Mrs Frost, her aunt, who'd inherited it from a relative a few weeks ago.

The dog was a dream to walk on the lead as he didn't pull or fuss at all. He also gained many admiring looks from passers-by. At first Emily had thought it was her daring short haircut that was attracting attention but soon realised it was the dog, not her.

They cut down a few backstreets into the field and once safe she let the dog loose. The boys threw sticks for him and after half an hour they were ready to go back to Nancy's, but Boyd would have been happy to stay out for another hour or more.

'Whose turn is it to hold the lead on the way back?' Emily asked.

'It's me,' Sammy said firmly so she tossed the lead to him.

They walked ahead of her, the dog in the middle, whilst she strolled along behind thinking how much had changed so far this year and it was still only May. Baby Grace had arrived in February and Emily was loving being a big sister. The boys were also devoted to the infant, which meant there was always somebody to watch or play with the baby. This gave Mummy lots of time to do her good works.

Normally Emily escorted the doctor's little daughter, Claire, who went to the prep school at Greyfriars, back and forth. Dr Cousins and his family lived next door on the other corner of

Alma Street. On Wednesday night, Mrs Cousins had to send somebody in to collect the five-year-old from school.

Another exciting thing was that Nancy wasn't Nancy Bates any more, she was now Nancy Brooks, as she'd married Dan after he'd nearly drowned when the Thames barge he'd been sailing on had sunk outside Harwich. He was now skipper of a new barge that sailed from the Hythe port which meant he could easily get home in between trips.

The boys collected their possessions and carefully hung their precious blazers over the back of a kitchen chair.

'Do we have to do our homework right now, Emily, or can we play with Boyd for a bit?' George asked hopefully.

'Let's all do it after tea. I'll call you in to wash your hands when Nancy and Daphne have locked up the shop.'

This was another part of her Wednesday evening that Emily loved. She was now a competent cook and it was her responsibility to make tea for the five of them. Not as difficult as making a main meal but it made her feel very grown-up. She'd be twelve in September, already had her monthly courses, so as far as she was concerned she was almost a grown-up. She just wished her parents didn't still treat her like a little girl sometimes.

* * *

Annie Thomas had settled in well at Harbour House and although she wasn't earning as much as she had been doing piecework at the sewing factory down the end of the road, she now had her own room in the attic and didn't have to listen to her in-laws finding fault all the time. The Robys had been only too pleased to take her when Nancy had left to work in the family shop in Colchester.

The boys were friendly enough, the baby cooed and smiled at anyone who paid her attention; however, Emily was still a bit distant. She wasn't there to be the girl's best friend but to do the cleaning in the morning, the ironing in the afternoon and make the children's tea and watch them when they came home from school.

Mrs Roby wasn't like the other mothers down this end of Wivenhoe, she was posh, spoke with a plum in her mouth, and didn't do any housework, cooking and scarcely any mothering neither. She was always out and about at some do-gooders' meeting or other – but then she had the time to do it. She was pleasant enough, just not Annie's cup of tea. She preferred a more down-to-earth sort of person. Any road up, she was a damn sight better off living here than with those miserable buggers she'd been forced to stop with after her Norm had died whilst working for the council digging roads or something.

She'd been told it had been an accident, not his fault, and that she was due some compensation. This was what had made his parents become even nastier – they reckoned they were entitled to half the money. Fat chance of that. Whenever it came, it was hers, they wouldn't get a brass farthing.

This was why she'd been so desperate to get away. She was intending to join the WAAF when she got the money. This live-in job wasn't permanent, but if she left before the compensation was paid her in-laws would cash the cheque and she'd get nothing.

From what she'd heard on the wireless, things weren't looking too good for the boys in France – that Hitler was charging through Europe and she didn't reckon this so-called Maginot Line would stop him. At least she didn't have to worry about her man being killed or captured when the Nazis overran the British Army.

'Annie, I'm up to my arms in pastry for tonight's rabbit pie,' Molly Bates called from the kitchen. 'Mr Roby asked me to post some letters for him when I was out earlier and I forgot. Would you take them to the post office?'

'Be happy to, Molly, could do with a bit of fresh air. I'll just finish this shirt and then I'm done with the ironing.'

The sun was shining; it was good to be outside for a bit. She got a couple of hours off in the afternoon and usually went for a walk along the river wall, especially now the weather was fine. It had been a long miserable winter, bleeding cold and knee deep in snow most of the time.

The letters were stamped correctly so she'd just pushed them into the post box and turned to head home when Mr Stoneleigh, the man who lodged at Harbour House and worked with Mr Roby doing something clever with boats, appeared in front of her.

'Annie, I've not seen you for a few days. Where have you been hiding?'

'I ain't been hiding nowhere, Mr Stoneleigh, just busy doing the work I'm paid to do. Have you got the morning off or something?'

His eyes flashed – he didn't like being answered back, thought his good looks and lovely hair made him God's gift. He wasn't her type; she preferred an ordinary sort of bloke, not one who spoke like him and couldn't talk to her without setting her on edge. She wasn't sure if he meant to be patronising – he just was.

'I'm on my way to Brightlingsea, I'm needed there for the next week or so.'

There was no need for him to tell her his business, she wasn't interested anyway. 'Right, I'll let you get on.' She grinned. 'You're going the wrong way for the station, Mr Stoneleigh.'

She walked off and she heard him laughing. This surprised her as she'd thought he'd have been cross at her for being cheeky. She glanced over her shoulder and he was still smiling. He was ever so good-looking, she couldn't deny that, but he was dangerous. Any interest he showed in her could get her into trouble and she wasn't having that.

She always used the back door. Mr Roby had said she could come in whichever way she wanted but she didn't think it right for her to use the front. That was for the family and visitors.

'Is Mrs Roby back for lunch, Molly?'

'Yes, as far as I know. She's taken the baby out in the pram – she and the doctor's wife are thick as thieves. It's nice that Mrs Roby has someone like her to spend time with.'

'It is. I was just thinking she's not like the women down this end, so it's good thing she has Mrs Cousins to spend time with.'

'You look more cheerful than when you went out, Annie.'

'I just met Mr Stoneleigh at the post office. He told me he's going to be staying over in Brightlingsea for the next few days. I'm just glad that I won't have to listen to his music any more – mind you, I quite like it – I think he said it was called jazz.'

Molly smiled. 'You don't want to get involved with a man like him, Annie, he's not interested in anything lasting.'

'Crikey, Molly, I wasn't born yesterday. I've been keeping me door locked, don't you worry.'

* * *

Richard Stoneleigh watched Annie walking away from him, her head high, her shapely hips swaying, making the skirt of her floral dress swirl outwards in an attractive way. He really shouldn't flirt with her, it wasn't fair, but she was so pretty and there was nothing he liked better than seeing the eyes of a lovely young woman light up when he spoke to them.

He smiled ruefully – not that he'd had any success charming this particular girl. Maybe because she was a widow, rather than someone younger and inexperienced, this had made her see through his façade.

He wasn't a Casanova, wasn't a seducer of innocents and, despite appearing confident, he'd only ever had one serious relationship. This had ended amicably enough when the young lady concerned had managed to snag herself the son of an aristocrat – a much better catch than him. If he was honest about this, he'd been relieved rather than heartbroken when the engagement had ended. His family were wealthy but not aristocratic which in this instance had proved to be of benefit.

His father was something high up at the War Office, his mother was running the placement of land girls throughout the Home Counties. He was an only child and for some extraordinary reason both his parents thought he could do no wrong. He'd been coddled and spoilt throughout his life. If ever he stopped to consider it, which he rarely did, he was quite sure that this added to his arrogance and sense of his own importance.

He picked up his suitcase, crossed the road, and took the back way to the station. The train to Brightlingsea arrived on that side, so this made sense even if it meant he got muddy shoes.

He knew all the men who worked at the station as he was a frequent traveller. What he really needed was a motorbike, then he could get to Brightlingsea and back more simply and not have to remain there for several nights as he'd have to do this time. Bit too far to use a push-bike.

He was waiting on the platform for the train to steam in

when someone hailed him from the other side of the rails. Startled, he looked up to see the stationmaster beckoning him to come to the edge of the platform so they could converse without having to shout.

'Morning, Mr Hatch, how can I be of assistance?'

'There's something coming for you on the train from London. I've just had a telephone call from Liverpool Street to say that a motorbike's on its way.'

'Good God! I was just thinking how much easier things would be if I had a bike. Dammit – if I wait then I'll miss the train to Brightlingsea and the next one isn't for hours.'

'You won't need to catch the train, Mr Stoneleigh, you'll be able to go on your new motorbike.'

'That's true – but I doubt that it's got any petrol in it. There's no fuel available for civilians.'

The old chap grinned, revealing he had more gum than teeth at the top. 'You work for the Admiralty, special rules apply. You stop where you are, Johnny will come across and help you get the bike out of the guard's van.'

'How long have I got?'

'An hour, I reckon. Plenty of time for you to go back to Harbour House and change into something more suitable.'

Richard chuckled. He wasn't sure he had anything hanging in the wardrobe that would be any better than what he had on now. A smart suit and polished brogues weren't ideal for being an Admiralty surveyor either, but that was what he preferred to wear.

'Okay, I'll nip down to the yard and let Mr Roby know my change of plans. Don't worry, I'll be back in good time.'

He found his quarry in his office. Jonathan slapped him on the back and congratulated him on his good fortune. 'Just the ticket, it'll be so much easier for both of us if you don't have to rely on the somewhat unreliable train.'

'There's something that neither my father – who must be the sender of this miracle – nor yourself or Mr Hatch have considered,' Richard said with a sheepish smile. 'I've never ridden a motorbike and was never all that stable on a bike. Are you an expert by any chance?'

'God no, hate the things. I can drive a car but you're on your own as far as motorised two wheels are concerned.'

'I'm going to make a complete fool of myself but so be it. I won't have to stay overnight now I've got my own transport. Jack Hatch seems to think I'll be allowed to get petrol from somewhere because I work for the Admiralty. Do you think he's right?'

'Absolutely. I tell you what, wheel it round here and I'll fill it up from our supply. Also, there's bound to be somebody here who can show you the ropes.'

'Great, I'll wander about and ask.'

Richard was in luck as the third person he spoke to, a carpenter, travelled from Colchester on a motorbike every day.

'Bring it round, mate, I'll show you what's what. Piece of cake as them boys in blue are fond of saying – nothing to it.'

Richard left his case in Jonathan's office and headed back to the station, hoping that everybody's confidence in his ability to ride a motorbike wasn't misplaced.

The bike proved less of a hazard than he'd feared and after a few false starts he was confident he could safely ride the ten miles to Brightlingsea without falling off or injuring other road users or pedestrians.

Sundays used to be sacrosanct, no working, no shops open, but things were different now. The yards worked seven days a week, the men were lucky to get an afternoon off and it was no different for him. This is why he was here, as was, it appeared, every able-bodied seaman in Brightlingsea. Stone's yard was even busier than usual. Richard was astonished at the feverish activity. Something was up. He'd scarcely got off the motorbike when a navy officer yelled at him.

'Stoneleigh, over here. Do you have navigational skills?'

'I do, sir, I have my first mate's ticket.'

'Good man. You're captain of that tug.' He pointed to the vessel bobbing on the water. 'Admiralty's sending all the small boats it can find across to Dunkirk this evening. We need to get the poor sods marooned there off the beaches before the Germans capture or kill them.'

A few hours later, dressed in appropriate gear, Richard found himself captaining a crew of three local fishermen on the tug. If the sea had been rough, none of this would have worked but by some miracle tonight it was like a mill pond.

His role was to tow small wooden rowboats, lifeboats from big ships and a couple of barges to Dunkirk so they could, being flat bottomed, be rowed in and collect as many soldiers as they could hold. No one complained, no one talked about the danger, the likelihood that many of them might not return, every man was focused on their task. The trapped men needed them, and they would do their duty even if it killed them.

2

Emily knew she shouldn't be sitting on the stairs listening to the news bulletin but from the way her parents had been talking earlier she just knew that there was something really bad going on to do with the war. They'd been looking very serious before they'd gone into the sitting room to listen to the latest news broadcast.

She was in her nightie and dressing gown, should have been in bed reading, not lurking on the stairs eavesdropping. They'd had their nightly hot drink and biscuits an hour ago.

There was a slight sound behind her and the boys slipped in on either side of her.

'Something's up in France, Emily,' George whispered. 'Our army's trapped on the beaches and there's hundreds of thousands of them waiting to be rescued.'

'We've been listening to the wireless in Mr Stoneleigh's room,' Sammy said quietly.

She was shocked the boys had gone in there and even more upset that they'd had the nerve to switch on the wireless without permission. Then curiosity at what they might have learned overcame her dismay.

'Quickly, let's go back there. Mr Stoneleigh won't know as he's in Brightlingsea,' she hissed and led the silent charge up the stairs and into the unoccupied bedroom.

The wireless was still warm which meant it crackled into life almost immediately.

A very well-spoken man was telling everybody that the British government was doing everything it could to bring home as many of the BEF who were trapped on the beaches as possible. It didn't say how this feat was to be achieved.

The newsreader continued to say that the RAF were protecting the troops, the navy was there in force, that the stranded men would soon be on their way home to a hero's welcome.

Then Daddy strode into the room and switched off the wireless. Emily froze in horror. There was nothing any of them could say which could make things less appalling. She put an arm around each of the boys and they sidled closer to her.

She waited, fists clenched, heart hammering for him to turn and tell them in that awful terrifying voice he used when he was truly angry exactly what he thought of them.

'Good God, children, you don't want to listen to this. You shouldn't be in here, but I don't blame you for wanting to know,' Daddy said. He wasn't furious, he was smiling but his eyes were sad.

She pushed the boys towards him first and he hugged them before pushing them gently out of the room. 'Run along, boys, there's extra cocoa and a slice of cake being prepared in the kitchen. Quietly now, we don't want to wake Grace next door.'

They vanished – the chance of extra cocoa and cake would make them forget about everything else.

'I'm so sorry, we shouldn't have been in here.'

'No, it's a gross invasion of privacy, sweetheart. However, I'm sure that Richard would understand if he was here.' He looked around as if expecting George and Sammy to be eavesdropping. 'Richard isn't in Brightlingsea, he's on his way to Dunkirk to help save the soldiers.'

'Is that why you and Mummy are looking so worried?'

'It is, sweetheart, but we really didn't want you and the boys to know. He's an experienced sailor, he knows what he's doing.' He put his arm round her shoulder and squeezed. 'Come on, Emily, let's join the boys for a late-night snack.'

Emily wanted to know how Mr Stoneleigh being a good sailor would help. He wasn't in the Royal Navy, like Daddy he was just working for the Admiralty. Neither of them went on the big ships, like the destroyers and sloops, they stayed on the shore making sure minesweepers and other small ships were built properly.

She wondered if other men from Wivenhoe and Brightlingsea were helping too. How could they help?

'Daddy, are little boats from around here sailing all the way to France to help with the rescue? Is that what Mr Stoneleigh's doing?'

He nodded. 'Clever girl. Yes, the big ships can't get in close enough to get the men from shore, therefore the smaller craft are essential.'

'Does that mean the Thames barges will go? Dan might be taking his barge there too.'

'He might very well be, sweetheart. Please don't mention this to the boys.'

'I won't, I promise.'

Emily no longer wanted cocoa and cake, her mouth was dry and her stomach churned. Poor Nancy, she must be so worried.

Dan had almost drowned a few weeks ago, what would she do if her new husband lost his life now?

Maybe because today was a Sunday, if there was a God, He would look kindly on the little boats, on the soldiers hoping to be picked up, and all the other servicemen involved in this dangerous rescue.

She mustn't let her brothers know what was going on. Daddy had trusted her with his news and she had to pretend everything was okay. She'd wanted to be treated like a grown-up but right now she truly wished she was still a little girl and didn't have this horrible information lodged in her head.

* * *

Annie had been round a friend's house for tea and they'd had a laugh, played a few games of Brag and not listened to the wireless. Mary's hubby was with the army in France and she was that worried about him Annie had spent all evening turning the conversation away from the war.

Mary had two little kiddies, Jed was three and the baby, Jill, was three months old. She'd been conceived just before Mary's hubbie had gone off to fight. Annie and Norm hadn't had children and now she was glad. If she'd been a mum she wouldn't have been able to up sticks and leave but would have been forced to remain and be abused by her in-laws.

'I've never understood, Mary, how my Norm could have been all right when both his parents are plain horrible.'

'Crikey, what's brought that on? You don't have to worry about them two any more. You're a free woman, unlike me.'

'You wouldn't be without your little ones, would you?'

Mary's face lit up. 'I love them to bits; if anything happens to my Fred then at least I've got them to remember him by.' She poured them both another glass of port and lemon. The wine was from last Christmas and the lemonade probably as old as it was a bit flat.

'Are you going to stop at Harbour House, Annie? You could go anywhere, join up and that.'

'I reckon the government will want women like me to serve; doing domestic work ain't a lot of help for the war effort, is it?' She frowned. 'I'm not going to work in munitions even if it is good money. No, I'll volunteer for the WAAF, I was a scholarship girl, remember, and they want clever girls like me.'

'Don't you fancy the Land Army?'

'No, thanks, too much like hard work. I'd thought I'd go for the army but I've changed my mind. I'll stay put until the money comes from the council. The last letter they sent they said I'd have it by the summer – been waiting more than a year now so I'm not holding my breath. I'm going to write to the WAAF recruiting centre in London and see if I'm eligible to enrol for one of the more interesting jobs when I'm free to do so.'

The evening was cut short when the baby started to wail – she was still being breastfed – so Annie gave her friend a hug and walked home. It was almost ten o'clock but still light. This new double summer-time malarkey was working a treat.

She was surprised to see Mr and Mrs Roby and the children in the kitchen when she went in. 'Shall I lock up, Mr Roby? Is Mr Stoneleigh coming home tonight?'

Mr Roby appeared in the passageway. 'No, he's otherwise occupied, Annie, so yes, please do lock up.'

She was about to walk past the kitchen – she didn't want to intrude on a family meeting – but he called her back.

'Join us for a piece of cake and a mug of cocoa, Annie. Have you been listening to the news by any chance?'

She shook her head. 'No, none of it's good at the moment and my friend didn't need to be reminded of what's happening to the army in France right now.'

'Probably wise. Richard's been recruited to captain a small boat and is part of a massive rescue operation. From what he told me when he telephoned before he left Brightlingsea there are literally hundreds of boats of all descriptions, fishing, barges, pleasure boats, lifeboats and so on that have been asked to help with the evacuation. Sounds a harebrained sort of scheme but just the kind of thing someone at the War Office would come up with. There's not a breath of wind tonight so hopefully it'll be calm as I don't think it could work if it wasn't,' Mr Roby told her.

Emily handed her a mug of cocoa and a piece of cake and Annie didn't have the heart to refuse, even though after the amount of port and lemon she'd consumed neither seemed a good idea.

'Ta, that's very kind of you. Excuse me, I'll take this up if you don't mind.'

Mrs Roby smiled. 'Of course, let's pray there's good news tomorrow.'

Annie had used the WC before she left East Street where Mary lived. She really didn't want the cake or the cocoa and decided to put it on her dressing table and heat up the drink when she went down the following morning. Fortunately, there were no mice anywhere in the house because of the big ginger cat. The cake wouldn't get nibbled if it was uncovered, although it would probably dry out a bit.

The clothes she'd been wearing would do for tomorrow as she just put a wraparound pinny on whilst she was cleaning. She wasn't one for saying prayers, thought that God had more important people to listen to than her, but tonight as she settled down she sent up a fervent wish that this crazy scheme would work and that this flotilla of little boats and navy vessels could manage to rescue the bulk of the British Army who were stranded on the beaches.

For some reason she couldn't settle and she always fell asleep as soon as her head hit the pillow. Images of a tall, smiling redheaded man filled her thoughts. She wasn't stupid – she knew that the German Luftwaffe would be bombing and strafing, not only the beaches but all the boats coming to rescue them. There were also mines in the Channel, mostly put there by the British Navy, and they would be an extra hazard.

She should be praying for Mary's man, Fred, after all, she knew him better than she knew Richard Stoneleigh. She mentioned them both by name and guessed that the Almighty would be bombarded with such prayers tonight. Maybe the calm weather was his way of showing he was listening.

* * *

Richard was at the helm and his role was to keep his trot of five boats safe. This meant travelling parallel to another similar row of linked vessels. It also meant remaining in the mine-free channel as soon as they got out to sea.

Thank God the sea was dead calm tonight – not a breath of wind so a sailing barge wouldn't have been much use. The boats he was towing were between twenty and thirty feet long and would be able to accommodate maybe forty sailors when they arrived at the beaches of Dunkirk.

They chugged to Southend Pier where they collected provisions – nothing fancy – just tinned meat and bread to eat and tea to drink.

'See that bucket, you two,' he said to the young men who

were on board in charge of catering. 'You've got to make tea in it and then pass it back full to the boats we're towing. They've got mugs and their own supply of meat and bread.'

'Right, sir, we'll get the water boiling. I reckon it'll take an hour or more,' one of them replied.

There was no more talking, they all knew that voices travelled across the water, especially at night. It wasn't dark, but the clouds were low, which should mean the Luftwaffe wouldn't be able to see them.

In the organised chaos, Richard steered his tug and its followers into Ramsgate where they were told they would wait until word came from above that they were to head for Dunkirk. They couldn't sail straight across, it wasn't safe, and he reckoned it would be hours before they reached their destination.

In fact, he didn't need his navigational skills – all he had to do was follow the fleet of small craft. He was impressed the Admiralty had managed to get this organised so quickly and so efficiently. His night vision was excellent and occasionally he saw larger navy vessels, destroyers and corvettes. The small boats were not alone on their journey.

'Pass the word back, boys, that we're almost there. Tell them to detach the tow rope and then row ashore. We'll be hanging around here ready to take them back at dawn.'

His instructions were passed and he hoped, unlike the game of Chinese whispers that he'd played as a child, that the information which arrived at the end of the line of boats would be the same information he'd given at the start.

He smiled in the darkness. Most of the men and boys crewing the small boats had some nautical experience and would be able to work out for themselves what they had to do.

He took the tug in as close as he dared and then cast off the boats. He heard the sound of oars dipping into the sea and one by one they slid silently past him and headed for the beach, which he could see was packed with men.

The big ships had remained some distance from the shore but he thought he could risk venturing a little nearer. From the light of the fires burning in Dunkirk it was possible to see what was going on.

Men were wading out and being heaved into the waiting boats. The troops looked exhausted. There were long columns waiting patiently and there didn't appear to be any disorder or panic.

There was the constant sound of bombs being dropped, of the bombardment of the navy ships on the German emplacements on the shore, the darkness ripped apart by the noise, shouts and screams of those injured.

'I'm going to go towards the mole, the one that sticks out at sea about a mile, we can collect a dozen or more ourselves.'

'Bloody hell, sir, those Nazi bastards have sunk two hospital ships, I can see stretchers floating in the sea,' one of the hands replied grimly.

A German fighter bomber screamed overhead. Richard instinctively ducked – not that doing so would make any difference. A small ship, it looked like a fishing boat, took a direct hit.

They managed to pick up half a dozen survivors, two crew and four soldiers, the rest were dead. Bodies were to be left, only the living to be rescued.

'I'm going to take you to that sloop. They'll take care of you,' Richard yelled to make himself heard above the noise of the bombs being dropped.

This nightmare continued until the first glimmer of dawn. They couldn't remain so close to the beach once it was light as they would be sitting ducks. He thanked God that the sea was calm and there were still low clouds, meaning Luftwaffe fighters had to fly low – become targets themselves – if they wanted to strafe the soldiers on the beach or the boats rescuing them.

He'd lost count of the number of men he'd hauled over the side, how many times he'd steered his tugboat to one of the big ships so the men could be transferred. They'd worked for hours and his crew had had enough. Time to return to Blighty for a few hours' respite before doing it all again.

'How the bleeding hell are we going to find the boats what we brought over, sir?' Richard didn't have an answer for the man who'd asked this.

'I don't think we can. I can navigate back to where I cast them off but whether they find us or not remains to be seen.'

He adjusted the helm and the tug responded.

'Look, I reckon that's a couple of ours rowing towards us,' another crewmember shouted.

Half an hour later, with two of the original lifeboats and four from another trot securely attached, Richard was ready to return to Ramsgate.

They'd eaten the bread and tinned meat but there was still water and tea – the bucket was filled and sent back but he doubted that the poor sods at the end of the line got anything but seawater by the time it reached them.

They were following the flotilla of small ships also heading back to Blighty. He had around twenty soldiers packed into his boat and the boats he was towing had a similar number. He thought they'd probably made at least half a dozen trips to the beach and back so each one of them had saved over a hundred chaps. A good night's work and if all the others had done the same, thousands would have been rescued that night.

Richard was talking to a couple of soldiers on the port side when the terrifying scream of a Junkers approaching at speed jerked him from his thoughts. There was little point in shouting 'take cover' – there was nowhere to hide.

A massive wall of water engulfed him and he was hurtled into the air. A fishing boat travelling alongside had taken a direct hit and disintegrated. He wasn't wearing a life jacket – nobody on his boat was. The water closed over his head and he kicked furiously. He was a strong swimmer, was pretty sure he was unhurt, and thought he might be able to rescue at least one of the men who'd gone into the sea with him.

His head broke the surface and from the light of the fierce fires burning in Dunkirk he looked around. He couldn't see his boat, but he could see two soldiers floundering in the sea just ahead of him. He'd already kicked off his boots and was able to swim strongly to them.

'Don't struggle, relax, and turn on your backs. You'll float. Once you're steady, I'll tow you towards the nearest vessel.'

Both men listened, thank God, and after a few minutes he was able to hook an arm around each of them and by treading water was able to keep them safely afloat. He wasn't sure how long he'd be able to maintain this and prayed that a passing boat would pick them up.

There was little point in yelling for help – the noise from the Luftwaffe, from the guns on the beach, from the naval vessels firing back made that a waste of breath and he needed every mouthful to keep his two comrades afloat.

Then it seemed from nowhere the prow of a boat came alongside and a rope was tossed down.

'Okay, hang onto this, you two, they'll pull you aboard.'

Richard continued to tread water and pushed the men from below as willing hands hauled the rope upwards. A few minutes later, the rope returned and he was able to scramble up the side of the fishing boat unaided.

He fell headlong over the side and for a few seconds lay there like a beached fish gasping for breath.

'Up you come, matey, bleeding hero you are. We've got three others from your tug, but it never sunk, and them soldiers you were bringing are tickety-boo,' a smiling fisherman told him as he pulled Richard to his feet.

'Thank God for that. It's a night for miracles.' This boat was packed with rescued soldiers who patted him on the back and wished him well as he made his way down the small vessel to the cabin. Inside he was given a rough towel and stripped off his wet clothes. It was a crush in there as the other five were doing the same. Warmer, and wrapped in an old blanket, he found himself a corner and drank the tea he was offered gratefully.

'We've stuck your clothes and that on the engine, matey, they'll be dry enough to put on by the time we get back to Blighty,' a helpful young man told him.

Richard nodded his thanks and fell asleep. If his tug hadn't sunk and was still seaworthy then there would be many more trips like this one before those poor bastards trapped on the beach were safe at home.

3

Emily slept poorly and was gritty-eyed and tired on Monday morning. No one mentioned the rescue at Dunkirk or Mr Stoneleigh and she didn't like to ask. Her brothers were more interested in playing cricket that afternoon at school and appeared to have forgotten last night's news.

She found it hard to concentrate at school and even her favourite subject, art, failed to engage her attention. Every time planes flew overhead she shuddered and wondered how many men had died in the rescue attempt. For some reason the fact that thousands of men were being saved didn't seem as important as the fact that many of them would have been killed.

That afternoon, after school, she was glad of the constant chatter from Claire Cousins, the doctor's daughter, who she escorted back and forth to the Colchester Girls' High School every day apart from Wednesday.

'You're not listening to me,' Claire whined and tugged hard on a leather satchel strap, almost strangling Emily. This certainly got her attention.

'I'm sorry, I've got a lot on my mind. What did you ask me?'

'It's going to be my little brother's birthday tomorrow. What are you giving him?'

'He's getting a gift from the family, it's just not possible for everybody to give him something. Anyway, he won't know if he gets presents or not as he'll only be one year old.'

'I need to get a present as well. It won't be fair otherwise.'

'I don't get anything when it's George's birthday and he doesn't get anything when it's mine. I did get a small gift when he was born, I expect you're muddling it up with that.'

To her horror, the child stopped and before she could put her hand over Claire's mouth an ear-splitting scream startled the pigeons who flew protesting into the air. Far worse than that, the elderly gentleman they'd just been walking past stepped into the road and was almost knocked down by a horse and cart.

The language the cart driver used was just awful, people were gathering around and at any moment someone would point at Claire and they'd both be in trouble. Emily grabbed the child's hand and wrenched her forward. They ran, satchels and gas masks banging painfully, until they reached the comparative safety of the station.

Her heart was thudding, her palms clammy, the poor old man could have been killed. Emily turned her anger on Claire.

'How dare you create a scene like that? If I was your mother, I'd give you a very hard spanking. You're a very, very naughty little girl. That old man could have been killed because of you.'

She was holding both of Claire's shoulders and giving her a little shake with every sentence. Then, to her shame, the poor little mite wet herself and stood shivering and crying in the resulting puddle.

'Oh, I'm so sorry, I shouldn't have yelled at you. Quickly, let's go into the ladies' room and get you cleaned up.'

The little girl couldn't stop crying and Emily knew this was her fault. Her worry about the war, something Claire wasn't aware of, had made her behave badly, be unkind, and that wasn't like her.

She knew there'd be spare knickers in the satchel and it didn't take long to put things right. She tucked the wet ones into the front pocket where they couldn't contaminate anything else.

Because they'd run down the hill, they were still in good time for the train. 'If you don't stop crying you'll make yourself sick. Nobody was hurt, everything's all right.' Emily picked her up and the little girl clung to her.

'Please don't tell my mummy or daddy what I did. I don't want to be spanked.'

'You won't be, I promise you that. I should never have said that as I know that your parents don't believe in smacking, mine don't either.'

'I shouldn't have screamed. Mummy made me go to my bedroom and stay there for hours and hours and hours when I did it last time.'

Emily was rather relieved that this wasn't the only time this had happened. 'Well, I hope that after this you won't ever do it again.'

'I won't, I'm very naughty, I promise I won't do it again.'

The shivering and sniffling stopped and as the train puffed in Emily was able to put Claire down, wipe her face and then lift her into the nearest compartment. By the time they reached Wivenhoe, it was as if nothing had happened – apart from the wet knickers, nobody would ever know. They certainly wouldn't hear anything from her.

* * *

Annie noticed that Emily was subdued when she left for school that Monday morning – it wasn't right that a little girl should be worrying about grown-up things. Mind you, children had been working full time fifty years ago at her age. Emily was mature for her age and looked a lot older, especially now she'd had her hair cut short.

As she was flicking around Mr Stoneleigh's room, she decided she'd be a bit more friendly to him if he came back safely. Not that she'd encourage him, let him think she was the sort of girl who hopped into bed with anyone, but after what he'd have gone through he deserved to be treated a bit special.

Mary must be beside herself wondering if her Fred had been rescued or was wounded, captured or even worse was dead – she probably wouldn't know anything for days. How would she manage with two little kiddies and no man to provide for her? It wasn't as if she could find herself another man as there weren't that many around. Fishermen, those that worked in the shipyard, were still here but most of them were spoken for.

Did she dare switch on the wireless and try and hear for herself what was going on? She glanced at the fancy clock on the mantelpiece – it was minutes to ten o'clock – she thought there might be news on the hour. There was a wireless in the sitting room but she didn't have access to that.

Vi, who came in to do the heavy work on Monday, was busy in the laundry room and wouldn't hear. Molly was out shopping; Mr Roby was at work and Mrs Roby had gone to a WI meeting and this time had taken the baby with her.

She pushed the door shut and switched on the wireless. It hissed and crackled for a few seconds and then the plummy voice of the newsreader filled the room. She listened and her eyes filled. If she'd been a man, she didn't think she'd have been able to do what they were doing – he didn't say how many soldiers had been brought back during the night but he did say the operation was going well.

Hastily she switched the wireless off and resumed her cleaning. She hadn't learned anything really, but then maybe the BBC didn't give bad news as it would lower morale. She doubted any newspapers would carry details either. This rescue couldn't be done in a day – it could be a week or more before they'd brought back the huge army that was stranded on the beaches.

She reckoned that Mr Stoneleigh wouldn't be back until the rescue was done. He might be toffee nosed and full of himself but somehow she didn't doubt that he was brave. However many little boats the Admiralty had managed to requisition, it wouldn't be enough for them to go to Dunkirk just the once, they'd have to go back and forth until the rescue was done.

The telephone jangled – she didn't like answering this but there was no one else as even if Vi was prepared to do it she wouldn't hear it in the laundry. She thundered downstairs and snatched up the receiver and recited the telephone number as she'd been taught to do.

'Thank goodness, I didn't think anyone was going to answer. To whom am I speaking?' The speaker was a very posh woman.

'I'm Annie Thomas, I work here.'

The woman interrupted. 'I don't wish to speak to a housemaid. Fetch Mrs Roby at once.'

'I'm sorry but Mr Roby's at work, Mrs Roby's out somewhere and Mr Stoneleigh has gone to Dunkirk.' As soon as she said that, she knew she shouldn't have. This sort of information shouldn't be bandied about as you never knew who was on the other end of a telephone call. Also, whoever it was didn't deserve to have any answers as she was rude.

There was a shocked silence. 'You are speaking to Mr Stoneleigh's mother. He never fails to telephone on a Sunday night and I was concerned that he hadn't.'

'I'm sorry, Mrs Stoneleigh, I shouldn't have told you that. I'll tell him you called when he gets back but I don't think it will be for a few days yet.'

Annie expected to hear sobbing, for there to be a flurry of questions, but the woman on the other end of the telephone sounded not upset at all.

'I am not comfortable conversing with a servant, but as I have no choice you'll have to suffice. Kindly tell my son to contact us as soon as he can.'

'He's a brave man, Mrs Stoneleigh, I reckon he'll come through this a hero.'

'It's not your concern, but I suppose you mean well.'

The line went dead and Annie stared at the receiver for a few seconds, puzzled by the abrupt disconnection. Thoughtfully she replaced the receiver in the cradle. Mrs Stoneleigh was a horrible woman, but she obviously cared for her son. Probably explained why Mr Stoneleigh was so arrogant, he'd been spoilt.

He was lucky to have even someone as unpleasant as her looking out for him. Her upbringing had been a shocker, which was why she'd been so keen to marry Norm when he'd asked her four years ago. Fortunately, her family lived in Alresford, the next stop on the Clacton line, and far enough away to mean that she didn't have to see her parents very often. She'd come on the train every day to work at the sewing factory and had met Norm at a village social.

Her two older sisters were married to farmworkers but she reckoned they'd probably been called up by now – she'd not bothered to find out. She'd got half a dozen nieces and nephews and avoided contact with them if she could. She'd never felt part of the family, didn't look like any of them, and her father actively disliked her. She'd discovered when she was fifteen that her mum had had a fling with a travelling salesman, and she was the unwanted result.

It had been a shock when she'd found out, but this had explained why she didn't fit in. She was lucky, she supposed, that she wasn't mistreated – just ignored. Mum could have put her into a home, so she was grateful that hadn't happened.

She was just putting the cleaning things away when she heard Mrs Roby opening the front door.

'Give her a hand, Annie, it's hard getting that big pram over the doorstep. You'd better tell her about the telephone call as well,' Molly said.

'I'll do that.'

She hurried down the passageway and smiled at her employer. 'Let me get the end, Mrs Roby, it's easier with two.'

'Thank you, Annie, that's very kind of you. Grace has been an absolute angel. She's a little restless now as she's due for a feed.'

Once the pram was safely inside, Annie slipped behind it and closed the front door. 'I'll put it away, Mrs Roby, if you want to take the baby up to feed her.'

'Thank you, I didn't like to ask as I know it's your lunch break now. We really do appreciate everything you do for us and hope you don't get conscripted too soon.'

'I know I'll have to join the services or go into a munitions factory, but I hope it won't be just yet. I want to join the WAAFs, not the ATS or the WRNS.'

Mrs Roby had the baby in her arms who was grizzling and nuzzling into her. 'I'm sure you'll do splendidly wherever you go, Annie, but as I said we hope it won't be for a while. I very much doubt we'll be able to find anybody else to replace you when that happens.'

* * *

Richard slept for hours and was eventually woken by a very welcome mug of tea and a spam sandwich. His clothes were damp but wearable and he hastily dressed, regretting the fact that he'd lost his socks and his Wellington boots. Being barefoot wasn't a good idea on board a boat.

'You look just the ticket, mate, after your kip,' the cheerful deckhand told him. 'We'll be docking at Ramsgate in an hour or so. I reckon you'll want to get home.'

'No, absolutely not. I intend to return to Dunkirk as long as my vessel's still seaworthy. You told me it hadn't sunk, so hopefully once they'd bailed out and got the pumps going it'll be just fine.'

'We ain't doing another run, saw our mates be blown to smithereens. That's enough for us – anyway catching fish for folk to eat's important too.'

'I just need to find some footwear. Don't suppose you've got a spare pair of boots, size ten, hanging about?'

The chap shook his head. 'Sorry, can't help you there. You're an Admiralty bloke, ain't you? They'll sort you out quick enough when they know you're stopping on your boat and not going home like what we are.'

'I hope you're right. Thanks for the tea and sandwich – I'm a new man now.'

In fact, he felt anything but fit and his clothes were wetter than he'd thought. If he didn't catch pneumonia he'd be surprised. He grinned. He spent a lot of his life nowadays out in the elements, was frequently soaked to the skin, and so far had suffered no ill effects.

The men who'd been fished out of the water with him were no longer in the cabin and he decided to go in search of them. He didn't even know their names and this mattered. After stubbing his toes twice before he'd reached them he gave up the attempt. If his bare feet were trampled on by the heavy boots of the soldiers packed in like sardines, he'd not be able to continue with the rescue work.

He'd spent hours rescuing some of the thousands of men who were waiting patiently on the sand. He'd watched them diving for cover when the German fighters flew low under the cloud cover, machine guns blazing. Then the soldiers had bravely waded out, sometimes up to their necks in the water, in order to be picked up and all this done without complaint. The men he'd hauled aboard had been dirty, tired, but still resilient.

With the arrival of dawn, a fresh armada had arrived to continue the rescue. He'd seen British soldiers being attacked from above. Their lips were dry and cracked, and they were covered in mud, but they were playing football with half a baguette whilst the bombs dropped around them.

He'd watched a warship fire hell and destruction at the Germans and three Nazi fighters fall from the sky. Having seen men die, shattered and bloody, having seen men killed ashore before they could be rescued, had changed him. Despite everything, he'd seen no fear, just a grim determination on the faces of those waiting and those rescued that had inspired him.

* * *

With a new pair of boots, new clothes and a fresh crew, Richard was ready to set out again. This time he wasn't towing a trot of rowing boats behind him – he was going to be used to transfer those rescued from the rowing boats and take them to the destroyers, corvettes and other larger ships anchored out to sea.

It didn't matter that it was daylight, the boats continued to collect the men and he and his hands worked tirelessly until he feared he would run out of fuel and not be able to get back to Blighty.

They'd been involved with the miraculous rescue operation for the best part of three days without respite. They'd done enough and with a final load of equally exhausted and filthy soldiers he headed for Ramsgate.

When the men had been unloaded at the docks, they'd been welcomed by the Women's Institute and the Women's Voluntary Service with food, blankets and cigarettes. Richard then shook hands with his three crew members.

'Thank you, we've saved hundreds of men, possibly thousands, now it's time to hand over to someone else to continue the good work.'

When the gallant little tugboat was secure and they'd wearily clambered ashore, he followed. As the captain of this little boat it was his job to report to the naval officer in charge.

If he'd been asked to file a written report he couldn't have done it, but a verbal account was sufficient.

'Good man, your heroism and dedication hasn't gone unnoticed. The Admiralty has sent a car for you – it's been waiting here since yesterday,' a naval officer told him.

Richard blinked. 'A car? Bloody hell – that's a miracle in itself. I thought I'd have to stagger up the hill with these other poor sods and find a corner in a train.'

'No, it's the Humber parked over there. Are you sure you can get there without falling on your face?'

Richard managed a weak grin. 'Just about, sir. I'm glad I've been able to be of assistance.'

A uniformed chauffeur who looked vaguely familiar assisted him into the rear of the car. 'There's a flask of tea and a couple of sandwiches, sir, on the seat. Then there's blankets and pillows so make yourself comfortable.'

'Thank you.' Richard devoured everything, drained the flask and settled himself under the blankets. He was asleep before the car had left Ramsgate and didn't open his eyes until someone spoke to him.

'My darling boy, we're so proud of you. Johnson will help you up to your room where there's a hot bath waiting. Get clean and sleep. We can talk after that.'

'Ma, I can't believe it. Home in leafy Hampstead – there's nowhere I'd rather be.'

4

Emily had been allowed to stay up to listen to Mr Churchill speaking on the wireless about the rescue of the stranded troops from the beach in Dunkirk. This amazing operation had been going on for several days. Mr Stoneleigh was still not back; they didn't know if he was alive or dead.

Mr Churchill was speaking and she listened carefully. She thought he was a wonderful man and that England was lucky to have him in charge of the war.

'It was in conditions such as these that our men carried on with little or no rest for days and nights on end, making trip after trip across the dangerous waters, bringing with them, always, men whom they had rescued. The numbers they have brought back are the measure of their devotion and their courage.

'A miracle of deliverance achieved by valour, by perseverance, by perfect discipline, by dauntless service, by resource, by skill, by unconquerable fidelity, is manifest to us all.

'We must be very careful not to assign to this deliverance attributes of a victory. Wars are not won by evacuations.'

When he'd finished speaking, her parents were silent for a moment. Then Daddy nodded solemnly.

'It's nothing short of a miracle that they've saved so many. But he's right, darling, an evacuation isn't a victory, whatever the papers might be saying.'

'I think that the families of the men that have come home safely would disagree with that, Jonathan. You can replace the tanks, guns and other equipment but you can't replace a human life.'

Emily put her hand up like she did at school in order to join in the grown-up conversation. Daddy laughed.

'You don't have to do that here, sweetheart, what do you want to say? Your mother and I think that you're old enough to have opinions on such things, although we don't want you to discuss this with your brothers.'

'I won't, I promise. I wanted to say that I read in your newspaper that twenty thousand motorbikes had been left behind. Don't you think that's quite extraordinary? I also read that there were nurses on the beach looking after the wounded men and they refused to leave until the end.'

'I don't see how the two pieces of information are connected, sweetheart, but both are interesting nonetheless,' Daddy said.

'I didn't explain that very well. It seemed an awful lot of motorbikes and I just thought it might be hard to replace those. I also thought how wonderful it was that women had been there alongside the men and were just as brave.'

'Women are proving every day that they are capable of doing jobs that previously were considered things only men could do. There are already women doctors and nurses, I'm sure in a few years' time they will be working in every profession.'

'I think I'd like to be a doctor, Daddy, so that's what I'm

going to work towards. I know I said I wanted to study art, but medicine would be so much more useful. I think being an artist would be rather self-indulgent.'

Her parents stared as if they didn't understand her. Then she giggled. 'Miss Baker at school used that word and I've been looking for an opportunity to bring it into a conversation ever since I heard it. Did I use it correctly?'

Mummy smiled. 'You certainly did, darling girl, and you never fail to surprise us. I'm quite sure that you can be whatever you set your heart on being, a doctor, artist or motorbike rider.'

'Maybe I can be all three – I don't see why a doctor can't ride a motorbike and paint pictures.'

Daddy leaned down and kissed her on the head. 'It's time for bed, sweetheart. I hope you don't have nightmares.'

'Thank you for letting me stay up and listen to the news, I really appreciate it. Goodnight, Mummy and Daddy.' As she reached the door, something else occurred to her, something nobody was mentioning. 'Annie said that her friend Mary's husband Fred has been rescued safely. Why haven't we heard about Mr Stoneleigh?'

Her parents exchanged a worried look. 'I'm sure we'll hear when he's back, sweetheart.'

'It's not that late, Jonathan, perhaps you could ring his parents' number. It's possible that they've heard something. I doubt anyone would think to contact us.'

Emily sat on the stairs whilst Daddy made the telephone call. Mummy joined her and she snuggled in, loving the closeness. They listened to the one-sided conversation but couldn't see his face as he had his back to them. All he said was things like, 'I see, yes, I understand, thank you.'

Finally, he turned round and he was smiling. 'I spoke to Mrs Stoneleigh and she said she was just about to ring us. Richard's safe and well and recovering at home in Hampstead after spending three days helping the evacuation.'

Emily squealed and clapped her hands. 'That's the most wonderful news. Excuse me, I'm going to tell Annie, she only went up a little while ago.'

* * *

Annie had gone into Colchester on her afternoon off and collected some pamphlets about joining the ATS, the WAAFs and the WRNS. She was busy reading each of them and still thought that being a girl in air force blue would be preferable to either of the others.

There were footsteps on the stairs approaching her attic room and she was on her feet and heading for the door when there was a timid knock.

'Annie, it's me, Emily.'

As soon as she opened the door, Annie knew it was good news. 'Is Mr Stoneleigh safe?'

'Yes, yes, he is. Isn't that absolutely marvellous?'

'Where's he been all this time, do you know?'

Emily nodded. 'He's been rescuing soldiers. He's a hero, don't you think?'

'I do, ta for coming up and telling me. I'll give his room a good going over tomorrow just in case he's back.'

'Mr Stoneleigh's staying with his family to recuperate for a few days so there's no need to do his room just yet.'

Annie never enjoyed being given instructions by this girl, it made her feel inferior and she was as good as anyone, in her opinion. She forced a smile and answered, 'I think he'll be better there, at least until he's well.'

'He certainly sounds as if he comes from a good home. I'm

supposed to be going to bed, so I'd better do that. Goodnight, Annie.'

Emily vanished silently down the stairs, leaving Annie to return to her pamphlets. She hoped these hadn't been noticed by her visitor. Not much escaped that child's eagle eyes.

She was glad that she'd told Mrs Stoneleigh that her son was brave. He'd just proved it, as had all those men who'd remained over there being bombed and that in order to bring back the soldiers.

As she settled into bed, her thoughts turned to the handsome young man that she wasn't sure she even liked. She smiled in the darkness. Being brave, even being a hero, didn't make him less of a danger to her. Some men just had that kind of magnetism, attracted girls like moths to a light.

Finally, she was forced to admit that she was attracted to him, that he made her pulse race and that, despite knowing the possible heartbreak, she wouldn't take much persuading to get to know him better.

Her Norm hadn't made her feel like this, he'd been a good man but dull and hadn't gone in for romantic gestures or even for much in the way of marital relations. Annie reckoned that was why she'd not got in the family way – you had to do it more than once a month to get pregnant.

She laughed out loud, the sound echoing in the big attic room. She knew of girls who'd only done it once and still got caught out, so either she was wrong, or they'd been very unlucky.

* * *

When she got up the next morning the house felt different, even the big ginger tom was purring and friendly.

'Morning, Ginger, no nasty surprises for me today, I hope?' The cat rubbed against her legs and she leaned down and stroked him. 'I'll get the range going, put the kettle on and then I'll find you some breakfast.'

'Annie, I didn't know you talked to him like we do,' Emily said from the kitchen door.

'Of course I do, be rude not to. You're up early, love, aren't you taking little Claire in today?'

When little Claire didn't go to school then Emily went in early and spent time in the art room. Annie thought that the girl sometimes went to see Nancy too, the girl whose job she'd taken. The Robys were very easy going with Emily considering she wasn't even twelve. But Emily looked fourteen at least, especially since she'd had her lovely, long golden hair cut short a few weeks ago.

'I woke up and it's such a lovely day I thought I'd go for a walk before breakfast.' She ran her fingers down the skirt of her pretty summer uniform dress. 'So pleased I don't have to wear a gymslip now. I even quite like the straw hat.'

'Better than the felt pudding basin you had to wear until this term.'

Emily giggled. 'If anyone wants to know where I've gone, please would you tell them I've gone for a stroll along the quay.'

The back door banged and she was gone. The cat meowed and nipped at her ankle. 'Okay, cat, I'll do it right now.'

Molly had the morning off and was going to spend it with her daughter Nancy at the haberdashery shop in Colchester. Dan, Nancy's new husband, had returned safely from Dunkirk and this called for a family get-together. Even the youngest, the boys, were missing school to go as well as the actual owners of this busy shop.

Annie sighed. She envied the Bates family and wished she'd

been born into such a happy one. God knows who her real father was, her mum had been tight-lipped about that. She knew she must have got her brains from him as her family were barely literate and for that she was grateful. He must have had dark hair and dark blue eyes, an unusual combination, like her. Everyone else in the Thomas family had mouse-brown hair and pale blue eyes. Small wonder she'd not fitted in there.

* * *

By the time Emily returned, the boys were in the dining room gobbling down their cereal and toast. Mr Roby had already gone to the shipyard and Mrs Roby was having her usual tray upstairs.

'Sorry, Annie, I got talking to some of the fishermen. Sadly, two men from one of the boats lost their lives at Dunkirk, but they weren't local, they came from Colchester.'

'Daddy said Mr Stoneleigh's safe and will be back at the weekend probably,' George said with his mouth full of toast and sprayed crumbs onto the table.

'Disgusting little boy,' Emily said with a smile. 'Have you got cricket practice after school?'

'We have, so we'll make our own way home,' George said. 'Sammy's better than me at batting but I'm better with the ball. I've got loads of boys out with LBW and caught behind.'

Cricket was a mystery to Annie so she nodded and smiled, didn't risk an answer, and put freshly made toast down for Emily. All the children drank tea, so the girl helped herself from the pot on the table.

Fifteen minutes later, the house was quiet. Annie cleared away and washed up before putting on her pinny to begin the daily routine of cleaning. The telephone in the hall rang twice, meaning the call was for this house and not the doctor's next door. She hesitated, waiting to see if Mrs Roby was coming down. She wasn't, so Annie reluctantly picked up the receiver.

* * *

Richard had spent three days being spoilt and fussed over at his family home in Hampstead and that was sufficient. He was fond of his parents but was beginning to feel smothered.

'Ma, I need to get back to work. I'm fully recovered and have loved every minute of being home but—'

'My darling boy, you don't have to tell me, I'm just surprised that you've remained here as long as you have. When do you plan to leave?'

'Today, that means I'll have the rest of the weekend to talk to Jonathan Roby, find out what I've missed and what I'll need to do on Monday. I'll call in at the Admiralty and speak to Pa as I also want to know how many of my friends perished.'

'Terribly sad, but despite the prime minister insisting it was a defeat and not a victory, the fact that almost 400,000 troops were safely recovered and will be ready to fight when necessary is nothing short of a miracle.'

'I agree, massive loss of equipment, of course, but that can be replaced eventually. The biggest problem is that Hitler might invade before we're ready to repel him. Every day counts, Ma, so I have to get back to work.'

'I'll get Johnson to drive you to London. No, don't shake your head at me and frown, whilst we have petrol in the car we can use it how we want.'

Richard knew it was fruitless to argue once his mother's mind was made up. He'd been quite prepared to walk to the station and go in on the underground and then, after seeing Pa, make his way to Liverpool Street station.

'That's kind of you, it will certainly make things easier. I'm not entirely happy about you living here as things are about to kick off. The Luftwaffe hasn't started bombing civilians but I'm sure that's going to happen soon.'

'Good heavens, Hampstead is almost the countryside, darling, we're perfectly safe here. If there was an air raid we've got a more than adequate cellar repurposed as a shelter.'

An hour later, he was on his way with a vague promise to visit when he had a chance. He'd also told his parents that his weekly phone calls had to stop as personal calls were now frowned upon by the government. Of course, in an emergency that would be different.

His father was in a meeting which was a shame as Richard had wanted to say goodbye and thank him for sending the car to Ramsgate to fetch him. He scribbled a note instead and left the building, wondering how long it would be before he saw Pa again.

As Colchester was an army town, he'd expected the train to be crammed with khaki and was surprised to find so many Brylcreem boys joining the press of travellers. He found himself jammed into a corner with three young pilots. He could feel their disapproval because he wasn't in uniform.

'I work for the Admiralty, in case you're wondering, and did my bit at Dunkirk, I can assure you. Spent three days back and forth collecting men from the beaches.'

The three men looked uncomfortable and then the oldest offered his hand. 'We shouldn't have judged, bloody horrible out there. We've been on crash leave and are just going back to our base.'

The journey to Wivenhoe passed quickly and he enjoyed

exchanging news with these brave fliers. Two of them were still teenagers, the one who'd initiated the conversation was a year younger than him. It appalled him that boys – that's what they were really – were tasked with keeping Britain safe. He wasn't exactly sure how many pilots there were – a few thousand at the most – and they now had this fearsome responsibility.

He shook each of their hands and wished them luck, and when he jumped off the train at Wivenhoe he'd almost decided that he'd enlist in the navy. He would be an officer and would then be doing far more to protect his country than he was at the moment. He felt guilty that these young men didn't appear resentful or afraid and were ready to die in order to protect everything they loved.

Jonathan Roby would be at work so Richard headed to the shipyard first – it was only a few hundred yards from the station. He nodded at the old man supposedly guarding the place from spies and headed for the office.

The men worked shifts, having an occasional afternoon off in turn, but basically there seven days a week. The noise of the saws, the hammering, the pneumatic drills made normal conversation impossible.

There were two girls working as secretaries in the office and they'd be able to tell him where to find Jonathan.

'Richard, I can't tell you how glad I am to see you. Well done, well done indeed, you've returned a regular hero,' Jonathan said from right behind him.

He was about to offer his hand but was embraced. 'Everyone at Harbour House is proud of you – we're basking in your reflected glory at the moment.'

'Hang on, Jonathan, don't overdo it. I was just doing my job, as were hundreds of others. I don't expect to be praised for doing that.'

'Your mother telephoned this morning to tell us that you were on your way which is why I'm taking the afternoon off. The family are preparing a welcome-home party. I can't tell you how excited the children are and I apologise in advance for the barrage of questions you're going to have to answer.'

Richard reached out and grabbed Jonathan's arm. 'No questions. I couldn't tell the children what I saw, what happened, none of it was glorious and I really don't want to talk about it.'

'Good God, man, I wasn't expecting you to give graphic details. I've told the children they can only ask the most general things. Surely you can talk about the journey, what you had to eat – if anything – things like that? I know you must have seen the most ghastly things and would prefer to forget them.'

'Thank you for understanding.' They were stationary just outside the shipyard and Richard continued. 'It's changed me, I'm not the same man I was just a few days ago. The heroism I witnessed from ordinary soldiers, no complaints, just a grim determination to get home and continue fighting was extraordinary.'

He was silent for a few moments and then thought it only fair to tell Richard his plans. 'I'm thinking of joining the navy. I'm qualified, and somehow being safe here overseeing these ships is no longer enough for me.'

'I can imagine that it isn't. I had a nasty feeling that you might have decided that being an Admiralty surveyor isn't sufficient in the circumstances.' Jonathan put out his hand as Richard was about to interrupt. 'I can assure you that without us there'd be no ships. Building weapons of war might not seem heroic but it's essential. You've got skills and training that a naval officer doesn't have – before you make the decision to leave, consider how valuable you are and how difficult it will be to replace you.'

5

Emily stood back to admire the glorious afternoon tea that Annie and Mrs Bates had prepared to welcome Mr Stoneleigh back. Goodness knows where they'd found all the rationed ingredients to make such a spread. Mrs Peterson from the farm had donated a dozen cracked eggs, some ham and cream. Other people had been turning up all morning with gifts and treats. Mr Stoneleigh was now considered the hero of the village and everyone knew how brave he was.

'Is he going to be much longer, Emily?' George asked. He'd been asking this since one o'clock and it was now just after two thirty.

Sammy had been standing at the dining-room window watching the gate. 'He's here, he's coming. Mr Stoneleigh's with him. I'm going to tell Mrs Bates it's time to make the tea.' He disappeared, forgetting he wasn't supposed to run or shout in the house.

Mrs Bates usually had Saturday afternoon and Sunday free to be with her family but as this was a special occasion she'd volunteered to work. Everybody was in their Sunday best and

Emily was wearing her new summer frock that Nancy had made for her – it was called a shirtwaister – and for the first time she wasn't embarrassed about showing off her new front. Only a girl with a front like hers could wear such a grown-up dress.

George had rushed off to tell Mummy the guest of honour was arriving as she'd gone upstairs to change herself and their little sister. Hopefully, baby Grace would be her happy gurgling self and not grizzling because she had teeth coming in.

It was Emily's designated task to open the door with a flourish and she was standing ready to do that. As the door had no glass in it, she had to listen carefully for footsteps so she could open the door at the right time.

She got it spot on. 'Welcome home, Mr Stoneleigh, thank you for your bravery. We have a wonderful afternoon tea made for you to celebrate.'

She'd expected him to smile, nod his head, stride in as if he owned the world like he usually did. Instead, he put his hand out to steady himself against the door frame. There were tears in his eyes, he'd lost a lot of weight and looked as if he hadn't slept for weeks.

'I didn't expect this, don't deserve it, but thank you. I can't tell you what it means to me.'

Before she could move aside, he reached down and hugged her, then did the same with the boys. Mummy received a kiss on the cheek which she didn't seem to mind at all. He dumped his suitcase on the floor and to everybody's astonishment – especially Annie's – he hugged her too. He then took both of Mrs Bates's hands – not really a handshake – released them and turned to view the laden table.

'Good God – this is better than tea at the Ritz. Thank you for making today so special. I did my duty as did hundreds, no, thousands, of others. I was one of the lucky ones and returned home in one piece. I don't deserve to be treated like a hero – the true heroes were the men who fought their way to the beaches and then waited without complaint until they were rescued.'

Daddy stepped forward and patted him on the back. 'Well said, Richard, but I hope your reservations won't stop you enjoying the tea.'

Mr Stoneleigh laughed. 'It certainly won't. Do we charge in and help ourselves or behave like ladies and gentlemen and form an orderly queue?'

Emily smiled shyly. 'I'm going to serve you, Mr Stoneleigh, then everybody can tuck in. What would you like to have first?'

* * *

It was the best afternoon ever, she decided, when she collapsed into bed at almost ten o'clock. The tea had been scrumptious, they'd all eaten themselves to a standstill and there had still been enough for Mrs Bates to take home a basket filled with goodies for her family.

Mr Stoneleigh had been relaxed and friendly and by the end of the afternoon she decided her initial opinion about him was wrong – he was not only a hero but a very nice man.

What had puzzled her the most was Annie, who Emily had heard say more than once, when she didn't know she was being overheard, that she didn't like Mr Stoneleigh, that he was patronising and toffee nosed – whatever that meant.

Obviously, Annie's opinion had completely changed like everybody else's where Mr Stoneleigh was concerned. She'd positively glowed whenever he spoke to her and he seemed to be looking at her in the same way that Dan looked at Nancy.

Emily bit her lip. It was different with Nancy and Dan as

they'd known each other for years, both came from the village, but she didn't think someone like Annie was quite right for Mr Stoneleigh. He spoke in the same way that her mummy and daddy did, but Annie sounded more ordinary.

She didn't know a lot about this sort of thing, but she did know that people from different worlds probably wouldn't make a good match. Then she shook her head. Sammy had come from the East End last year but now you couldn't tell him apart from George when he spoke. He fitted in just perfectly – maybe if Annie and Mr Stoneleigh were to fall in love it might work out after all.

* * *

Annie had volunteered to do the washing up so that Molly could go home in time to serve her family the basket of treats for tea. The house was quiet which was the way she liked it. Then she could pretend she belonged here, that she didn't come from a dilapidated little cottage full of noisy, unpleasant people, that she wasn't an uneducated, common sort of girl.

It had been a wonderful afternoon – neither she nor Molly had been made to feel like they weren't part of the celebration. The children had behaved and the baby had been passed from person to person, smiling and waving, obviously enjoying the extra attention.

It had been a shock when Richard – he insisted that she call him by his first name in future – had hugged her and initially she'd thought he was just being friendly. But during the afternoon she'd found him by her side more often than not and never in a threatening way either. He helped clear the table, refused to be waited on and was like a different man. Something had changed him and it must have been whatever he'd experienced at Dunkirk. He'd left the house last Sunday a cocky young man with a tendency to be patronising and had returned quieter and more genuine somehow.

She'd been up to her elbows in sudsy warm water washing the glasses for the past half an hour but they were now polished and ready to be returned to the cupboard in the dining room. It hadn't only been tea they had drunk that afternoon. The children had had fizzy pop and the adults had had red wine. She'd never had this before, thought it rather dry and bitter, but had been pleased to be offered it so didn't refuse.

The scullery window banged. Usually, the cat stalked in immediately but this time something heavy banged against the sink in there. If he'd fetched in a mouse, she'd happily deal with that but she wasn't going to touch a rat.

'Don't you dare come in here with that, keep it in the scullery with you,' she called out, hoping he'd understand from her tone of voice that whatever he had wasn't welcome in the kitchen.

There were footsteps in the passageway and Richard walked in. She thought he'd gone to bed a while ago.

'Ginger up to his usual tricks? Do you want me to have a look?'

'Yes, please. It sounds as if he's fetched in something big this time and I just can't be doing with a rat, dead or alive.'

He smiled and made a pantomime of creeping to the door as if he too was afraid of what he might see. 'Bloody hell! It's not a rat, it's a rabbit. How do you feel about them?'

'If it's dead, I don't mind. I've skinned and gutted a few in my time and would be happy to do the same for this one.'

She thought that perhaps the cat would refuse to give up his prize but she was wrong. Richard returned holding the rabbit triumphantly by its back legs and it was quite definitely deceased.

'I promised to give him the offal and he agreed that was a reasonable exchange.'

'That means I'll have to do it tonight. Not in here though, in the scullery in that sink would be best.'

To her surprise, he shook his head. 'Leave it to me, I've prepared game more than once for the table. I just need a sharp knife and a pair of kitchen scissors.'

She was only too happy to hand these over. 'Can you butcher it as well? Then it can go in the meat safe and should be all right until Molly gets here Monday morning to cook it.'

'I'll do my best. That sort of thing was generally done by Cook. I just skinned or plucked whatever we'd shot.'

Whilst he banged about in the scullery, she finished putting everything away. She paused for a few moments to look around the dining room, satisfied it was ready for breakfast tomorrow. On a Sunday the family sat down together and it was her job to cook whatever was available.

It would be a feast this time as someone had kindly given them slices of bacon and there were still half a dozen eggs to use up. Eggs, bacon, tomatoes, field mushrooms and fried bread – it would be a real treat preparing such a feast for Richard and the family.

He was at the gas cooker now, putting on the kettle. 'I'm desperate for a pot of coffee – I'm not sure if you drink that so I'm happy to make you cocoa or tea if that's what you prefer.'

'Richard, you don't have to make me anything. That's my job. You're a guest here – well – more a member of the family really.'

He looked at her directly. Her heart thudded and she wasn't

sure if it was a prickle of fear or anticipation that ran down her spine.

'I want to make you a hot drink. As far as I'm concerned you're as much part of this family as I am. You didn't answer my question. Do you like coffee?'

She swallowed nervously. 'To be honest, I've only ever had that horrible Camp liquid made with chicory and probably acorns as well. I do like the smell of coffee, but I've never had any myself.'

'Then coffee it shall be. I know we stuffed ourselves silly a few hours ago but I hardly ate anything for three days and seem to be permanently hungry now. Do you think Molly will mind if we raid the larder?'

She smiled. 'You make the coffee; I'll find you something to eat. You're the man of the hour, probably the year, so can do no wrong. If you even ate the last rasher of bacon I'm quite certain nobody would complain.'

'I wouldn't dream of doing anything so dastardly. I also hope this nonsense regarding my heroics is forgotten.'

'It soon will be but enjoy it whilst it lasts. It's the only reason I'm being pleasant to you.' This was obviously a joke but his expression changed. Suddenly he looked young, vulnerable, and without thinking she rushed forward and took his hands.

'I was joking, silly, don't look like that.'

His long, strong, tanned fingers closed over hers. She held her breath. If he kissed her she wouldn't stop him but she hoped he wouldn't. Things had changed in society, but not that much, and like chalk and cheese the two of them were too different to ever have a life together. She liked him a bit more now, found him attractive, but she'd be wise to avoid getting involved with him. He might think she was suitable but his mother would soon put him straight.

* * *

Richard desperately wanted to kiss the lovely young woman holding his hands but recognised the hesitation in her eyes. He hadn't realised he was so attracted to her until he lay semiconscious in his own bed in Hampstead. In the worst moments at Dunkirk she'd been in his thoughts, her lovely face keeping him focused on the awful job. He'd almost died, and that changed him. Life was fragile. He didn't want to wait to fall in love when Annie was right here.

He knew that she wouldn't resist if he did make a move, but he wasn't going to rush things. She had become someone special to him in his thoughts, but she didn't know this. In fact, he rather thought she didn't even like him all that much. He hoped one day they could be something special together. He'd changed, but had she?

Would she think that somehow she was inferior to him? She didn't sound like him, but she was intelligent and would soon lose her accent and fit in if they were together. There were obstacles to overcome but he was determined to try, to show her that they could be more than friends.

'I'm sorry, of course you were joking. Annie, I want to apologise for the way I behaved before. I shouldn't have flirted so outrageously. I treated you with disrespect. Can you forgive me?'

She still looked uncertain, as if she didn't quite understand what he was saying – more likely she didn't believe him and he didn't blame her.

'You don't have to apologise to me, I suppose I was flattered that you noticed me. I'm not blind, I know how handsome you are, I didn't mind you flirting with me, but I absolutely don't want to have any sort of fling with you or any other man. I'm about to volunteer to be a WAAF – I won't be here for more than a few more weeks anyway.' She nodded and he thought things were progressing, then she continued. 'I'm not the girl for you, I'd not fit into your world. I've been unhappily married once; I'm not going to risk that a second time.'

'I understand. I think you'll make an excellent WAAF. I wasn't suggesting anything untoward, wasn't suggesting anything really, I just wanted to apologise if I'd offended you.'

Finally, she smiled. 'Then everything's tickety-boo. I'd suggest that we be friends but obviously that's not possible. Whilst I'm working here as a domestic and nanny it wouldn't be right for someone like you. The Robys would disapprove.'

'Then we'll be casual acquaintances, share a few conversations over a cup of cocoa sometimes. I can't see anyone would disapprove of that.'

'It's late, Richard, I have to be up really early. I do the cooking on a Sunday.'

'What about church?'

'I reckon God can hear my prayers just as well at Harbour House as he can in a church. He'll understand why I can't go. Since the war started, the vicar stopped doing Evensong or I'd go to that.'

'That's a shame. I wasn't entirely convinced about religion but my time at Dunkirk has changed my mind. It could only be divine intervention that allowed us to rescue so many soldiers.'

'I agree. It says in the Bible that Jesus could calm the waters and I reckon that's what he did. Goodnight, God bless.'

Richard stood aside to allow her to go past and thought he'd made a complete hash of it. He'd wanted to tell her that it was thinking of her that had kept him going at Dunkirk, that he thought they might work well together, but instead had now agreed to be not even a real friend, just a 'casual acquaintance'.

It took him a long time to fall asleep despite being bone weary. His head was full of what ifs, regrets and he eventually drifted off, determined to demonstrate to Annie that his intentions were genuine, that in today's modern world it didn't matter that they came from such different backgrounds. He wasn't sure if they could be more than friends, but he wanted to try. Didn't want to die at sea, which was likely to happen if he was in the navy, without having someone of his own on shore.

* * *

Richard thought that being waited on by Annie wasn't going to help him persuade her to at least go out with him.

'I'm going to accompany you to church this morning, Jonathan, Elizabeth, if that's all right with you. I've a lot to be thankful for.'

George grinned. 'Will you sit with us, Mr Stoneleigh? Sammy and I would really like that.'

'Of course, if your parents have no objection.'

'The boys tend to fidget,' Elizabeth said with a fond smile at the two looking pleadingly in his direction. 'However, I'm sure your good influence will keep them stationary for once.'

Immediately after breakfast, the six of them set out, joining dozens of others in their Sunday best walking to the church. The bells were no longer rung – they were to be kept to warn if there was an invasion or when victory was announced – Richard thought the former unlikely and the latter wouldn't happen for years.

The boys were marching side by side ahead and Emily walked beside him.

'Is it always this busy?'

She shook her head. 'Like you, Mr Stoneleigh, everybody's

come to give thanks. I'm an agnostic, you know, so is my daddy and Dr Cousins and Mrs Cousins.'

'I was until a week ago. I'm still not 100 per cent sure, but it won't hurt to add my prayers of thanks to all the others being sent heavenwards today.'

'I think it's a shame Annie can't come – she's the only one in the house, apart from the boys, who truly believes there's a god taking care of all of us.'

'Does she always have to work on a Sunday morning?'

'Yes, Mrs Bates doesn't work on Sunday or Saturday afternoons.'

There was no time for further conversation as the church was only a couple of minutes from the house. Richard became aware that he was getting a lot of attention; families were nodding and smiling at him, the children were gawping as if he was something special.

Could he plead a sudden headache and retreat? Then the vicar was there, offering his hand, and he was obliged to take it.

'Welcome, Mr Stoneleigh, you honour our congregation today. I don't believe we've ever had a real live hero attend one of our services.'

Richard removed his hand. 'Thank you for your kind words, Vicar, but they are unwarranted, I assure you. I apologise, but I can't attend the service, it would be totally inappropriate. People are here to thank God, not me.'

He spoke to the boys. 'I'm sorry, lads, I just can't go in. I'm going home.' He then turned to Mrs Roby. 'I hope you understand, Elizabeth. This is a place of worship, my being in there will distract from the true purpose.'

His words were sincere and she nodded sympathetically. 'We understand, Richard, I didn't realise it would be quite as bad as this.'

He stepped aside and walked briskly down the path that ran along the side of the church and out through the gap between two houses which led him into East Street. He was back at Harbour House in minutes.

He went in through the back door as it was closest. 'Annie, I can take over whatever you're doing, you can go to church. I wasn't comfortable being hero worshipped so came home.'

She appeared in the kitchen door, a smudge of flour on her nose. 'Ta for the offer, Richard, but I'm also looking after baby Grace. But when you're out of your Sunday best you can give me a hand with the spuds if you like.'

Her smile was warm and for the first time he believed there might be a real connection between them. He reached out and rubbed the flour from her nose. An instinctive gesture. Her eyes widened and he thought he'd offended her.

'I always get it everywhere. Ta for that, Richard.'

'Always ready to help. I'll get changed and be back in a jiff.' He flew upstairs knowing, praying, that this small exchange had moved things on, that he could persuade Annie to go out with him.

6

Annie waited eagerly for Richard to return, surprised with herself that she'd had the cheek to give him orders and even more surprised that he'd followed them. Her mouth curved, having him offer to cook the Sunday lunch was unexpected and if Grace hadn't been in her pram in the garden watching the apple tree she might have taken him up on it.

She could see and hear the baby from the kitchen and Ginger was sitting on the small iron table watching the infant as if protecting her. The rabbit was in a lovely pie that just needed to go in the oven to cook the pastry. The spuds would go in at the same time to roast and there were carrots and a nice salad to go with it too.

Richard strolled in looking relaxed and dressed casually. No tie, sleeves rolled up, and the top two buttons on his shirt open.

'Sous-chef reporting for duty,' he said.

'What's one of those, then?'

'You're the chef, I'm your helper. Shall I peel these potatoes?'

'Do you know how to peel one? Posh blokes like you must have had a cook to do everything.'

'Actually, my mother encouraged me to spend time in the kitchen. She loves to cook, although, you're correct, we do have a cook who does most of it.'

She smiled. The first genuine smile she'd given him. When he was on his own, in his shirtsleeves, she could almost imagine he was a man she could go out with. 'Okay, then please peel those and cut them into bits. The water's ready on the stove. I've already salted it.'

He then did the carrots, whipped the cream for the strawberries that were for afters, and happily peeled and sliced the precious onion for the gravy.

The dining-room table was laid, everything ready to serve. The baby was fussing so she had to bring the pram in.

'Ta for helping, Richard, I'm impressed. I thought Mr Roby was the only man around here who's a dab hand in the kitchen.'

He followed her into the garden and whilst she soothed the baby he fetched the pram into the passageway for her. 'I'm going upstairs to change her. The family will be back soon. I saw someone going past the house a moment ago so people must have started walking back from church.'

'It smells delicious, Annie. I think I'll go for a walk and then eat with you in the kitchen if you don't mind. I don't like being waited on.'

She smiled. 'If you're going out then you'd better smarten up a bit. You'll give the old ladies a funny turn if they see a gentleman's bare arms.'

His laughter followed her up the stairs and she wished he wasn't interested in her. She wasn't sure she'd have the common sense to resist him as it could only end in tears – most likely hers, as a man like him would soon find somebody else.

By the time she'd changed Grace, the family had arrived

home. Mrs Roby came into the bedroom and Annie had heard Richard leaving to go for his walk a few minutes before.

'I'll just feed her; go ahead and get everybody seated for dinner, she doesn't take long.'

'Yes, Mrs Roby. Mr Stoneleigh said he'd eat later as he needed some fresh air.'

'He really isn't enjoying being the centre of attention. I've a feeling he'll move to Brightlingsea in order to get away from all the fuss.'

Annie hoped he wouldn't, she was beginning to enjoy his company. Then she frowned as she turned away. Maybe it would be for the best, nothing could ever come of it.

* * *

The children were upstairs doing their homework, the adults in the sitting room reading the Sunday paper and listening to the wireless, the baby was probably asleep. The dining room was done, the washing up waiting in the scullery.

Annie's stomach rumbled – she was going to eat and Richard would have to eat on his own when eventually he returned. She dished up his lunch, put a plate over the top and was about to put it into the oven when the back door banged and he came in.

'Excellent, I've timed it perfectly.'

'It's probably ruined by now and so's mine. I thought you'd fallen into the river.'

He grinned. 'No such luck, I was forced to hide behind bushes and houses to avoid being interrogated by passing pedestrians. I'm sorry if my being late has ruined your meal. That wasn't my intention.'

'Go on, sit down and stop blathering. We can just put extra gravy on it and then we'll not notice if it's a bit dry.'

She hadn't put out any cutlery but he didn't sit down and wait for her to find it, he went to the cutlery drawer and got out what was needed for both of them.

There'd been nothing to worry about as the pie, roast potatoes and vegetables were still lovely. The strawberries and cream finished it off just right.

'You're an excellent cook, Annie, what other talents do you have?'

'I'm a trained seamstress, a dab hand with kiddies, and even better with a mop and bucket. I'm not bad at ironing either.' As she was speaking, she collected the plates – there was nothing to scrape into the pig-swill bucket – and was about to take them into the scullery to join the others waiting to be washed and dried.

'Are you going to wash or dry?'

'Don't be daft, I'm doing both. It's not your place to do my work.'

'I insist.'

She looked at his face and knew that whatever she said he was determined to help. She just hoped none of the Robys wandered in and found him.

'Then you dry – it'll be quicker that way. Thank you. Once this is done I'm finished for the day. Mr Roby makes the family tea on a Sunday.'

'I suppose there's no point in asking you to spend the afternoon with me. I've got to go down to Brightlingsea and collect my motorbike – there's a train at three we could catch.'

Annie had intended to refuse but found herself nodding. 'I've never been on a motorbike – I've got a nice pair of slacks upstairs which will be perfect for riding on the back.'

His eyes flashed and his smile made her feel special. Just this once – then she'd post off her application to join the WAAF in the morning and remove herself from temptation.

* * *

Emily didn't have much homework to do and she'd already had permission to walk up to the farm when it was done. The door to the boys' room was open and they were playing with their soldiers on the carpet.

'I'm going up to the farm – why don't you come with me? It's far too nice to be lying about on the carpet.'

The little soldiers were back in the box in seconds and the boys were jumping up and down in excitement.

'We finished our homework ages ago. We didn't have much as we did most of it after school on Friday. Can we take a couple of apples for the bull?' George asked and Sammy nodded.

'We can't give good food to animals as it's against the law. Don't look so disappointed, boys, I'm sure there'll be something we can take him. I can't see there'd be any objection to feeding a bull vegetable peelings instead of giving them to the pigs.'

George screwed up his face – he always did this when he was thinking. 'I expect it's all right to feed the pigs because they feed us. But we don't eat that bull so I don't think the same rules would apply.'

Sammy shoved him. 'Spoilsport, who's going to know what we give him? We can take some vegetable peelings, can't we, Emily?'

'I think it would be better if we took a pair of scissors and cut him some lush grass from the other side of his hedge. Actually, I'm pretty sure he'd prefer fresh grass to vegetable peelings anyway.'

'Right, I've got scissors in my art box,' George said and was about to get them.

'No, it had better be the kitchen scissors. But we must make sure we bring them back and give them a good scrub before we hang them on the hook.'

The sitting room door was ajar and Emily poked her head around it. 'The boys and I are going for a walk to the farm. We'll be back in time for tea. We've all finished our homework.'

Before they could escape, Mummy was on her feet and pushing the pram towards them. 'In which case, children, you can take your baby sister with you. You know how much she loves going for a walk.'

'It'll be too bumpy going down Hamilton Road and up Anglesea Road, Mummy. It's also a very steep hill,' George said.

Daddy looked up from his paper. 'He's right, Elizabeth, let them go on their own. Why don't we take the pram for a walk?'

Mummy laughed. 'As long as the baby's in it then that sounds like a plan.'

* * *

The three of them were out of the front door before either of the adults could change their mind.

'That was a close call, good thing Daddy intervened,' George said. 'Sammy and I don't want to spend the afternoon with the pram.'

Emily giggled. 'Actually, I'm hoping that when our sister no longer needs it, we could make it into a go-kart. Imagine how fast it would go down Hamilton Road with all three of us in it.'

The thought of being able to make their own go-kart was the only topic of conversation all the way to the farm. Emily still looked after Mrs Peterson's three children occasionally, but now Mrs Peterson had more time to do things for herself since they had the three jolly land girls working there.

They went to the gate to the field in which the bull lived but they couldn't see him. 'Let's cut the grass before we call him. I don't think he'd be very pleased if he arrived and we've nothing to give him,' she told the boys and they agreed.

They'd brought a basket and as soon as it was packed full of fresh green grass they climbed onto the fence and the boys called the huge animal. There was an immediate response and seconds later he appeared in the gap between the bramble bushes at the bottom of the hill.

'Look, he's seen us. I do hope he decides to come,' Sammy said.

Emily waved the basket and that did the trick. He didn't charge, just trotted up to them, nodding his huge head as if he recognised them.

When he leaned against the gate it moved and Sammy fell off.

'Blooming heck, I wasn't expecting that,' Sammy said as he scrambled up, laughing.

'Our big friend here thought it very funny, and so did we,' George said solemnly.

When the grass had gone, the bull allowed them all to pat him a few times and then with a dramatic snort he tossed his head and trotted away, dragging the chain and big stone behind him.

'Golly, do you remember when we were chased by him? When he tossed the chain and stone over his shoulder so he could charge?' Emily said as she watched him go.

'We do, and to think he was only after our blackberries,' George said.

'Shall we walk across the fields and come back down the lane? It's too soon to go home,' Emily said.

'No, we want to get back to our soldiers,' George said. 'You made us put them away when we were halfway through our battle.'

Emily was about to protest that this was unfair but the boys had already run off. They were allowed to be out on their own. Since they'd transferred last year to the Colchester Royal Grammar School, they no longer mixed much with the local boys. They did join in football and cricket games occasionally when the down-streeters played the up-streeters – good players were always in demand.

She'd no friends her own age in Wivenhoe and since Nancy had moved to Colchester Emily was lonely. The boys had each other, so did her parents, the baby was too small to care about such things. She was the only one with nobody special to talk to.

'Hey, stranger, I hope you weren't going to walk past without calling in to say hello,' a familiar voice called from behind her. She looked round and saw Jimmy Peterson approaching on his bicycle. He was fourteen but looked older.

'I don't like to drop in without an invitation nowadays. I'm always happy to come if your mother invites me.'

He wheeled his bike up to her. She spoke without thinking. 'Goodness, I think you've grown since I last saw you.'

He chuckled. 'Probably, Mum says I'm growing like a weed. I'm not the only one. Your new hair's smashing. It really suits you.'

Emily flushed. 'Thank you, my parents were horrified, but they've got used to it now. It's so much easier than having hair down to your waist to deal with every day.'

'Not something we blokes have to worry about, thank God.'

They'd reached the entrance to the farm and she accompanied him. She hoped Mrs Peterson would be as pleased to see her as Jimmy was.

* * *

Richard didn't attempt to hold Annie's hand; in fact he made a point of not touching her at all. She was clearly nervous around him and he wasn't going to do anything to scare her away. He sat opposite her on the train which didn't seem contrived as this meant they both had window seats.

'Have you been to Brightlingsea before?'

She laughed. 'My husband Norm liked Brightlingsea and we went weekends when it was fine. I've not been since he died last summer so this is a real treat.'

Richard was shocked. He hadn't realised she was so recently widowed. A year wasn't long enough to get over such a loss. Small wonder she was shy with him.

'I'm sorry, I'd no idea you'd lost your husband such a short time ago.'

'No need to be sad, Richard.' She hesitated as if unsure whether to tell him.

'You don't have to say any more, Annie, we don't know each other that well, do we?'

'That's true, but if we're going to be good friends then I want you to know.'

'Okay, I'm listening.'

'I was fond of my husband, but to be honest it was a relief to be free. I only married him to have my own home.' She paused, frowned and again seemed reluctant to continue.

'Go on, please tell me. But I'll understand if you don't want to.'

'Not much more to say really. Norm said he'd found a nice little house for us, but after we got back from a weekend in Clacton I discovered he meant it was to move in with his parents. He knew I didn't get on with his mum, not well with his dad either, and he'd deliberately tricked me.'

'That's appalling. I'm not surprised you were pleased to be able to move away from your in-laws.'

'That's why I'm working and living at Harbour House. There just wasn't a room free after the evacuees and their mothers arrived here. I can't leave Wivenhoe because I'm waiting for the compensation for Norm's accident to come through from the council.'

'Why couldn't you have moved and then sent your new address to the council?'

'I didn't dare risk it, especially now, as things get lost in the post. If those two get their hands on the cheque they'll keep it. They deliver it by hand, to make sure it arrives, and as I'm just a street away the council have agreed to bring it to Harbour House.'

Richard was somewhat reassured by this explanation but being an intelligent chap he realised that as soon as the money came through this lovely girl would be leaving Wivenhoe. This didn't give him very long to persuade her that he was worth taking a punt on – especially after her less than successful first marriage.

Fortunately, the train had slowed to trundle over the wooden bridge across Alresford Creek and he was able to recover his composure before having to respond to her explanation. Until she'd mentioned her first marriage, he'd not understood that this was possibly more than he'd thought. He knew in that moment she was someone he could fall in love with.

He turned his face to the window to pretend that he was enthralled by the somewhat precarious progress of the train.

'I heard a funny story about this train, Annie, would you like to hear it?'

She sat back and nodded. 'Go on then, I'm all ears. It had better be a good story to make me miss the crossing.'

He grinned. He was pretty sure she'd love it. 'Businessmen travel on this train to London. A few months ago, when it was dark, the train slowed down to go over the bridge. Some silly fool thought they were at the station and opened the door and stepped out. He ended up falling through the bridge and up to his shoulders in the mud.'

'I don't believe you. If that had really happened everybody would have been talking about it. Did he drown?'

'No, you weren't listening, Mrs Thomas. I clearly said that he fell into the mud, so the tide was obviously out. Please pay attention to my fascinating tale.'

She sat up straight and was trying not to laugh. This was going even better than he'd dared hope. 'The train was blacked out, obviously, but the other passengers called out to him and shone their torches down. They couldn't reach him but the engine driver had a rope and between them they managed to haul him out. He was none the worse for his experience, apart from being covered in mud and having lost his precious briefcase.'

The train was now safely on the other side and rattling towards Brightlingsea station. The three other passengers in the compartment had been listening. The young woman with two well-behaved girls sitting beside her was laughing too.

'That's a true story! Mr Culley hasn't been to London since. He decided to retire.'

The children were giggling and one looked at the young

woman for permission to speak and she nodded. 'Go ahead, Sally, but don't ask anything silly.'

'Please, mister, are you the hero who my dad was talking about? You look just like what he said, with your red hair and all,' the older one asked.

Richard was about to deny it but Annie answered for him. 'Yes, he was at Dunkirk and rescued hundreds of men but he doesn't like to talk about it. Real heroes don't boast about what they've done, now, do they?'

The child nodded. 'No one likes a show-off, that's what my teacher says. Sorry to have asked you that, mister.'

'I can tell you a funny story about my adventure if you like.' They did like and he entertained them with the difficulty they'd had sending a bucket of tea down the line of towed rowing boats.

Annie listened and laughed along with the others. He was good with children, and she began to look at him a bit differently.

When they disembarked, the woman and her children hurried off, leaving him to escort Annie to Stone's shipyard, which was fully functioning despite the fact it was Sunday.

'My motorbike's tucked away behind some timber. It wouldn't be a good idea for you to come in with me, but it'll not take me long to collect it.'

He managed to retrieve the bike without being seen. The men working today wouldn't be wandering about and the navy chaps – the ones he was most worried about – must be in their office.

The main reason he didn't want to be waylaid wasn't because Annie was waiting for him but because he didn't want to hear the names of the men who'd accompanied him so bravely and lost their lives. Time enough for that when he returned to work tomorrow.

He heaved the bike off its stand but didn't kickstart it. Doing that would draw attention to himself and that he wanted to avoid at all costs. He wheeled the bike out into the road and Annie walked beside him. Few people knew it was in the yard as he hid it under a tarpaulin.

'Has it packed up? Are we going to have to walk all the way back to Wivenhoe?'

'Crikey, I hope not. I didn't want to start it in the yard, and you can guess why. I managed to collect it without being seen.'

He had a pilot's helmet and goggles – he dreaded to think where his father had found those – but had forgotten to bring anything for her to wear. Her hair was going to get pulled out of its neat arrangement by the wind and there was nothing he could do about it.

'I'll get it going now,' he said unnecessarily as he got astride the bike. It roared into life immediately. He wasn't going to wear the helmet and goggles as that wouldn't be fair. When he looked around, he saw that she'd obviously thought about what riding on the back of a motorbike would be like.

She'd got a headscarf tied tightly around her hair and put a pair of dark glasses on. 'You look like a film star, Annie, just the ticket.' He twisted and reached into one of the side panniers and removed his own headgear.

Going down the steep hill by the church was exciting but he kept his speed down, not wanting to frighten her and put her off agreeing to come out for another jaunt when they were next both free.

7

Annie clung on for dear life as Richard raced through Brightlingsea, down the steep hill, and up the other side. She wasn't scared, she was exhilarated and trusted him to get her home safely.

He turned down the Cut and rolled smoothly into the back yard of Harbour House. She didn't want to get off, for the excursion to be over.

'That was wonderful, Richard. You're a real expert on that bike.' She somehow scrambled off the back without embarrassing herself and he kicked the bike onto its stand and turned to face her.

'I'm not sure I should tell you this, Annie, but I'm an absolute novice on a motorbike. This is only the second time I've ridden it.' He was laughing and she thought he was joking.

'Go on, don't tease me.'

'Sorry, it's true. I'm relieved you felt safe, that's why I travelled so slowly.'

'Blimey! I thought we were tearing along. I'd not want to go any faster.'

'Then I promise that next time we go out for a ride I'll stay at the same speed.' He was smiling but his expression was watchful.

'If you take me to the pictures in Colchester then I'll come with you. But only as friends, nothing else.'

'Is there a film you particularly want to see?'

'Anything really, I've not been to the pictures many times. *The Wizard of Oz* sounds good, or a Charlie Chaplin film. I know that the Regal in Crouch Street or the Playhouse in Head Street have afternoon showings.'

'I'd love to escort you but I'm working most days and only get a few hours off a week. It's doubtful we'll be able to coordinate our time off.'

'Never mind then, better we don't go out, even as friends. As you know I'm hoping to join the WAAF in the summer so I'll be leaving Wivenhoe anyway.'

'Yes, I did know you were intending to do that. Women don't have to serve, so why would you want to leave a good job?'

She guessed he was referring to himself, not her job. 'Anyone can work as a domestic help, look after children, but I want to do something useful. I want to try for one of the technical trades, something that will use my brain.'

They were talking quietly outside the scullery but she thought someone could be listening. Emily had her bedroom just above them.

'Shall we go for a walk along the river? It's high tide soon and the barges will be coming up.'

He nodded. 'Good idea, we can continue our conversation and maybe tell each other a little more about ourselves.'

It couldn't do any harm to spend a bit more time with him as she was going to leave in a few weeks. She wasn't a silly girl likely to have her head turned by him, was she?

* * *

They were just coming out of the end of Alma Street when Annie's mother-in-law stepped out from the corner. Too late to turn back – Mrs Thomas senior spotted them.

And even though they weren't holding hands, just strolling along chatting, that was enough to set the horrible woman off.

'Well, well, what do we have here? My son will be turning in his grave to see his wife walking out already with another man.'

There was no point trying to explain that Mrs Thomas had got it wrong, as she never listened.

'Don't toss your head at me, you can't deny it. I always knew my Norm was too good for you. You couldn't even give us a grandbaby to love now he's gone.'

Annie intended to walk around the woman, ignore her, but Richard decided to get involved.

'Mrs Thomas has kindly agreed to accompany me to the river. She is worried I'm not well enough to be on my own.'

'Suppose you like being with a bloke what thinks he's a hero, that you're too good for us now.'

Annie could feel his tension, see that his hands were clenched. They were gathering a bit of a crowd who had come out to watch the fun.

He continued and for the first time she saw Mrs Thomas silenced.

'If I hadn't insisted and Mr Roby hadn't agreed, Mrs Thomas wouldn't have come. She's showing me kindness, ma'am. Something you seem to know nothing about.'

Those watching murmured their approval and her nemesis was defeated and stalked off clutching her basket to her chest and vanished into the house next to the church where Annie had been forced to live for almost four years.

Richard smiled down at her. 'What a particularly unpleasant woman. No wonder you were so pleased to move into Harbour House.' His smile made her feel a bit better. 'Shall we continue our walk, Mrs Thomas?'

'No, I'm going back. I'm sure you'll enjoy your walk a lot more without me tagging along.' Not allowing him time to disagree without making another scene, she headed back down Alma Street and was relieved to find sanctuary in her own room back at Harbour House. No one had seen her come in, so she could remain invisible in her attic room until tomorrow.

Annie didn't eat tea with the family, but came down later and got herself something when they'd finished. Perhaps the miserable old cow's interference was for the best as now she would make sure she didn't go anywhere with Richard again.

She settled down to read the book she'd borrowed from Emily; it was a children's book of fairy tales but she was enjoying it. From now on she would keep Mr Stoneleigh at a distance.

Until she received the compensation for Norm's untimely death, she needed to stay in Wivenhoe and not cause any further upsets. Her in-laws had every intention of taking her money and had insisted that it should come to them as she'd lived under their roof, and, according to them, had been totally dependent on them.

Annie wasn't going to give them any reason to appeal the council's decision by appearing to be courting another man a few months after she'd been widowed. She hadn't been beholden to them at all. Norm had paid for their board and lodging and she'd worked full time at the sewing factory. Half her wages had gone into the post office account towards getting their own place one day. The rest she'd given to her husband. So really, she'd been the one paying for their keep, not him.

Later that evening, before blackout, she took her filled-in application to join the WAAF to the post office and slipped it into the post box. The information leaflet had said that an applicant might have to wait several weeks before being called for an interview in London. Then, if deemed acceptable, it would be a further week or two until they actually got the warrant to travel to wherever they were going to be trained.

This, hopefully, would be enough time for the much longed-for cheque to arrive from the council. Three hundred and fifty pounds was a fortune, more than enough to put away for her future, whatever that might be.

She smiled as she curled up on the bed with her book again. She would go into Colchester on her afternoon off and open a bank account. There was almost £100 in her post office book, she'd get half that out to open an account. She'd get a decent bit of interest when there was eventually £400 to put somewhere safe.

She was startled to her feet by a knock on her door. She knew who it was. Only Richard would have the front to come up here and disturb her.

'I'm not decent. I can't open the door.'

'Then I'll talk to you from out here but I'd prefer to speak to you face to face.'

'I don't want to talk to you at all, Mr Stoneleigh. We can't be friends, that's obvious, and so it's better to go back to how things were.'

* * *

Richard hesitated for a moment, tempted to insist that she opened the door but then reconsidered. If she was in fact in her night clothes it would be unconscionable for him to be standing outside her bedroom door.

'If that's what you want, I accept your decision. Goodnight, Annie.'

It would have been more respectful to not to have used her first name but if things were to go back to the way they were, before they'd become slightly more than friends, she must remain as Annie. He didn't like the idea of calling her Mrs Thomas – the obnoxious woman he'd met earlier would forever be the only person in his mind to have that name.

The children were asleep as far as he knew and so were Jonathan and Elizabeth. He'd deliberately waited for the house to be quiet before venturing up to the attic. He fiddled with his wireless until he found the evening concert and then stretched out on his bed and closed his eyes.

He enjoyed his job, was bloody good at it, but after his experiences in Dunkirk he no longer felt he was doing as much as he could to help Britain win the war. There was nothing to keep him in Wivenhoe now that Annie had made it abundantly clear she didn't feel the same way about him as he did about her.

Living under the same roof as a young woman he'd fallen in love with wouldn't be good for either of them. No – better to remove himself from the situation and become a naval officer rather than an Admiralty surveyor.

Probably a sensible decision as he could just imagine his parents' reaction if he told them that he'd fallen for Annie. She was intelligent, kind and tough which were all qualities they'd admire. She was also beautiful, which would help. However, the fact that she was uneducated, worked as a domestic help and had been married before would outweigh her advantages in their eyes.

He was fond of his parents and wouldn't deliberately

displease them if he could avoid it. If Annie had shown the slightest interest in him then he'd have ignored their disapproval, but it was clear now that his feelings weren't reciprocated.

He wasn't quite sure if he'd be allowed to transfer from his present employment to become a serving naval officer. He'd heard the fishermen and bargemen talking disparagingly about the quality of the naval officers working at Brightlingsea. If they were to be believed then the majority of them had little or no experience of the sea and were learning on the job, so to speak.

He yawned loudly. He was torn, not sure whether he'd be doing his duty by becoming a naval officer or by remaining where he was. This wasn't something he could discuss with Jonathan as obviously his opinion would be heavily biased.

If he got an afternoon free then he'd go to Admiralty House and speak to somebody there before he rocked any boats in Wivenhoe.

* * *

Returning to Brightlingsea was difficult for Richard as he knew that some of the men who'd died under his command were locals and folk would be grieving their loss. The village had only just recovered from the loss of the Thames barge, the *Lady Beth*, and two of the crew – the captain and the boy – and now had to deal with this.

Almost certainly there'd been husbands, brothers, fathers and sons from here who'd been lost at Dunkirk or who were now POWs somewhere in Germany. It was a depressing thought to think that things could only get worse. Invasion was a definite possibility, but first Hitler would have to destroy both the navy and the RAF. Richard had every confidence that this wouldn't happen.

To his surprise, nobody was talking about Dunkirk. There were certainly no glum faces, the men working at Stone's shipyard were as cheerful as ever and working just as hard.

It didn't get dark until ten o'clock so the shipyard continued working until then. This meant that when he eventually arrived in Wivenhoe the time was after eleven and he'd just the moon to help him see. He'd stayed late so that he could take the following day off. The house was dark as everyone was asleep. He'd worked for fourteen hours today and was exhausted.

Molly had left him a ham salad and a bowl of strawberries in the pantry on the slate shelf but he was almost too tired to eat them. As he'd had nothing since breakfast he pulled out a chair and sat alone at the kitchen table. After taking his used crockery and cutlery into the scullery, he checked that he'd locked the back door.

He was halfway up the stairs when he froze. The hair on the back of his neck stood to attention. There was someone in the dining room. He'd definitely heard a sound coming from there.

He was in his socks so moving quietly wasn't a problem. He was a big man and more than able to confront whoever had come in to rob the place.

He was at the bottom step, one hand resting on the newel post, when there was a second noise from behind. The huge cat stalked past him and he reached down and stroked his head. He didn't purr, which was odd.

Richard erupted into the dining room, flicking the light on as he did so. A tall, scruffy boy was cowering in the corner.

'Keep that bleeding cat away from me, mister, it near killed me last time.'

The cat had followed and was now growling like a dog. A

terrifying noise. Before he could stop Ginger, the animal launched himself at the boy and was biting and scratching his legs. The intruder was yelling and swearing, fighting a losing battle to dislodge it.

Richard didn't hesitate. He snatched up the chenille cloth from the table, sending the vase of flowers crashing to the floor. He flung it over the hissing, snarling cat. It took all his strength to remove Ginger. With it struggling in his arms, he backed out and threw it, still enveloped in the cloth, into the sitting room and slammed the door.

'What the bloody hell's going on down here?' Jonathan said as he arrived in bare feet and pyjamas, his usually immaculate hair standing on end.

'I found a boy in the dining room and your cat attacked him. You don't need a bloody guard dog with that cat here to protect your property. I didn't know a cat could behave like that.'

'Daddy, why's Ginger yowling and throwing himself at the sitting room door?' Emily said from the landing. She was peering nervously from the top of the stairs.

'Nothing for you to worry about, go back to bed, sweetheart, Richard and I will deal with it.'

* * *

Emily knew who it was hiding in the dining room. She'd recognised the yelling. It was Pete – Sam's brother – the one who'd tried to strangle her last year when Ginger had saved her. Her wonderful cat must have sensed the boy was in the house and rushed down to protect her.

She retreated to her bedroom, not to go back to bed, but to dress quickly. She put her ear against the boys' room when she came out, relieved that they were quiet. Both of them slept like logs, thank goodness. She didn't want Sammy to know his brother was here. The only reason Pete had come must have been to see Sammy and persuade him to go back to London.

Shouldn't the boy still be in detention? Was she wrong? Had he escaped and come to seek revenge on her and his appearance was nothing to do with Sammy?

There was no sound from Mummy or Grace either so she could creep downstairs and collect her cat without her daddy or Mr Stoneleigh knowing.

She waited until she could hear the two men dealing with Pete's injuries.

'I never came to steal nothing, mister, I wanted to speak to me brother. I was let out early and came back with Reggie and thought I'd give it a go.' Now her suspicions were confirmed. That was definitely Pete speaking. She wasn't scared of him now she had Ginger to keep her safe.

The cat was still creating a terrible noise in the sitting room and if she didn't stop it the rest of the house would be up. If Sammy knew his big brother was here he might want to leave them. She wasn't going to let that happen.

She didn't stop to speak soothingly to the cat before opening the door in case her father heard her. She'd intended to slip in without him escaping but completely misjudged the situation.

The door was only open a few inches when a ginger ball of fury shot between her legs and straight back into the dining room. Now she'd made things worse and she'd only been trying to help.

Daddy was swearing – really rude words – and Mr Stoneleigh wasn't much better. She could hear Pete swearing too and wished she'd minded her own business.

A very cross voice from the landing called her name. 'Emily, go back to your room immediately. I can assure you there will be serious repercussions for your interference tonight,' Mummy said.

Emily fled past her and bolted into her bedroom, closing the door firmly behind her. She'd promised to behave herself after the haircutting incident and now she'd let herself and her parents down a second time.

If Ginger had seriously hurt Pete, or even worse Mr Stoneleigh or Daddy, would they want to get rid of him? Ban him from her bedroom? Her eyes prickled but she blinked the tears away; only little girls cried, and she wasn't one of those.

She didn't know whether she should get back into her night things or remain dressed. Would Daddy want to reprimand her tonight or would he leave it until tomorrow? Mummy had sounded so angry. She swallowed the lump in her throat. She really didn't like upsetting her parents and especially not her mother.

She was dithering at the door when she heard the distinctive wail of the baby. It didn't matter if she was disobeying, she wouldn't leave her little sister to cry. She walked into her parents' room and hurried across to the crib.

'Now, now, little one, no need to cry. Emily's here to look after you.'

She scooped the screaming baby up and sat in the special chair Mummy used to feed Grace. Then she rested the baby over her shoulder and rubbed her back. 'It's all right. Mummy will be back soon.'

After a few minutes, Grace stopped crying and relaxed. Emily never walked about holding her little sister, Mummy didn't like her to. This wasn't really fair as Emily knew she was old enough to carry Grace without dropping her.

After a few more minutes, Grace was sound asleep. Slowly Emily stood up and gently put her back in the crib.

She waited for a minute or two more to be sure she was settled and then crept out. As she was opening her own door, her mother came up the stairs and saw her.

'I told you to remain in your room. How dare you disobey me?'

Emily tried to explain but Mummy shook her head. 'No, I'll hear no excuses. I'm bitterly disappointed, Emily. Go to bed immediately. Your father will be speaking to you tomorrow.'

Things might have been smoothed over if Emily had remained silent. Mummy never listened to her. It wasn't fair. Anger made her say the most dreadful things.

'I'm disappointed in *you*, Mummy. You didn't even ask why I was out here. I don't care what Daddy says, I don't care what you say. Goodnight.'

She didn't wait to see Mummy's reaction but stepped into her bedroom and hastily grabbed the wooden chair and shoved the back under the door handle. She was shaking and thought she was going to be sick. With a groan, she collapsed onto the rug and this time gave in to her tears.

No one tried to come in and eventually she crawled into bed fully clothed and fell asleep. She'd never spoken to anyone so rudely, and didn't know why she'd done it tonight. Her last thought as she fell asleep was that her parents would most likely decide to pack her off to boarding school and it would serve her right.

She woke up later when it was still dark with tummy ache and had to get up again and find her horrible ST belt and a pad. Having her monthlies just made her feel even more miserable.

8

Annie had heard the commotion last night but stayed in her room as it was nothing to do with her. She'd listened at the door in case anyone wanted her and had heard the baby crying before Emily went in to the infant. She wasn't exactly sure what had happened but knew the cat was involved and that somebody had been found in the dining room.

She was still awake when she heard the angry exchange between Mrs Roby and her daughter. Emily shouldn't have been so rude, but Mrs Roby had blamed the girl when she should have been praising her.

None of her business, but after listening to Emily sobbing for hours, she decided she'd explain to Mrs Roby what had actually happened.

* * *

Annie liked to be in the kitchen before Molly although she didn't have to be on duty until seven o'clock, which was when the children got up so they could be ready to catch the train to

Colchester just after eight o'clock. Her first job was to riddle the range and put the kettle on.

The house seemed the same as usual, no sign of any disturbance or damage by whoever had got into the house. She was washing up the few things left in the sink when Richard walked in. He was obviously on his way out to his motorbike.

'Annie, I expect you heard the racket last night. The evacuee who caused all the problems last year came in hoping to see his brother. The back door was open so he didn't actually break in and he didn't steal anything or do any damage.'

'Where's he gone? Surely Mr Roby didn't turn him out in the dark?'

'The boy didn't want to stay, apologised, and said he wanted to be far away before the cat came back and finished him off.'

This last comment got her attention and she turned to face him. 'What do you mean?'

He grinned. 'Ginger doesn't like him. In fact, that's the understatement of the year – the cat went for him like a guard dog when he saw him in the dining room. He scratched the boy's legs but not too badly. Emily let the cat out of the sitting room and it tried to attack the boy again. Jonathan had bare feet when the cat came back to finish the job so got the worst of it.'

Only then did she notice the scratches on his hands. 'I hope you put disinfectant on those. Cats' claws can cause nasty infections.'

'Well doused, don't worry. I just wondered if you'd give Molly a message for me. There's no need to leave out any supper – I'm going to stay in Brightlingsea. Doesn't make any sense to come home to sleep when I can find decent digs there.'

'Does that mean you're going to move out when you find something permanent?'

'I think that would be for the best, don't you? I know you

don't reciprocate my feelings, and I don't want to make you feel uncomfortable.'

She froze. Feelings? They hadn't talked about them, until he'd said he had them for her she'd not realised. It was as if she was seeing him clearly for the first time. He was special to her too.

Her legs moved without her permission and she was in his arms. For the first time in her life she felt safe, loved, wanted. His heart was pounding. She tilted her head and his eyes blazed then everything changed between them.

She didn't know that a kiss could be like this. She leaned into him, her fingers dug into the curls at the back of his neck, and she pressed closer.

'Good God – what next?' Mr Roby said from behind them – he didn't sound too pleased either.

Instinctively she tried to pull away but Richard kept his arms around her. His smile melted the last of her reservations about him.

'Go away, Jonathan, you're *de trop*.'

Mr Roby laughed. 'I'll leave you to it then. God knows what Elizabeth's going to say about this development.'

She heard him backing out of the scullery. Then he spoke again.

'I don't suppose you'd make me a bit of toast and a cup of tea, Annie? I know you don't start work for another fifteen minutes but I've got to leave for work. Don't keep Richard here too long as he's supposed to be in Brightlingsea by half past seven.'

'What's does *de trop* mean?'

Richard kissed her again before answering. 'It means unnecessary, unwanted and in the way. He's right, I need to get off. I'll see you when I get home – I'm not going anywhere now.'

He kissed her again. 'I've got to rip down to Brightlingsea to get some papers signed, but then I have the day off so will be back in an hour.'

Then he was gone and seconds later the roar of his motorbike woke the street. Annie smiled. Everything was happening so fast, maybe too fast? How could things have changed so suddenly between them? Was one kiss enough?

She needed a cup of tea; everything would be clearer after that. Whilst she was busy with that she tried to make sense of what they'd done, what had been said. With a mug clutched in her hand she leaned against the table, trying to organise her thoughts.

Annie considered herself a sensible sort of woman, not given to making rash, impulsive decisions and here she was thinking she and Richard were in love after one kiss.

As she sipped, she understood that the strange bubbling feeling inside was new to her, it was happiness.

She'd never been happy. It didn't matter if things didn't work out, she was going to enjoy this novel sensation for as long as it lasted. It didn't matter what anybody thought, she and Richard could make it work. She hadn't understood that she had feelings for him until he'd said he was moving away.

The kettle was gently hissing and she hastily made a second pot of tea. It didn't take long to toast a couple of slices of bread under the fancy grill on the gas cooker. Mr Roby would be quite happy to eat his breakfast in the kitchen but today she put it on a tray and took it through to him in the sitting room.

He nodded his thanks but didn't look up from his briefcase where he was riffling through some papers.

'Excuse me, Mr Roby, I need to tell you something and it's nothing to do with Richard.'

He looked up. 'Go ahead, I'm listening.'

'It's about last night. Emily went in to see to the baby, who was screaming, and that's why she was out of her room. I just thought you needed to know.'

'I guessed that was the case. I suppose you heard all of it?'

'I did, and she shouldn't have spoken to Mrs Roby like that.'

'No, the whole thing is a damnable mess and I don't have time to sort it out this morning.' He smiled sadly. 'I tried her door but she'd jammed a chair under it and I couldn't get in.'

'She was sobbing for an hour last night.' She heard the children coming downstairs. 'I've got to make their breakfast, Mr Roby.'

* * *

Emily was quiet, pale, ate nothing but she did drink her tea. The boys, who'd slept through the kerfuffle, looked at their sister anxiously a couple of times but didn't ask what was wrong.

The three of them politely thanked Annie for their breakfast, put on their outdoor shoes, collected their satchels and gas masks and left the house. Annie wondered if Emily would tell her brothers what had happened and how Sammy would react if he knew that his big brother had been in the house.

* * *

Richard arrived at the shipyard without knowing how he'd got there. The ride had been a blur as his head had been whirling with possibilities and happiness. There were going to be obstacles, his parents wouldn't be happy, but he didn't care. He loved Annie and she loved him and that was all that mattered.

It took an annoying amount of time to get the papers signed that hadn't been ready last night and he told the foreman he was leaving and would be back at seven thirty the next morning. He sprinted to his bike and was out of the yard moments later.

With complete disregard for his own safety and that of other road users, he sped back to Harbour House. He strode into the house but instead of being greeted with delight he found Annie in tears. He embraced her and she leaned into him.

'What's wrong? What happened? Why are you upset?'

'It's Emily, she's disappeared. She didn't go to school. They just rang and nobody knows where she is.'

'Doesn't she take next door's little girl to school?'

'Claire's not well so Emily didn't have to do that today. The boys walk to school on their own once they get off the train but it's a different way to her.' Annie sniffed. 'I think she might have run away. She had a dreadful row with Mrs Roby last night and she's a very sensitive girl.'

'She's also highly intelligent – I don't think she'd do anything so stupid. Where the hell would she go anyway? I've a nasty suspicion it's something to do with that boy who was here last night.' Richard hugged her and stepped away. 'I'm going to speak to Elizabeth – I take it Jonathan knows.'

'Yes, he's in the sitting room right now.'

The sitting room door was open and the Robys both looked distraught. Elizabeth's eyes were red rimmed and she was clutching a handkerchief.

'I'm so sorry about Emily. What did the boys say?'

Jonathan answered. 'I rang their school but no one answered the telephone. I'm going to try again now.'

Richard heard him speaking to someone and then he came

back looking even more worried. 'The boys didn't turn up either.'

'I knew it. It's something to do with that boy who was here last night. Emily hasn't run away; he's involved somehow.'

'Can we ring the police, Jonathan?'

'I did that from the office but they weren't particularly helpful. They think she's run away because of the argument we had and will come home on her own eventually. I agree with you, Richard, it's something to do with Pete – I don't believe in coincidences, do you?'

'I don't,' Richard said. 'Might one explanation be that this Pete persuaded his little brother to go back to London with him and George found Emily and they've both gone after the other two?'

'Sounds far-fetched, but it could be right. We need to go into Colchester. I checked and they all got on the train as usual. If we go door to door in Queen Street we might find a shopkeeper or pedestrian who saw something.'

'Fortuitous I'm here as we have my motorbike and can get around the town easily. I'm going to change; I'll be ready to leave in a few minutes.'

The telephone jangled in the hall. He hesitated. It rang twice which meant it was for them. Richard snatched up the receiver. 'Harbour House, Stoneleigh speaking.'

'Mr Stoneleigh, it's Nancy Brooks, I've just given Emily and George money to catch the train to London. Pete and Reggie persuaded Sammy to go back with them and they've gone after him. I'm sorry, I did try to stop them but they were determined.'

Nancy disconnected, leaving him appalled but not surprised by her news.

Elizabeth was standing beside him. 'Was that Emily? Where is she, why hasn't she come home?'

'No, it was Mrs Brooks. She gave them enough money to go to London on the train. Emily and George are fine, but we were right, Pete persuaded Sammy to go back to London with him and they've gone after him.'

Annie was hovering further down the passageway, listening to the exchange. He held out his arms and she ran into them. He hated to see her so distraught.

'Annie, darling, Emily's perfectly well and she's with George.'

Elizabeth spoke from behind them – they'd both forgotten that she didn't know about his new relationship with Annie.

'How could Emily think this was a sensible thing to do? Why didn't she contact us immediately and not try to sort things out on her own?' She nodded at the two of them. 'I rather thought you two might make a go of it. But you cannot share a bed under this roof – I hope you understand that.'

* * *

Emily regretted not eating any toast as her stomach was rumbling and it was a long time until lunch. She had gym today and hadn't got a letter to be excused. Whatever the games mistress said, Emily wouldn't be doing gym. She'd have to face the music when she got home but until then she was going to pretend nothing had happened last night.

She was halfway up Queen Street when she heard George calling her. Sammy wasn't with him. Her stomach lurched. She ran towards him.

He was crying. 'That Pete, and Dan's horrible brother suddenly came up to us and persuaded Sammy to go with them. They told him that his mum's dying and wants to see him one last time. He didn't want to go but they said he had to.'

'That's dreadful. Poor Sammy, I'm sure he doesn't really want to leave us. We have to go after them but I don't have any money. If we go to Nancy, I'm sure she'll help us.'

'We can't play truant; I'll get the cane.' He scowled at her. 'Sammy wanted to go. He didn't have to leave us.'

'If you aren't worried then why did you risk being beaten to come and find me?'

She gave him a shake. 'Listen to me, George. By the time we've told the adults it'll be too late. We'll be heroes when we save our brother. Pete was in the house last night and if Ginger hadn't found him I expect he'd have tried to take Sammy then.'

'Why do we need money?'

'For the train fare, silly. I expect those boys will already be at the station by the time we get there.'

They ran towards Head Street where Nancy lived. The back gate was unlocked and Boyd greeted them with enthusiasm. Emily left her brother fussing the huge dog and rushed in to speak to Nancy.

Quickly she explained why they were there and what they needed.

'I'm not sure this is the right thing to do, love, but I'll give you a pound in change. I'm going to telephone Harbour House and let them know where you both are though. You do realise that your schools will have contacted them to find out why you didn't turn up this morning?'

'We do, we're in the most dreadful trouble but finding Sammy and bringing him home's more important than that. We don't know where he lives. Once they get off at Liverpool Street station he'll be lost forever.'

They were lucky and caught a bus from just outside that took them directly to the station. Emily glanced down at her uniform. She wasn't quite as conspicuous as her brother in his royal purple blazer, but they were still recognisable. She wasn't sure if that was a good thing or not.

'When we find them, Emily, how are we going to get Sammy to come with us?'

'I'm sure he doesn't really want to go, he's very happy with us. We just have to convince him that Pete has lied about their mother.'

They ran up the slope to the ticket office on the upside of the station. Nobody was taking any notice and she realised people probably just thought they were on their way to school and late for some reason.

'What about asking to speak to the stationmaster? I bet he's going to take our word over Pete's,' George said as he tugged at her sleeve.

'That's an excellent plan, well done. That's exactly what we'll do.'

The station was busy, not with businessmen as they'd already have gone to work on the earlier trains, but with housewives and smart ladies going up to London to shop. Not that there was much in the shops nowadays but she'd heard her parents say that if you had enough money you could buy anything at something called the black market. Maybe this market was in London and that's why everybody was going there.

She went to the guard clipping the tickets as people went onto the platform. 'Excuse me, sir, we're looking for our foster brother. His actual brother who is just out of detention is trying to take him back to London.'

She'd spoken loudly and clearly so that all those standing nearby could hear and was satisfied by the general chorus of shock and support that was coming in their direction.

'Would the boy you're looking for be dressed the same as

you, young man?' a smart woman in a mink coat asked George, who nodded vigorously. 'In that case, I think he's on the platform as I just saw a flash of purple a few moments ago.'

The guard blew his whistle – Emily wasn't quite sure why but it certainly drew everybody's attention. Two guards appeared from somewhere.

'There's a boy being kidnapped by two ruffians. They've got onto the platform without tickets.'

'He's wearing the same uniform as my brother here,' Emily said helpfully. 'The other two are poorly dressed and can be violent.'

'You two wait here. We'll get hold of him for you and arrest the other two,' one of the new guards said.

The ticket inspector gestured that they stand to one side so he could deal with the people queueing up behind them. Emily would much rather be on the platform but didn't want to create a scene.

'What if Sammy says he doesn't want to come?' George asked.

'They'll bring him anyway as he hasn't got a ticket. Once he's back here we can talk to him. I think if I say that we think that Pete's lying, but even if he isn't Daddy will make arrangements for him to visit his mother safely, he'll agree to come home with us.'

'I don't want him to go, Emily, he's my brother now and I know that he wants to be adopted so he can stay with us forever.'

There was the sound of shouting on the platform and ignoring the instruction to remain where they were Emily and George dashed past the ticket collector. They weren't called back which was a relief.

At the far end of the platform, where the guard's van would be when a train stopped, she saw the two guards holding onto Pete and the other boy. There was no sign of Sammy.

'Quickly, we've got to find him or he might run away thinking he's in trouble,' Emily said.

With her satchel and gas mask bouncing painfully in the small of her back, she raced towards the altercation. Sammy couldn't be far away and must be hiding.

'I can't go in the gentleman's WC, you go and check, George, he might be in there.'

Her brother ran in whilst she hovered nervously outside, getting several funny looks from the men who wanted to use the facility themselves. Then she smiled. George emerged with his arm around Sammy, who was crying bitterly. There was no sign of his satchel or his gas mask.

'Are you all right? We've got you now, we'll take you home.' She hugged him and he cried even harder.

'I didn't want to go, I didn't really believe him, but, but...'

'Never mind, we've got you safe now. Come on, we'd better get off the platform as we don't even have platform tickets, let alone a ticket to catch a train.'

The stationmaster was waiting for them. 'I've just had a telephone call from Colchester police station. You're to wait with me in my office. Those two villains will be back in detention by tonight.'

'Thank you, sir, that's very kind of you,' Emily said.

They were escorted to a big room, told to sit on the wooden bench against the wall, and then left to their own devices.

'What happened to your satchel and your gas mask, Sammy?' Emily asked.

'They took them. They said they'd sell them for a bob or

two. That's when I knew I'd made a dreadful mistake agreeing to go with them.'

She hugged him and he sniffed against her shoulder. That Pete was an evil boy; whatever happened to him served him right.

9

Annie kept smiling when she knew she should be looking serious because of what was going on with the children. Richard had roared off to Colchester station with Mr Roby on the back of his motorbike – she prayed they would get there before those horrible boys from the East End managed to drag poor Sammy onto the train.

Mrs Roby had taken the baby next door in the pram so Annie didn't feel guilty being happy as nobody could see her smiling. She still couldn't believe that despite all the reasons why she and Richard shouldn't be in love, they were. When she'd spoken to Mrs Stoneleigh on the telephone she'd been horrible. His parents wouldn't be happy that their son had fallen in love and would most likely mind that his chosen partner wasn't one of them.

She had a moment's worry when she realised she'd sent off her application to join the WAAF but until she'd been accepted and signed the necessary papers she was free to change her mind. She thought at the moment that in any of the armed services, because a woman was a volunteer, even those that were already trained and working could leave if they wanted to.

Anyway, nothing was settled, and she could still join up if she wanted to. Even married women would have to do war work soon, unless they were expecting or had small children. She and Richard weren't anywhere near that point in their new relationship so no chance of her being excused war work. No, becoming a WAAF was still a good option.

Molly was busy in the kitchen preparing lunch without actually knowing if anyone was going to be there to eat it. Annie heard the grandfather clock in the passageway downstairs strike eleven. It wasn't even lunchtime; that didn't seem possible when so much had happened today.

The telephone rang again and she ran to answer it – Molly refused to do it even if she was there.

'Good morning, Harbour House, how can I help you?'

'Annie, is my wife not there?' Mr Roby said.

'No, sir, she's gone over to see Mrs Cousins with the baby. I'm sure you could speak to her there. Have you found the children?'

'Yes, thank God. Emily and George got the station staff involved and Pete and his friend have been arrested. I'm just about to get on the train to Wivenhoe with the three of them. Richard's on his way back on his motorbike.'

'That's the best possible news. I'll tell Molly there'll be six for lunch.'

He disconnected without answering and she hastily replaced the receiver in the cradle. She headed back to the kitchen to give Molly the good news. She also thought it might be sensible to tell the housekeeper about her and Richard.

'Everything's tickety-boo, Molly, all three children are about to get on a train for Wivenhoe and Richard's on his way on his bike.' She deliberately used his first name, hoping this would make it easier to explain that things had changed.

'I thought the children would go back to school for the afternoon, but Mr Roby knows best.'

Molly hadn't noticed Annie's use of Richard's name or if she had wasn't going to say anything.

'Richard and I are walking out, Molly, I hope that's not going to make things awkward here for either of us.'

'Bless you, it's none of my business. I learned my lesson interfering between my Nancy and her Dan. I don't reckon you want to let your in-laws know, though – they'll have plenty to say about it.'

'I don't care, they're nothing to do with me now. I know my husband only died last summer but we weren't close, hadn't been sleeping in the same bed so, as far as I'm concerned, I think that we were separated for a year before he died.'

'People can be a bit sticky about things like that, Annie, especially with your new young man being who he is. He's not one of us, is he?'

Annie didn't answer – there was no point in doing so as what Molly said was true. Maybe it would be better for her and Richard if she did actually join up and then nobody would know their business.

She'd just put away her cleaning things, removed her apron and put a smudge of lipstick on when Richard arrived. She didn't wait for him to come in but met him in the garden.

'I've told Molly about us. I don't have a family to tell but I suppose you're going to have to tell your parents. Do you think they're going to be upset?'

'I don't care what they say. I've made my choice and they'll just have to accept it.'

'Anyway, we've only been going out together for a few hours.

I don't suppose you need to tell them anything for quite a while.'

'You're right, we're worrying unnecessarily. Something has occurred to me though about our situation, my darling. I don't suppose the Robys will be very pleased.'

'I've been thinking about exactly that. I've sent in my application to join the WAAF and think it might be better if I do join up.'

'Absolutely not – you could be posted anywhere in the country and we'd never see each other. There must be a better way to arrange things.'

Annie blushed. 'Mrs Roby made it quite clear we can't sleep together – not that I intended to do that anyway. If I'm not going to join up then perhaps I'll go back to working at the sewing factory and try and find a room somewhere in Wivenhoe. That is if you think it will be awkward me being here when we're going out together.'

He frowned. 'That's not going to happen either. I can think of one solution. Why don't we get married, then we can share my room and you won't have to work at all.'

'I already told you I'm not sleeping with you. That's not why I think I should leave.'

If he'd got down on one knee, said that he loved her, then maybe she'd have answered differently. But he sounded so matter of fact, offering to marry her to solve a problem, not because he really wanted to. She wasn't even sure that he meant it.

'No, Richard, getting married would only add to our problems. We don't know each other well enough to even consider it.'

He didn't have the opportunity to answer as Molly banged on the window. Annie stepped around him and rushed in. Probably a good idea to let him digest what she'd said and this evening, when the children were in bed, they could sit down and have a sensible discussion. Hopefully one or other of them would have come up with a solution to this problem. Normally she'd have the afternoon free but as the children were at home she thought that might not be the case today.

* * *

Now the excitement was over and they were travelling back to Harbour House on the train, Emily began to feel queasy. Not only did she have to face the repercussions from her dreadful outburst last night, she'd also played truant and not told her parents anything. George had also skipped school, but he wouldn't be in trouble for that. She was pretty sure her parents would make sure neither of them were punished for rescuing Sammy.

'Daddy, did the police get Sammy's gas mask and satchel back from Pete?' George asked.

'They did, son, and we'll have them both eventually. They're evidence that those boys not only coerced Sammy into going with them but also stole from him.'

'I'm sorry, Uncle Jonathan, I should have refused to go but they took me by surprise,' Sammy said.

'Well, your siblings came to the rescue and saved the day,' Daddy said. 'If Emily and George hadn't gone straight to the station it could have been catastrophic.'

She closed her eyes and let their words flow over her head. At least the boys weren't in any trouble. But her horrid rudeness last night wouldn't be so easily forgotten. Her tummy hurt and it served her right.

The train arrived at Wivenhoe too quickly. Before she could

stop them, the boys vanished over the footbridge, leaving her alone with Daddy. To her surprise he put his arm round her shoulder and hugged her.

'Sweetheart, are you feeling poorly? You're very pale.'

She nodded. 'I've got my monthlies and I never feel well then.' She paused and decided to mention last night. 'It's no excuse for what I said to Mummy. I just don't understand where those awful words came from. Will Mummy ever forgive me?'

'After rescuing Sammy, what happened last night will soon be forgotten. Do I have your word you won't speak to your mother like that again?'

Instead of promising, Emily broke down. He gathered her close and bent to pick her up. 'Come on, little one, I'll carry you home. Please don't cry, I can't bear it.'

She shook her head. 'No, I'll walk,' she managed to gulp. 'I can't promise not to say dreadful things as I didn't know I was going to say them. I think I'm a horrible person inside.'

Daddy said one of the very bad words she'd heard him use last night. This dried her tears and she stared at him.

'Darling Emily, I'm sorry, I shouldn't have said that. Don't look at me like that. I love you; it doesn't matter what you say or do, I'll always love you. You're the kindest, best daughter a man could have.'

She forced a smile. 'I do try to be.'

'You will feel a lot better when you've had some lunch. I'm quite sure you haven't eaten anything since last night.'

'I'm not hungry, Daddy. I'll go straight to bed if you don't mind. I'm sure I'll feel better in the morning.'

He didn't answer immediately but then squeezed her shoulder. 'Yes, you do that. Probably the best thing in the circumstances.'

They hurried down Station Road and all she could think

was that he'd said he'd always love her whatever she did, but he'd not said that her mummy would. That was why he'd just agreed to her creeping off to her room – it would give her mother another day to stop being cross with her. This reinforced the idea that things would never be the same between her and Mummy.

She flew past him when they reached the gate, burst into the house and ran straight upstairs. She'd never undressed so quickly in her life and was under the covers before anybody could come and look for her. She'd pretend to be asleep and then whoever it was would go away.

She was tense, waiting for a knock on the door, but time passed and nobody came. She was being ignored because of what she'd done, nobody cared if she was feeling unwell, or if she was hungry.

When she opened the door a fraction, she could hear laughter and loud voices downstairs. Nobody missed her. It was her fault. Nasty people deserved to be ignored.

She couldn't fall asleep, was too miserable and hungry and needed the WC. She wasn't going down until everybody had gone to bed and she definitely wasn't going to use the commode. How was she going to manage to wait for hours and hours?

Someone was bound to come and knock on her door; the boys would want to know how she was even if her parents didn't care. Daddy had said he'd forgiven her but now she wasn't sure about that. If he really loved her then he wouldn't leave her on her own with nothing to eat or drink... would he?

* * *

Richard wasn't sure if Annie understood that his proposal was genuine. She'd rather brushed it off and announced that she thought things would be difficult if they both lived at Harbour House.

In the circumstances, it would be better if he didn't go in via the back door but made his way to the front and entered that way. Elizabeth was standing at the sitting room window watching the front gate and saw him coming.

'Too much excitement in the past few hours, Richard, don't you think? I'm quite exhausted and it's not even lunchtime yet,' she called as he stepped in.

After kicking off his shoes, he joined her. 'Thank God Emily had the sense to go after the boys immediately and not wait to ask permission. If the train had left Colchester with the boys the chances of getting Sammy back would have diminished rapidly.'

'I'm so proud of her. Although she looks like me, she's exactly like Richard in character. I just wish she hadn't grown up so fast – I was still a little girl until I was thirteen at least. Happy to have pigtails and be taught by a governess.'

'She's a formidable combination of beauty and brains – Jonathan will have his hands full keeping her safe from eager young men.'

'Oh, please don't remind me. She intends to go to university, wants to be a doctor, or an artist or possibly both. We're 100 per cent behind whatever decision she makes.'

Elizabeth smiled and glanced at the baby sleeping peacefully in the pram. 'With her big sister as an example, I'm sure that Grace will want to do the same. Did you know that we're in the process of becoming Sammy's legal guardians? Mrs Bryant – his mother – is only too happy to sign the papers in return for a substantial sum. I'm sure she doesn't know anything about Pete's attempt to abduct Sammy.'

'More or less selling him then? It'll be easier for the boy when he has your name. He already looks like a Roby, extraordinary how alike he and George are.'

The boys suddenly erupted through the front gate and raced up the path. Elizabeth was at the door to meet them. Richard decided to retreat to his bedroom so the family could have this time together.

Jonathan and Emily arrived a few moments later and Richard was just closing his bedroom door when the girl flew up the stairs and into her own room. He frowned. Why hadn't she remained downstairs to be praised and fussed?

None of his business – one of her parents would come up and see how she was in a while. Having been an only child, he wasn't really an expert on children but he definitely liked them and hoped he'd have some of his own one day.

Despite Annie's apparent rejection of his proposal, he decided to write to his parents and tell them that he'd met the woman he wanted to marry, that he was about to get engaged.

He wouldn't say who it was initially, he'd only tell them his intentions and say that he'd give them more details when the matter was settled.

The letter was surprisingly difficult to write and it took him several attempts before he was satisfied. If he was confident that Annie's background made no difference, then why was he so reluctant to tell his parents everything?

Was he suppressing doubts about this because being in love was so new to him? He loved her, that was absolutely certain, what was less so was whether being in love would be enough to make the marriage successful.

Richard tapped his fountain pen against his teeth as he

thought about the pros and cons. Annie was intelligent, beautiful, kind and loved him as much as he loved her – at least he thought she did. But would she be able to fit in with his world? Would she want to? The way she spoke would immediately single her out as coming from a different background.

Would marrying her mean that he had to give up his friends and family or would she have to adapt and fit in?

He was surprised nobody had come up to tell him that lunch was served – this was very strange. Did they think he'd gone out for some reason? He could hear voices in the dining room so they'd obviously started without him.

It would be embarrassing for them to discover he'd been overlooked so he decided to wait until they'd finished and then go down and find himself something. As he turned to go back into his bedroom, he heard Emily crying.

He knocked on the door, but she didn't answer. He opened it and spoke from the door.

'Emily, is there something I can do for you? You shouldn't be here on your own, you should be downstairs with your family.'

She emerged from under the blankets looking wretched. 'They don't want me down there. Nobody has come to see how I am. I was so rude to my mother, she won't let my brothers come up and she and my daddy don't want to see me.'

This wouldn't do. He left the door open and strode across the room to drop down beside her bed. 'You've got this all wrong, Emily; your mother told me how proud she is of you. I think there's been a misunderstanding. They're giving you your privacy, respecting the fact that you can make your own decisions, not ignoring you.'

She'd been listening carefully and managed a watery smile. 'What about you, Mr Stoneleigh? Are they respecting your privacy too?'

He laughed. She really was intelligent. 'Actually, I was respecting theirs. I'm not family and didn't want to intrude.'

'I need to go downstairs. Will you check the coast's clear?'

'I certainly will. Hang on a minute.' He went halfway down the stairs and peered over the banisters. The kitchen door was shut and the family were busy eating in the dining room.

'Okay, Emily, you can come down now,' he whispered.

She fled past him – her need must indeed have been desperate. He followed her down and decided that the child's well-being was more important than the embarrassment he might cause by appearing so late in the dining room.

10

Annie had been asked to prepare a tray for Emily but not for Richard. Why hadn't he joined the family for lunch as he usually did? Mrs Roby had said she would take the tray up when she'd finished her own lunch – it was ready under a tea cloth for when she came in.

'You finish now, Annie, you don't want to be working when you're supposed to be free. You won't get paid for that, you know,' Molly said firmly.

'I've got a few things to do so if you're sure I'll go now.'

She wanted to be out of the house before Richard came down as she wasn't quite sure what to say to him. If her visit turned out as she hoped then she'd have good news.

If she hurried, she'd be able to catch the next train to St Botolph's. Nancy might be able to offer her a room and it would be easy enough to get to work from there. If there wasn't a train that suited her then she could catch a bus as those still ran quite frequently to Wivenhoe, Alresford and Brightlingsea.

The haberdashery shop that Nancy ran for her Auntie Ethel was closed for lunch so Annie went round the back. She'd visited a couple of times and she and Nancy were now good friends.

She knocked on the back gate and called out, more to let the big dog know she was there than expecting Nancy to hear her.

Boyd woofed and scratched at the gate and Annie opened it, ready to greet the huge dog. 'Hello, big boy, I'm pleased to see you too. Out of the way, silly fellow, let me in.'

Nancy appeared at the kitchen door. 'Boyd, stop that. I'm just sitting down for a sandwich, Annie, do you want one?'

'I'd love one. I'm not staying long and hoped you'd still be having lunch.'

Daphne, the girl who lived in and worked for Nancy, had the afternoon off so wasn't there which made things easier. Whilst the sandwich was being made, she explained her reason for coming so unexpectedly.

'Last time I was here you showed me that you'd got one of your rooms ready – if it's not already let, do you think I could have it?'

'It's not and you can, but why? You get free board and lodging at Harbour House – are you leaving there and looking for something else?'

Annie told Nancy about Richard and why she thought it might be best if they got to know each other whilst not living so close together. 'I do love it there, but it's not home. I don't like cleaning his room and so on, it's not good for our relationship. If I was here, just going in to work, it will change things. Not make me feel as if I'm not good enough for him.'

'Marriage to someone like him won't be easy for someone like you. He'll expect you to adjust – you realise that, don't you?'

'I do; don't forget I was married before. That's why I'm hesitating. I don't want to have to pretend that I'm something I'm not and if that's what he wants then even though I think I could love him and I know that he thinks he loves me, I just don't know if it'll work.'

'Wait until you've met his parents. If they accept you, if you get on with them, then things will be tickety-boo.'

Annie grimaced. 'I spoke to his mum on the telephone, she was snooty and I didn't like her at all. She'll never accept me if I'm a servant.' Nancy understood. 'Then I can be your first female lodger. The children are old enough to get themselves ready for school so I don't need to be there for that. My main job is to clean and to get the children's tea and look after them in the evening. Mind you, Mrs Roby's got nothing to do so it wouldn't hurt if she did that.'

Nancy shook her head. 'You're talking yourself out of a job, Annie. You'd be better off working at the factory than just spending a morning cleaning. What you'll get for doing that won't be enough to live on.'

'To be honest, I only took the job to get away from my horrible in-laws. If you'd had a room ready back then I'd have come here immediately. I've sent in my papers to join the WAAF. Richard doesn't want me to go.'

'I'm not surprised, you'd never see each other. Do you want to move in right away?'

'I don't have much to bring, so I'll come after work tonight if that's all right? I have my own bedlinen and that. I think it'll be better if Richard comes to see me here. He's got a motorbike which will make things easier.'

'So, you'll carry on working full time at Harbour House until you hear about your application?'

'I think so. I told Mrs Roby ages ago that I was going to join up at some point this summer, that I'm just waiting for my compensation. I need to keep my address at Harbour House until I've got that.'

'Are you sure you don't want a few days to think about it? It's a bit sudden, this move, isn't it?'

'I never make quick decisions but this time I know I'm right. Also, if I don't do it now, I'll allow myself to be talked out of it.'

Nancy's eyes suddenly widened and she clapped her hands. 'I want to start selling clothes as well as haberdashery. If you worked mornings in Wivenhoe, would you sew for me in the afternoons? I found a trunk full of materials and another of clothes that can be altered. I've been doing a bit after work but when my Dan's home we want to spend the time together.'

Annie couldn't believe things were working out so well. 'What about I work in the afternoons doing whatever you want me to in return for my board and lodging?'

Nancy laughed and held out her hand. 'That's a deal.'

* * *

Annie was back in Wivenhoe by mid-afternoon and the first person she needed to speak to was Mrs Roby, then she'd find Richard and explain how things were going to be.

'I think that's an excellent solution, Annie. In fact, having that attic room available couldn't have come at a better time. Richard can move into it so the other Mrs Roby, my mother-in-law, can come and stay.'

They agreed on Annie's new schedule and wages. Her employer had no objection to her keeping Harbour House as her address until the long-awaited letter and cheque arrived from the council.

'Is Richard in his room?'

'He is.'

'Then do you have any objection to me visiting him there?

Then I need to pack so I'm ready to leave when I finish this evening.'

'Would you mind very much explaining to Richard that he's being transferred to the attic room?'

'I'm happy to do that. He was intending to move to Brightlingsea a few days ago so I'm sure he won't object to being in the attic instead of the grand room he's got now.'

As she was about to go up, she reconsidered and thought it might be best to speak to Molly first and then Richard.

'Well I never, it's going to be ever so strange with you not living here and Mr Stoneleigh in your room. I wonder why the older Mrs Roby has suddenly decided to visit. None of my business, but I do like to know what's going on,' Molly said as she put the last peeled potato into the water ready to be cooked for supper later.

'I won't be working in the afternoons any more so I suppose I ought to tell the children,' Annie said.

'I shouldn't bother, they don't really need you to supervise them. You'll be better off doing sewing for my Nancy than acting as nursemaid to those three. I think being at posh schools and having to travel backwards and forwards to Colchester on their own has made them old for their age – even the boys seem a lot older than nine years of age.'

* * *

Annie could hear Richard moving about in his room – she could also hear the boys playing a noisy game of some sort, but Emily's room was silent. She knocked on his door and to her surprise the girl opened it instead of him.

'Goodness, I didn't expect to find you in here, Emily. I need to speak to Richard privately so I'll have to ask you to go to your bedroom.'

'That's all right, Annie, I was just going anyway.' The girl smiled warmly at Richard and pointed to the tray. 'I'll take the remains of our lunch down. Don't look so worried, Mr Stoneleigh, I'm quite capable of carrying a tray without dropping it or falling down the stairs.'

He smiled. 'Then off you go, thank you for keeping me company. I hope you feel better tomorrow. Don't forget what we said.'

Emily nodded but didn't say anything. As soon as the girl had gone, Richard was beside Annie and she was thoroughly kissed. A few breathless minutes later she pushed him away. 'I've come to tell you what I'm going to be doing.'

He sat on the bed and she took the armchair. He listened without comment until she'd finished. 'So, it's a *fait accompli?*'

She raised an eyebrow and he chuckled.

'It means it's already been decided. I'm not being given a chance to have an opinion.'

'I'm sorry, but what I do isn't any of your concern really, is it? I haven't really explained why I feel I need to move.' She did so and he nodded.

'I understand now, and I think it's a good idea. Not ideal for me, but much better for our future plans, if we do decide we want to move things on.'

'I'm glad you agree. This is the best possible alternative, don't you think?'

'I suppose so. I don't get much time off, as you know, but when I do get a few hours I'll make sure it's the afternoon. Then I can give you a lift back to Colchester.'

'I don't want to be engaged at the moment but if you still want to marry me then you can ask me again in a few weeks. I need to meet your friends and your family before I make my decision.'

'For God's sake, Annie, you'd be marrying me, not my family or friends. Are you suggesting that I need to vet your family and friends before I make *my* decision?'

His suggestion was so awful that she laughed. 'I'd better tell you exactly who I am before we take this any further. I'm the illegitimate daughter of someone my mother had a brief relationship with. My half-sisters married farmworkers but I reckon they've been conscripted. I think they were sent to France, but I don't know if they're back, dead or POWs. So I have no real family for you to meet.'

* * *

Richard managed to hide his shock at this revelation. He wasn't sure which was the most difficult to accept, her complete lack of concern for the welfare of her siblings or that she was illegitimate.

'I'm sorry if I sound unfeeling, but if you'd met them, you'd know why. Those two are bullies who made my life a misery, as did my father. My mother at least made sure I was fed and clothed reasonably well.'

'Is that why you married someone you didn't love?'

'To be honest, I'm not sure I even liked him. You know why I agreed.'

'I see. Thank you for telling me. I told my mother that you were a young widow. I don't think she needs to know the details of your past.'

'She won't want you to marry someone like me, we both know that. However, if we still feel the same way later on this summer then perhaps you can take me to meet your parents.'

Richard was beginning to wonder if being in love with her was going to be enough. He didn't enjoy being told what to do by anyone and certainly not by a female. But she was being realistic rather than romantic and he admired her for that at least.

'Then we're in agreement. You move to Colchester and we'll snatch whatever time we can together over the next few weeks. If you get here before seven then I'll still be here.'

Annie looked at him as if he was talking a foreign language. 'Good grief, I'm just going to be the cleaner, I'm not nursemaid to the children any more, I won't need to start until eight o'clock.'

'Oh, sorry, I suppose I didn't really take in all the details. Will you still join the WAAF?'

'I expect so. Are you still going to apply to be an officer in the actual navy?'

He patted the bed beside him. 'I don't know, we don't need to make that sort of decision about our future right now. Things are going to be different enough.'

She joined him and before she could object he swung his legs onto the bed, taking her with him so they were stretched out, leaning against the headboard.

'I was expecting you to ask me what Emily was doing in here – aren't you curious?'

'I am, but what we had to say was more important than hearing about her.'

'Right, she was very distressed as she thought her mother hadn't forgiven her for being rude. She didn't tell me exactly what she said but it must have been pretty bad.'

'I overheard. It certainly was – not at all like her.'

She obviously wasn't going to elaborate and he didn't intend to ask for more details. 'It was fortunate that Elizabeth had actually said to me how proud she is of Emily and how sad she and Jonathan are that their oldest child is turning into a young woman too soon. I was able to reassure Emily and she's just on her way to apologise.'

'I'm glad things are going to be smoothed over. I'm sorry, Richard, I can't lounge about here with you, I've got to pack. I'm catching the train at five o'clock. I'm sorry, I forgot to tell you that you've got to move into the attic as Mrs Roby's mother-in-law will be taking this room.'

'Bloody hell! My life's being upended and there's absolutely nothing I can do about it. I'm not used to being manipulated like this.' He hadn't meant to use that word and she flinched.

'How can you say that? I've not been manipulating you. You've been the one who's made the moves and it's me that's had my life upended. You've got to move from this room to one upstairs – you'll still be a lot better off than most of the people you work with and certainly far better than if you become a naval officer.'

She scrambled off the bed but he was too quick for her. He blocked her exit but didn't touch her. 'I'm so sorry. I'm not very good at this, am I? It's just that this morning I was so happy, was planning our life together and from nowhere it's been taken away from me. It's not your fault – I really do understand your reasons. I'm a romantic but sadly you're a pragmatist.'

He was about to explain what this meant but she shook her head. 'My grasp of English is excellent, thank you.'

'I apologise again. I'm constantly underestimating you. I love you, Annie, and want to make this work because I know that I'll never feel the same way about any other woman.'

He smiled; he thought that she was already sounding more like him than she had when she'd started working here. Hearing well-enunciated English all day was rubbing off on her. Not that it mattered to him but it would to his parents.

* * *

Emily took the loaded tray into the scullery and decided to wash up the things. She wasn't quite ready to go into the sitting room. Mr Stoneleigh had almost convinced her she was forgiven but until Mummy actually said so she wasn't totally sure.

When the very last teaspoon was dry and returned to the cutlery drawer she had no option but to go. Her feet seemed to drag as she made her way along the passage. The door was ajar so she didn't need to open it.

'There you are, darling girl, I was about to send out a search party. Are you feeling better now?' Mummy had jumped up and rushed to hug her.

'I am better, thank you, Mummy. I'm so sorry about what I said last night.'

'Forget about it, Daddy and I have. I want to thank you for showing such courage and initiative rescuing Sammy. We might have lost him if you hadn't.'

'Did you speak to our schools? George and Sammy were worried they'd be punished.'

'Of course, all done. You can return tomorrow with no repercussions or late marks.'

'That's a relief. Nancy lent me money which I've got to return to her.'

'Annie is moving in as her lodger this evening so I'm sure she'll be happy to take it for you.'

'Gosh, I didn't know that. Is it because she's in a relationship with Mr Stoneleigh and they can't be under the same roof?'

'Yes, that's right. Now, I've had the most exciting news today. Sit down with me and I'll tell you what it is.'

Emily thought that Annie moving out was enough excitement for now and really didn't want any more today. 'What is it, Mummy? Is it that Sammy is now my real brother at last?'

'No, but that will be happening soon. The news is that your grandmother, your daddy's mother, is coming to stay for a few weeks. Mr Stoneleigh is moving into the attic and your grandmother will have his room.'

This puzzled Emily. 'How can she be coming if you didn't know there was going to be an empty room?'

'Clever girl. We had decided to get one of the other attic rooms ready and then you would have moved up there next to Annie. Such good luck that Annie's moving out and now Mr Stoneleigh can move instead of you.'

'No, he can't do that. He needs electricity for his wireless and there isn't any up there. I'll move into Annie's room, I can read by oil lamp, it will be very historic.'

'What a good girl you are. Please run up and tell him before he starts to pack up his things.'

11

Annie was folding the last of her clothing into her battered cardboard suitcase when Emily appeared at the open door.

'Mr Stoneleigh's staying where he is and I'm having this room. Is there anything I need to know?'

'Goodness me, why is that?'

Emily told her and was so excited about moving into the attic that Annie just nodded and didn't voice her concerns. Emily was only eleven, too young to be more or less on her own up here with candles and oil lamps. Mrs Roby thought the girl was growing up too fast but was actually encouraging this herself.

'I'll show you how to light the oil lamps – it's not hard. It doesn't get that cold up here because of the warmth from the chimneys. I've been very happy in this room and I know that Nancy loved it too.'

'My grandmother's coming to stay and she's going to have my room. I'll do my homework in the kitchen like I used to.' Emily was looking around the room, her eyes wide. 'Moving up here, being allowed to light oil lamps, must mean that my parents now consider me to be responsible, almost a grown-up girl.'

'I'm sure they do. Now, I've just got to pack my bedlinen and then I'm ready to leave. I'll help you bring your things up before I go.'

Richard was going to take Annie to Colchester on the back of his motorbike so she didn't have to worry about train times. She wasn't exactly sure how two suitcases, a gas mask and handbag were going to fit on the bike but that wasn't her worry.

He appeared – as always in his socks – to offer his assistance. 'I expect you want to take your bookcase up with you, Emily, as well as your clothes.'

'I'm not sure I'm allowed to do that, Mr Stoneleigh, won't my grandmother want to put her books on it?'

'She's coming for a few weeks' visit so I think it highly unlikely she will have any books of her own. Come on, let's get this done.'

An hour later, her belongings crammed into the side panniers of the motorbike, her gas mask and handbag around her neck, Annie climbed onto the pillion and left Harbour House. She'd not been living there very long so wasn't too attached – being in Colchester was going to be far more exciting. She could finally leave the memory of her miserable marriage and her horrible in-laws behind and start again.

Richard expertly negotiated the narrow turning that ran behind the row of shops which included Mortimer's Haberdashery, the one that Nancy was now in charge of. He killed the engine and waited for Annie to hop off.

'I'll open the gate and then you can wheel the bike inside. I don't think anyone would pinch it but you can't be too careful. This isn't Wivenhoe where everybody knows everybody else.'

She opened the gate, completely forgetting about the big dog, who flung himself joyfully against her, sending her reeling backwards. She collided with Richard just as he was getting off the bike and all three of them ended up in a heap. Richard's leg was trapped against the red-hot exhaust pipe.

Richard was swearing and there was a strong smell of burning. 'For God's sake, idiot dog, get off before I burst into flames.'

Annie was already on her knees and grabbed the dog's collar. He just thought this was part of the game and licked her face enthusiastically. Richard was laughing as he scrambled up.

'Look at this – my trousers have been singed.' He snapped his fingers at the dog. 'Sit, Boyd, sit down at once.'

The dog obeyed instantly and calm was restored.

Then Nancy arrived. 'He's like that with Dan too, I think he must have belonged to a man before he became a stray. I'm sorry – has he caused much damage?'

'No, just to our dignity and my trouser leg,' Richard said with a grin.

* * *

It didn't take long to carry Annie's belongings up to her new room and Richard looked around approvingly. 'This is adequate. You've got electricity, a wardrobe instead of nails on the wall and plenty of space.'

'I'm not going to unpack now. It won't take me long as I don't have a lot. I'm far more excited about going to the pictures. I don't care what's on, it'll be such a treat and you did promise to take me, didn't you?'

His answer was to put his arms around her and hold her close, her back pressing against his front. She relaxed into his embrace for a few seconds then thought it wasn't a sensible thing to do when they were alone in the bedroom.

'That's enough of that, Mr Stoneleigh. I haven't eaten since breakfast – do you think there might be a fish and chip shop open somewhere?'

'Let's go and find out.'

* * *

After a delicious fish and chip supper they headed for the cinema. The film 21 Days with Vivien Leigh, Laurence Olivier and Leslie Banks had been showing. It was a drama and Annie had enjoyed every minute. The *Mickey Mouse* cartoon and the newsreel were just as enthralling.

Richard had had his arm around her shoulders and she hadn't minded because there was no one here to comment or criticise. When they came out they were holding hands and that was even better.

'Shall we go for a drink? Is there a curfew at Nancy's house?'

'She didn't have a spare key for me so she's getting one cut. Until then I have to be back before ten o'clock when she locks up. Instead of going for a drink, what I'd really like to do is take that silly dog for a walk. I've never ever had anything to do with dogs and I love him already.'

His smile said everything. 'I just don't want to say goodnight, so as long as we stay together for a bit longer, I don't care what we do. Walking the dog sounds absolutely spiffing.'

'That's what Emily says – I suppose I'm going to have to say spiffing, and golly gosh, and things like that now I'm walking out with someone as posh as you.'

'I don't want you to change, I love you just the way you are.'

Nancy was delighted that they offered to take the dog for his final walk and with Boyd on his lead, walking perfectly beside them, they headed down to the river. They let him off in the fields and he raced about chasing imaginary rabbits – at least she thought they were imaginary.

'I hope he comes back when you whistle, Richard, I'd hate to lose him the first time I take him out.'

'I don't know if you noticed, darling, but every few minutes he turns to check that we're still here. He's been abandoned by his owners once and is always going to be nervous about that happening again.'

'I don't understand why anybody would do that to such a lovely dog.' Then she answered her own question. 'I suppose for some families he was just too big to feed. At least they didn't have him euthanised.'

The sun had set, it would be dark soon and she didn't want Richard to be riding his motorbike in the dark. Ever since he told her he was a relative beginner she couldn't help worrying that he'd have an accident.

She was about to say something when a pair of nightingales started to sing. She stood in his arms, listening to this magical sound. The moment was ruined when Boyd bounced up to them holding something wriggling in his mouth.

'Leave, leave, Boyd, put it down,' Richard said sternly and to her astonishment the dog did exactly that.

The somewhat damp rabbit appeared unharmed and vanished into the long grass.

'What a clever dog, but we really don't want that sort of present,' Richard said as he stroked the animal's ears.

'Actually, you just let a perfectly good meal go.'

'Are you saying that you could have killed that little bunny rabbit?'

She giggled. 'No, that's a man's job. You would have had to kill it, but I would have skinned and cut it up.'

'Good God! I've shot a few pheasants in my time but never broken the neck of a rabbit and hope I never have to.'

'Big softy. We'd better go. I don't want you riding that bike in the dark.'

'I'm just as safe at night as I am in the day,' he said solemnly but his eyes were laughing.

'Exactly what I'm talking about. I don't really know why I agreed to go on the back of that vehicle with someone so inexperienced.'

He leaned down and clipped the lead on Boyd's collar and then the three of them headed back up the hill.

'I've a spotless record. I've never had an accident so I must be an excellent rider.'

'Ask me again in a couple of months and I'll give you my opinion.' Hand in hand they strolled to Head Street and she couldn't help wondering when they'd be able to do this again.

'I won't come in, darling, I'll get off straightaway. I promise that I'll come to see you whenever I can – even if it's only for an hour.'

'I hope you do. We won't get to know each other better otherwise.'

He cupped her cheek and her expression softened. 'You're going to be there five mornings so I can leave you a note if you like.'

'I'd like that. I'll write one to you on the back. I was going to suggest that you write to me as well as the notes, I don't get many letters. I know we're not supposed to clog up the post with personal stuff but one letter a week's acceptable, don't you think?'

***

Richard now had a key to the front door of Harbour House – the back door was now locked from the inside to avoid any further intrusions. He couldn't remember having enjoyed himself quite as much as he had this evening. Somehow Annie had seemed different, less guarded, and had become more fun as soon as she'd dropped her cases in her new room in Colchester. The fact that she had a large double bed hadn't gone unnoticed.

Lots of couples barely saw each other since the war had started so they were lucky in that regard at least. If they were going to exchange a letter each week, as well as daily notes, he'd get to know her much better. Maybe she'd admit that she loved him, that would be a result and worth having her move out.

After locking the door, he hung the key on the hook, removed his shoes, put them in the box and then tiptoed upstairs.

***

He was inundated with work and had forgotten all about his promise to write until he saw a letter propped up next to the telephone when he got home a few days later. The few lines they'd exchanged every day had been almost enough as she was an amusing writer and he often left for work smiling. He'd not had a chance to eat since breakfast so took the letter into the kitchen and dropped it on the table; he'd read it whilst he devoured whatever was on offer.

He made a pot of tea, cut himself several slices of bread and collected his egg salad from the pantry. Only then did he allow himself the pleasure of examining the envelope. Annie's handwriting was better than his. Initially he'd been expecting her to be unable to write legibly. Maybe even write in pencil and not ink. Her notes had proved she was as literate as he was.

He slit open the envelope carefully and withdrew two sheets of immaculately written paper.

Dear Richard,

What a treat it is to be able to write a letter as I don't think I've ever written a personal one before. The little notes don't count. I've written business letters, to the bank, to the council and so on but this is the first one to a friend.

I wasn't sure if I was to write and then you would reply or the other way round but as I've not had one from you, I'm writing and hope that you send me one back.

In fact, I hope you don't because that will mean you're going to come and see me soon. I had such a wonderful time when you were here and can't wait to repeat it.

I've settled in well, don't find the travelling backwards and forwards to Wivenhoe too much of a problem. Having to pay the train fare's a bind, but there you are.

Mrs Roby arrived yesterday with so much luggage I think she's come to stay indefinitely. I've only spoken to her a couple of times, but she's nice enough and the children seem to like her too. They don't need me at all as they have a grandma there to talk to them.

I've made three frocks and altered half a dozen other garments for Nancy. You won't believe it, but she's insisting that she pays me – that I'm earning her double what I'd be paying her for board and lodging.

Imagine that! I'm a woman of means now – I've put two pounds into my post office savings book already.

I take Boyd out every evening and when I do I think of you.

Fondest wishes,

He read the letter a second time and there wasn't a single inkblot or spelling mistake – even the punctuation was perfect. His wouldn't be as neat.

The work that had been keeping him so busy would be completed the next day and he'd told Jonathan he was taking a day off – he'd been working more than twelve hours a day and had clocked up a week's work in four days.

He read the letter again and then carefully replaced it in the envelope and put it in his waistcoat pocket. He didn't need to reply this time as he'd be seeing her tomorrow evening.

He left the kitchen tidy; knowing that Annie would be washing up his things made him feel more connected to her. He stopped at the door to give the kitchen a final look and then turned to leave.

He almost walked into the older Mrs Roby, who was waiting to come into the kitchen for some reason.

'Good heavens, young man, you almost had me off my feet. I didn't expect to find anybody down here at this time of night.'

'I apologise, ma'am, I too wasn't expecting to find anybody downstairs. Is there something I can do for you before I retire?'

'I couldn't sleep and thought if I came down and made myself some hot milk then maybe that would help.'

'I'll gladly do that for you. If you'd care to wait in the sitting room then I'll bring it through.'

To his surprise, she laughed. 'I don't expect to be waited on by you or anybody else. I'm perfectly capable of making myself some hot milk. I might be old but I'm not senile. Off to bed with you, Mr Stoneleigh, and please don't call me ma'am again as I'm not the queen.'

'Understood. Goodnight then, Mrs Roby.'

He was smiling as he undressed; he now had something interesting to tell Annie when he saw her tomorrow. This new Mrs Roby was charming, and he'd liked her immediately. He hoped Annie was wrong about why Jonathan's mother had joined them, but he couldn't think of any other explanation than that she'd left her husband. Not something he could ask his friend either.

* * *

He'd packed an overnight bag as he intended to stay at a hotel so he didn't have to travel back and forth from Wivenhoe. Hopefully he wasn't too late to find a room as it was already after eight o'clock. He was a free man for the next thirty-six hours. Elizabeth had said that Annie didn't have to come in tomorrow morning so they could spend the entire day together.

She wasn't expecting him, but he knew the drill. He called over the fence to let the dog know he was coming in and then opened the gate. This time he was braced and fended off the excited animal without being sent flying.

'I'm pleased to see you too, Boyd, but you've got to learn not to jump up at people. Down, get down.' He spoke sternly and moved his hand towards the ground to emphasise his order. The dog immediately flattened and looked up at him with adoring eyes.

He was about to shut the gate when Dan, Nancy's husband, stepped out of the kitchen.

'Annie didn't mention you were coming but she'll be

delighted. I don't think we've met officially but I'm Dan and I know that you're Richard.'

'Good to meet you. I'm not back at work until the day after tomorrow and Elizabeth has given Annie the morning off as well. I can't wait to give her the good news.'

'Come in, she's sewing in the sitting room. I'll take you up. Do you have somewhere to kip tonight?'

Richard shook his head. 'Not yet, I'm hoping one of you can recommend somewhere not too expensive.'

'You can stop here if you like. You could sleep in the sitting room – Annie can't object to that as she's on the floor above.'

'That would be terrific. However, I won't bring in my bag until I've spoken to Annie and you've checked with Nancy. Sometimes I don't know what Annie wants.'

Dan slapped him on the back. 'Join the club. Women are a mystery. But I wouldn't be without my Nancy, she means the world to me.'

'Are you home for a bit, Dan?'

'Yes, I've got to collect grain from Marriage's mill at high tide the day after tomorrow. Free until then.'

'Then why don't we make an evening of it tomorrow? It's too late to do anything today. My treat. We can go to the cinema, have a fish and chip supper and then go for a drink perhaps.'

'Nancy will love that. She's doing some stocktaking in the shop so I'll nip in and tell her you're here and make sure she's happy with you staying.'

Richard bounded up the stairs and knocked on the sitting room door. Annie yelled for him to come in.

'Good evening, my darling, I hope you're as happy to see me as I am to see you.'

'Bugger it, you made me jump and I've just stitched up this man's trouser leg. He won't be able to get it on now.' She was laughing and threw herself into his arms and a very enjoyable few minutes later they both came up for air.

'Dan has said that I can sleep in here on the floor if Nancy's okay with it – are you? If not, I'll go now and find myself a room if it's a problem.'

'If Nancy's okay with you staying then so am I. I trust you. When do you have to be back at work?'

They sat together on the sofa whilst he explained. She was even more excited than he'd expected, and this made him believe that maybe they'd turned a corner in their relationship.

12

Emily and her brothers were overjoyed to have their very own grandmother living with them. She'd asked her daddy why Grandma had come without Grandpa and he'd looked sad and just said that sometimes grown-ups needed a break from each other when they'd been together a long time.

Having had no experience at all with grandparents she'd no idea what to expect but had been delighted to find Grandma was good fun and happy to spend time with them.

Their new relative had now settled in as if she'd always lived at Harbour House with them and was taking them to the cinema today. George thundered up the attic stairs and burst into Emily's bedroom without knocking. He was up really early for a Saturday morning.

'Grandma's already downstairs and making us breakfast. She says we can leave immediately afterwards. She wants to meet Boyd and take him for a walk down to the river.'

Emily was pretty sure no grown-up wanted to do that and especially not an old grown-up like their grandma. 'That's good news. I'm sure Nancy will be very pleased to have us take him out for a walk.'

'Mr Stoneleigh didn't come home last night – I expect we'll see him and Annie too.'

'Quite possibly, but we're not all trooping into Nancy's home especially if she's already got extra people staying there. Maybe Grandma might want to buy something in the shop and that would mean I could go in with her and ask Nancy about taking the dog out.'

'Sammy and I don't want to go in any sissy shop. We'll wait outside.'

Emily wasn't exactly sure what sissy meant and didn't like to ask. Sammy had taught George a lot of the words he'd known when he was living in the East End and most of them were a bit rude.

'I'm just coming, could you please tell Grandma I won't be a minute?'

He thundered down the stairs, making the floor shake, and Emily knew he'd be in trouble if their mummy heard him. Running about the house was absolutely forbidden even in an emergency.

This was the first time that her grandma had seen her in her grown-up clothes – she was wearing a pair of grey cotton slacks, a pretty floral blouse with a Peter Pan collar, and the new pink cardigan that Grandma had given her. The boys had got pullovers. They weren't nearly as happy with their gifts as she was.

As she walked past her parents' bedroom the door opened and Daddy came out carrying Grace in his arms. 'Here, sweetheart, will you take her down and give her breakfast? Your mother's not feeling well and I've got to go to work.'

Emily's excitement fizzled out like a dead firework. 'Of

course I will, Daddy, the boys will enjoy their trip to Colchester just as much without me.'

'Dammit! I'd forgotten Ma was taking you out today.'

'It doesn't matter, there'll be plenty of other times. I know how to make Grace's bottle and mix up her rusk for afterwards. Don't worry, I'm really happy to be looking after my baby sister.'

'Right, I'm sure Mrs Bates will help out if you need it. I've absolutely got to be at the yard this morning but will come back at lunchtime if I can.'

He kissed the baby, squeezed Emily's shoulder, and was out of the front door with his briefcase in one hand, and absolutely no sign of his gas mask, moments later.

'Come along, little baby, I expect you're hungry.'

She had Grace firmly over one shoulder and was about to descend the stairs when she hesitated. What if she dropped her sister? Could she negotiate the stairs without holding onto the banister?

'Good heavens, child, don't dilly-dally. I've got Grace's bottle ready for you in the sitting room.'

Grandma didn't offer to take the baby but waited smiling at the bottom of the stairs. This gave Emily the confidence to come down – if an adult thought her capable then she obviously was.

Although she'd fed the baby a few times since Mummy had stopped feeding Grace herself a couple of weeks ago, this was the first time she'd done it without supervision. Grandma left her to it and Emily glowed with pride that she'd been trusted to do this.

Once the milk had gone, the wind had been brought up, she spooned the gloopy rusk into the infant's mouth and that too vanished.

'Good girl. All gone. I'll leave changing your nappy for half an hour as I know you might fill it up now you've eaten.'

The baby was lying on her back on a blanket waving her feet in the air. She was a happy little thing and Emily didn't understand why she hadn't loved her the moment she'd set eyes on her in February, because she loved her so much now.

* * *

Grandma brought her in a tray with a boiled egg, soldiers and a mug of tea. 'Here you are, my dear, it's time for you to have breakfast.'

'Thank you, I didn't want to leave Grace on her own especially as she'd only just finished eating. As soon as I've had this, I'll fetch the changing bag from the pram. Do you know what's wrong with Mummy?'

'I've no idea, Emily, but as they haven't called in the doctor it can't be serious so don't look so worried. We can leave our trip to the cinema until another day – your brothers don't want you to miss the treat.'

'That's so kind of them, but no, it wouldn't be fair. I'm sure I'll have another opportunity. Are you sure that you can manage two boisterous boys without my assistance?'

'They're perfect young gentlemen with me so I'm quite certain I'll have no problems. However, I've vetoed visiting Nancy and taking a large dog for a walk. That certainly needs you to be there.'

'Are you going to be here when the holidays start next month, Grandma?'

'I rather think that I am. Being in the countryside with my grandchildren and my son is far more enjoyable than being in a busy town with just your grandpa for company.' She paused and then continued. 'He's in charge of the local home guard –

I'm sure you know who they are – and having the time of his life. But I think I deserve to have a little fun too, don't you?'

* * *

Annie went to bed half-hoping that Richard might visit her and half-dreading that he would. He'd given his word and she trusted him. Having been married before, she knew how a man's body worked when he was eager to make love and Richard definitely was.

Intimacy with her husband had never been exciting, it hadn't been exactly unpleasant, but not really enjoyable either. When Richard kissed her, touched her, even just looked at her, her pulse raced and all she could think about was falling into bed with him.

Doing that would be the wrong thing for both of them. There was always the possibility she could end up pregnant and then they'd have to get married.

If they ever did tie the knot one day it would be because they couldn't live without each other, that their love was too strong to be denied, not because they had to. She giggled into the darkness. She was thinking like one of the heroines in a Mills & Boon romance and not the sensible young woman that she was.

* * *

Daphne, Nancy's cousin, lived in and worked with Nancy in the shop and was downstairs when Annie walked in the following morning.

'Shall I take Boyd out or has he already been for his walk?'

'Oh, that would be just the ticket. Mr Stoneleigh's in the you-know-what but I'm sure he'll want to come with you.'

'Has Nancy gone to the bakers?'

'She has, not sure what she'll bring back but it's always something tasty.'

The dog was already bouncing about outside and as soon as he saw the lead in Annie's hand was at her side, politely sitting, wagging his long plumy tail, knowing exactly what this meant.

'Come along, Boyd, we'll wait outside for Richard.' She deliberately spoke loudly. She didn't want to address Richard directly when he was sitting on the lavatory but he would have heard her.

She'd only been outside for a couple of minutes when he came out looking as happy as she felt. 'Down to the river? This time if he catches anything we'll hang onto it.'

'Unless you know how to kill a rabbit cleanly then we blooming well won't.'

Laughing, they left the yard with the dog walking beside her and headed down the narrow passageways that led to the fields at the bottom of North Hill.

Boyd was soon galloping around on the grass but so far hadn't caught a rabbit. 'What are we going to do today, Richard? I know that we're going out for a fish and chip supper, cinema and the drink with Nancy and Dan but what about the rest of the day?'

'We could wander around Colchester; it's market day and I quite enjoy browsing the stalls even though there's not much on them nowadays. Or perhaps you'd like to go for a ride?'

'I don't want you to run out of petrol, it's supposed to only be used for work. I'm quite happy to stay in Colchester. I wouldn't mind walking down to the Hythe and watching the barges and other boats coming and going.'

'Breakfast first and then we'll meander around the town,' he said as he threw another stick for the dog. Sometimes Boyd returned with it but more often he collected it and then kept it for himself.

They found a log by the hedge and sat down. 'Do you think Italy joining Hitler is going to make things much harder for us to win?'

He frowned as if he didn't want to talk about serious things with her. 'Let's not spoil this wonderful day by talking about the war. I won't pretend that we've nothing to worry about, that an imminent invasion's possible, and that by some miracle the war will be over by next year.'

'I haven't decided yet whether I'm going to go for the interview when I hear. Have you decided about transferring to the navy?' She'd deliberately turned the subject to something that would be even more difficult to talk about.

'Going for the interview doesn't mean that you have to sign on the dotted line, does it? At the moment you would be a volunteer so could change your mind at any time.'

'I know that, but you haven't answered my question.'

He shrugged. 'I suppose my decision will depend on yours. If you leave me then I'll transfer.'

She stiffened. 'That's not fair, you can't put this on me. We're not engaged, and have only been seeing each other for a week or two, that means that both of us are free to make decisions for ourselves.'

'I don't see it like that, Annie. I'm in love with you, I want to spend the rest of my life with you at my side. As far as I'm concerned, whether we're engaged or not is immaterial. I'd hoped that you were beginning to see things the same way as me but I'm obviously wrong.'

Then he was on his feet and walking away from her. He was going off in a huff like a child.

She whistled for the dog and then ran after Richard. For some reason, instead of being cross, she thought his behaviour endearing, it made him seem more approachable, less formidable.

'Don't stomp off, that's just plain silly. Adults talk things over – children do what you're doing.'

Before she could react, he spun round and in two strides was beside her. She was crushed in his arms and being kissed with such passion her knees almost gave way.

Several minutes later he raised his head, his eyes blazing down at her. 'I don't think that was childish, was it, my darling?'

'I don't know why I like you, Richard Stoneleigh, you're infuriating, dogmatic and—'

His answer was more growled than spoken. 'And you love me, I know you do and the sooner you admit it the happier we'll both be.'

This time his kiss was gentle, less demanding, and her last reservations about the relationship evaporated.

When they finally moved apart, the dog had flopped down on the grass and was looking at them in a puzzled sort of way.

'I'm sorry, Annie darling, I shouldn't have—'

'You didn't do anything I didn't want. I never felt like this with my husband. I think I'm beginning to understand that intimacy could be a wonderful thing between two people who love each other.'

'I won't press you to become engaged to me. All I wanted was to know that you felt the same way and now I do, I'm content.' His grin was somewhat lopsided as he continued. 'Mind you, I'm tempted to go headfirst into the river to cool off.'

She giggled. 'Things will settle down by the time we get back so don't worry. You're not going to embarrass yourself.'

His laugh sent a flock of pigeons swirling into the air. 'I keep forgetting that you've been married before – that you know the ins and outs of it all.'

She choked and laughed. For a second, he stared at her in bewilderment then realised what he'd said, how his innocent remark could be misinterpreted. It took several minutes for them to recover.

Annie knew that things had changed between them. She had to decide whether that was enough to agree to marry him and put aside her intention to help the war effort. Was it possible she could do both?

* * *

Richard was learning so much about this amazing young woman happily holding hands with him as they made their way back. He'd always known she was intelligent, anyone could see that she was lovely, but he now knew she had a wonderful sense of humour and a fierce independence that he found admirable but was having difficulty adjusting his expectations. Like most men, he'd grown up thinking he'd be in charge of any relationship, that his decisions would be the only ones that counted, that his wife wouldn't want to work or do anything but run the home and bring up the children whilst he provided for them.

The war was changing everything. Women were now doing jobs that had been reserved entirely for men and doing them very well. He couldn't help but think that when the war was eventually over, he wouldn't be the only man wanting things to return to the status quo.

'You're looking pensive, Richard, what's wrong?'

'Nothing at all, my darling, I'm still digesting the fact that eventually I'm going to be able to marry the woman of my dreams.'

Instead of being impressed by his hyperbole, she giggled. 'Goodness, you just compared me to eating a meal and then said that you've been dreaming about me. Which is it? I don't think I want to be eaten or dreamed about, to be honest.' She shook her head when he was about to interrupt. 'I'm a down-to-earth, ordinary young woman and don't want to be considered as anything other than that.'

He ignored her last comment and continued with what he'd been about to say. 'I said I was digesting a fact, which is not the same thing, as you very well know. If I dream about you that is entirely my business.' He tried to look stern and disapproving and failed miserably as she poked him sharply in the ribs with her elbow.

'I've never been able to talk to anybody the way I can with you. You actually listen to what I say, which is more than any other man has done.'

He nodded, trying not to smile. 'I listen, but it doesn't mean that I agree with you or that I understand half of what you say. I hope I still pass muster?'

'Then that makes us equal. You sprinkle your conversation with words I've never heard before as well as French. I also listen carefully but frequently don't agree with what you say.' She smiled and he caught his breath. She'd never looked at him like this before.

His hand tightened on hers. 'I don't know if you feel the same way, my darling, but I want to make love to you, show you just how much I love you.'

'I feel the same, but we can't sleep together at Nancy's. I don't know how we're going to arrange this, do you?'

'Would you be prepared to stay in a hotel with me?' He grinned at her expression. 'Good God, not anywhere either of us are known. I thought London – we could take in a show, have a decent dinner somewhere, would you be prepared to do that? It would mean signing the register as a married couple.'

'I don't think we can do that now. Surely we'd be asked to show our ID papers. They're not going to let us have a room together as soon as they see that we're not married.'

'Good point. Leave it with me, I'm sure I'll come up with a satisfactory solution.'

'I'll have to take a day off at least when I get my interview. Nobody will think twice about my being away for that. If you can manage to get the same time off then we could meet in London and nobody will be any the wiser.'

He nodded and was about to answer when a skinny tabby cat jumped down from the gate they were passing right in front of the dog and then raced away. Boyd barked and took off after it, ripping the lead from Annie's hand.

'Boyd, bad dog, come back here. Leave that cat alone,' Richard called despairingly but for once the animal ignored him. They were left dogless, alone on the path. The barking had stopped. Was that an ominous sign or a good one?

An old chap on an ancient bicycle pedalled past. 'Your dog's at the end of the path. I've never seen the like.' He cycled off, leaving them mystified by his cryptic comment.

Richard grabbed Annie's hand and they raced down the path. They exchanged a worried glance. He didn't need to voice his fear that Boyd had caught and maimed the cat as he guessed she was thinking the same.

They rounded the corner at speed and almost fell over each other as they skidded to a halt.

'Good God! I thought we'd arrive to mayhem, not that daft dog playing silly beggars with a cat,' Richard said.

'He just wanted to play; I think he's lonely. Maybe he had a feline friend in his previous life,' she said, laughing.

Neither the cat nor the dog stopped their nonsense as the two of them walked over. Boyd was licking the cat which was rolling about on its back waving its legs in the air. No wonder the old chap had been astonished.

'Boyd, you shouldn't have run off,' Annie said as she retrieved the lead from the ground. 'You gave us both a scare.' She bent down and tickled the cat which was purring loudly.

'Do you think this is a stray? It's a male, and apart from this one being a tabby, he reminds me of Ginger. He's very thin under all that fur, don't you think?'

Richard squatted beside the cat who was now weaving in and out of his ankles, obviously enjoying the attention. 'I think you're right; he could do with a good meal. I doubt that Nancy and Dan want a cat so we'd better hope he doesn't follow us.'

They arrived at the back gate with the cat walking beside Boyd as if he'd always known him. There was no way of stopping the animal from coming into the yard as he jumped over the gate in one bound.

Dan was sitting outside in the morning sunshine with a mug of tea in his hand. 'Brought a friend back, Boyd? I'm not sure what my Nancy's going to say about that.'

Annie unclipped the lead and Boyd rushed over to Dan and dropped his head in his lap as if asking for the cat to be allowed to stay. Richard watched open-mouthed as the stray nudged Boyd before standing on his hind legs and staring pleadingly at Dan.

'Blooming heck, I can't resist him,' Dan said. 'Nancy love, come and see who's just joined our family.'

13

Emily changed the baby, relieved it was only a sopping wet nappy, and then decided to take her for a walk. The weather was warm, the tide would be up so she couldn't take her sister along the quay, therefore she'd brave the unmade-up lane and walk to the farm.

'Mrs Bates, I'm going out with Grace in case Mummy gets up and wants to know where I am. I'm going to go up Anglesea Road.'

'All right, love, I'll tell her if she comes down. Take a spare nappy, you might need it.'

'I have everything in the pram bag. I'm going to put the canopy on; I hope I can work out how to do it.'

'Let me, love, it'll be quicker.'

Ten minutes later, Emily was happily pushing the pram along Alma Street towards Brook Street. Grace was cooing and gurgling as she watched the fringe on the sun canopy fluttering in the breeze. Feeling very grown-up, Emily turned into Brook Street and wandered down the narrow road and up the other side of the hill.

She viewed the stony road ahead and thought that maybe she'd not manage to push the heavy pram as far as the fields.

'Are you ready, Grace? It's going to be a bit bumpy.'

It wasn't as difficult as she'd feared and, although a bit red in the face and puffed, she arrived at the bull's field in no time. Mrs Bates had given her some lettuce and a couple of shrivelled carrots to feed the bull.

She parked the pram carefully and then checked that she'd put the brake on. The baby had dozed off so Emily knew she could clamber onto the gate, had a while before she'd be needed. She was about to call out, hoping the huge black bull would recognise her voice and come and see her. She almost tipped headfirst into the field when Jimmy Peterson spoke from behind her.

'He's not in there, Emily, he's busy with the cows if you get my drift.'

'Oh, thank you for telling me. I'd have felt a bit silly waving my carrot at an empty field,' she replied. Jimmy had grown since she'd last saw him but then so had she.

He peered into the pram and grinned. 'Pretty little thing, it doesn't seem long ago that my little sister Gwen was like that and now she's almost five.'

'This is the first time I've taken Grace out. My mother's unwell and my father had to go to work so I'm in charge this morning.'

'Good for you, you were a godsend to my mum last winter. Why don't you come and say hello? Even if you can't play with my sisters and brother today, they'll be pleased to see you.'

'If you're sure we won't be in the way, I'd love to. By the way, the dog that Nancy rescued from your farmyard is doing really well in Colchester. Why didn't you take him in?'

Jimmy shrugged. 'My dad doesn't hold with domestic pets.

We've got three collies for the sheep and a herd of farm cats keeping down the vermin. To be honest, it was touch and go that he didn't shoot that dog. We were all relieved when your Nancy collected him.'

Emily was shocked that Jimmy's father had been prepared to shoot a healthy, friendly animal. But then, if the government had said domestic pets should be euthanised because they were an unnecessary expense, it was hardly surprising.

'Well, I'm glad Nancy took Boyd away before that happened. How are your jolly land girls getting on?'

'Crikey, they work hard, do a good job, but never stop eating. My mum's spending too much time in the kitchen and has no time for the children.' He looked at her hopefully. 'She said the other day that she'd be prepared to make your visits official, employ you to entertain the children of a weekend, if your parents would let you do that.'

'I'd be happy to come on a more regular basis, but I don't think my parents would allow me to be formally employed. I'm just happy to have the eggs and things from your farm to take home occasionally.'

'When does your little sister need her next bottle?'

'I'm not exactly sure, in a couple of hours I should think. Sometimes she goes longer without crying. I didn't bring one with me as it's too hot and the milk might curdle. I do have a bottle with boiled water in it in case she's thirsty.'

'Then could you stay?'

'I'm not sure I should stay out much longer. I tell you what, I'd be happy to take the children with me. I'm sure that my mother will be up by lunchtime and I'll bring them back then. I think that playing with new toys is always more interesting.'

He beamed at her and she felt very grown-up. She liked to be approved of. 'Mum will be delighted for them to do something different. Neil's old enough to play out but the other two aren't, and they won't let him go alone.'

* * *

At eleven o'clock, Emily pushed the pram into the front garden and the three children, eyes wide, followed her.

'There's a big box of garden toys over there you can have a look at. There's quoits, a couple of skipping ropes, a bag of marbles, a ball and a sack full of wooden bricks. I'm sure you can find something to play with whilst I tell my mother that I'm back and that I've brought you three with me.'

Neil had risen to the occasion. He was usually the naughty one but today he was being especially helpful. He'd even pushed the pram up Hamilton Road with her. Grace had slept through the bumps but was now grizzling and ready to be fed.

'Come along, sweetheart, you need changing and feeding. You're in charge, Neil, make sure your sisters don't leave the garden.'

She thought that if the boys were home then she'd introduce them. Neil was only a year younger than them and would probably enjoy raking about with her brothers.

The pram was left in the garden whilst she carried her baby sister inside. Neil had rushed to open the door for her, which made her smile. He was going to be a lovely, polite boy like his older brother.

'You're an absolute star, my darling girl,' Mummy said as she reached out and took Grace from Emily's arms. 'Thank you so much for stepping in and taking care of your baby sister for me.'

'I've loved doing it, Mummy. I need to tell you that I brought back the Peterson children as Mrs Peterson was desperate and I couldn't stay and play with them. I hope that's all right.'

'Of course it is, I'm delighted you had the initiative to do that. I'm going to feed and change your sister – why don't you ask Mrs Bates if she could make you and your charges a sandwich and a glass of squash?'

* * *

The four of them ate their impromptu lunch sitting on the grass in the front garden and were joined by George and Sammy halfway through. Emily introduced them and they seemed to like each other.

'If you come back with us after lunch then I'll show you properly around the farm,' Neil suggested.

'That sounds super, thanks. We'll go and ask Mummy if that's okay,' George said and dashed off. Although Sammy was now officially a Roby, had even changed his surname to theirs, he was finding it hard to behave as if he belonged here. He didn't say mummy and daddy either but had stopped using uncle and auntie.

George was back minutes later, beaming. 'We can go, Sammy. Mummy's pleased we've got a friend in Wivenhoe now. You can come down to see us next time, Neil, and we'll do things as a threesome.'

'That's good, George. I can go out with Jimmy sometimes but my dad says I get in the way. It'll be better having you two to mess about with.'

'Would you like to go to the park before we go back to the farm? There's often a game of football, Neil, and you could all join in. The three of us will watch,' Emily said as she licked the last of the jam tart from her lips.

'That would be just the ticket, Emily. I'm good at football but can't stop and play after school because I have to take my sisters home,' Neil said grinning. 'Mum doesn't like me coming back after school or at weekends either, more's the pity.' He was on his feet and the three boys headed for the gate, not waiting for her to follow with the girls.

The two little girls didn't mind what they did as long as they could each hold onto one of Emily's hands. There was a match being played between up-streeters and down-streeters, those who lived above the railway bridge being the up-streeters. It always seemed odd to her that there were more down-streeters when there weren't as many houses. Emily thought it must be because the families at her end of the town had more children than those that lived in the bigger houses at the other end of Wivenhoe.

She wondered how this was possible – she knew how babies were made but didn't understand the mathematics of it all. It wasn't something she was prepared to ask either of her parents about. Maybe next time she and her brothers went for tea with Nancy after school she'd find a moment to ask her.

* * *

Annie enjoyed every minute of the time she spent with Richard and was as eager as he was to spend the night with him. He'd suggested that maybe she'd be happier if they were engaged if that happened but she still wasn't sure – wanting to sleep with him wasn't the same as wanting to spend the rest of her life married to a man whose parents would hate her. She'd done that once and needed to be absolutely sure her love was strong enough.

She'd no idea when he'd be coming to see her again but that was all right. They'd packed so much into their time together she'd got plenty of memories to keep her going.

Things were different at Harbour House and she thought it was the arrival of the older Mrs Roby. It didn't really matter to Annie what was going on there as she no longer lived in Wivenhoe. She thought if Richard wasn't still living there and she could wander in and out of his room once or twice a week tidying up and so on, she'd have already handed in her notice and be working full time doing sewing and alterations for Nancy.

* * *

Annie received and replied to two letters from Richard over the next couple of weeks but didn't see him. It wasn't until July that anything of importance happened. She finally received a date for her initial interview in London. Her post was still going to Harbour House apart from those from Richard. As soon as she read the letter from London, she went in search of her employer.

What was even more exciting, and the real reason she was about to hand in her notice, was that the cheque for £350 from Colchester Council had finally arrived. Not much really for the life of a man, but more than enough to set her up, to give her a head start in life.

'Mrs Roby, I'm sorry but I've got to hand in my notice. I've got my interview on Friday and probably I'll be joining the WAAF in a couple of weeks. I'll work until Thursday but that will be my last day.'

'I'm sorry to hear that, Annie, but not surprised. Somehow I thought you might have changed your mind about volunteering because of your relationship with Richard.'

'We're thinking of getting engaged, so no, it's because I want to do my bit for the war effort. I've enjoyed working here, and hope you find somebody else to replace me,' Annie said.

'Molly thinks she might know someone. What are you going to do about your mail? It can hardly continue to come to this address if you no longer work here.'

'That's all right, Mrs Roby, I've got the letter I was waiting for. That was with my interview letter.'

Annie was putting away her cleaning things, happily thinking she only had to do this twice more and then she wouldn't be anyone's servant, but her own woman. If she did join the services then of course she'd belong to the WAAF, but that was different.

Mrs Roby senior must have overheard the conversation. 'I don't think we need anyone to do the cleaning – my daughter-in-law and I can take care of that between us. Molly keeps the kitchen spotless, and the children are old enough to do their own rooms.'

'I'm not sure that Mrs Roby will want to do anything herself, but the children certainly could help out. They seem more settled now you're here and I don't feel so bad about leaving.'

'My dear girl, it wouldn't matter if I wasn't here. This isn't the Victorian age; you don't owe your employers anything apart from doing your job when you're here. Does Richard know?'

'I'm going to leave a note in his bedroom as always.'

'He doesn't eat with us and is usually gone by the time I come down for breakfast with the children, but he definitely still sleeps here. He'll get your note, don't worry.'

* * *

When she arrived the following morning, Richard's motorbike

was still there. Her heart skipped a beat and she flew into the house and straight into his waiting arms.

'Darling girl, I've missed you and apologise for not having been able to come and visit.'

'I've missed you too.'

Their kiss was as passionate and wonderful as always and they were both reluctant to step away. 'I've been working flat out so Jonathan won't object to me taking time off. You can finish today – I've squared it with Elizabeth – and we can go to London this afternoon.'

She wasn't sure if she was cross that he'd done this without consulting her or thrilled that they could finally spend the night together.

'Then I'd better get on. I take it you're going to work this morning and will be back to take me to Colchester when I finish at midday?'

His grin was wolfish. 'I certainly will. I can't talk now, I need to get off, but I'll tell you everything I've organised later.'

The morning sped by as Annie was determined to somehow cram all Thursday's work into this morning. She didn't stop for a second and at twelve o'clock when she heard the motorbike turn into the Cut everything was spick and span and she was ready to leave. She hoped she never had to earn her money by cleaning other people's houses ever again.

* * *

Richard rammed his overnight case into one of the panniers on his motorbike and was ready to leave. Annie had to go home first to change and collect her bag, then they could head for London. Not on two wheels but on the train, the bike would be left parked outside the station.

As soon as they arrived at Nancy's home, he explained what he'd got planned. 'Train to London, then the underground to Kensington.'

'Why are we going there?' Annie asked.

'We're staying in a flat belonging to a friend from Oxford. Well, to be more exact, the friend's parents. They've decamped to Wiltshire for the duration and the place is empty.'

'That's perfect. No need for lies or unpleasant innuendoes from hotel staff.' She smiled and continued, not embarrassed or at all hesitant. 'I'm not sleeping with you unprotected. I assume you've taken care of that?'

'Of course. Neither of us want to start a family at the moment, although I hope you'll want children when the war's over. I certainly do.'

A lot depended on her answer. He'd deliberately tossed this into the conversation to get her honest reaction. He wanted a family; this was important to him.

'I wanted a baby initially but I didn't get pregnant when I was with Norm. I was glad I hadn't when he died. Mind you, my husband wasn't exactly keen in that department so probably not safe to assume I can't have children.'

Annie hadn't answered his question directly but saying she'd hoped for a baby with her husband was good enough for him.

'We'll settle in then go for lunch, plenty of decent places in Kensington. I didn't know which you'd prefer to do after dinner – a film, a show or dancing?'

Her eyes lit up. 'Dancing. I've heard there are lots of palais de danse in London. I'm not fussed about a posh dinner, am happy with fish and chips.'

'Now who's using French?'

'I know, get me.'

Whilst she rushed upstairs, he sat on the old chair in the yard and threw a stick for the dog. The cat, now unoriginally named Tabby, hopped onto his lap. He was enjoying the animals when Annie returned looking almost unrecognisable.

'That's a terrific dress. You look amazing.'

'Thank you, I made it myself, copying a picture in a lady's magazine. Nancy found this lovely navy-blue spotted cotton in a box in the attic.'

Her hair was up in a more elaborate arrangement, she had dark red lipstick, and apparently silk stockings. She laughed when she saw him looking at her legs.

'Old Mrs Roby gave me these. I've never owned silk ones before.'

'Perfect with that frock. Are you ready? Can we leave?'

She nodded. 'Yes, I've got a blue cardi, nighties and spare underthings. Don't need anything else.' She pointed at his battered leather suitcase sticking out of the pannier.

'Do you have a dinner jacket and dickie-bow in there?'

'Hardly. Like you, clean shirt and so on, nothing else.' She was going to be cold on the back of a motorbike in only a thin cotton dress, even though they were only going a couple of miles.

'You'll need to find a coat, Annie; we can stuff it in a pannier so you don't have to take it with you, just wear it to get to the station.'

Her expression made him laugh. It was as if he'd made an improper remark. What she said wasn't amusing at all.

'Put my only coat somewhere anyone could find it? I'd rather be cold than lose my coat.'

If she'd stopped there he'd have been able to laugh it off but she continued. 'That's the trouble with rich people, they think money grows on trees and everybody's like them. That we all have spare coats and can afford to lose one.'

He'd got up when she came out, had been smiling, now he turned his back, afraid of what he might say. How could she think that he was like that? She was right – maybe they didn't really know each other well enough to be engaged.

'In which case, you can either wear my jacket or be cold. It's up to you.'

There was an ominous silence behind him. 'Yes, it is up to me. I think I'll catch the bus.'

He faced her, couldn't hide his shock, thinking she meant she was going to London on her own.

'Don't look so upset, Richard, we're still going to London together, I'll meet you at the station.'

He moved closer and held his breath, waiting to see if she stepped away or came into his arms.

'I'm sorry, I shouldn't have said all that. I know you're not like that. You wouldn't be going out with me if you were. I do love you, but it's going to be a bumpy ride for both of us until we know each other well enough not to misunderstand things.'

He kissed her gently and she responded and the knot in his stomach unwound.

'In which case, my darling, we'll both go by bus. It makes more sense really as I don't want my bike to be stolen.'

He wheeled it into the far corner of the yard where it was out of the way, removed his suitcase from the back, and they were ready to leave.

* * *

Travelling on a country bus was a novel experience for him – he had, naturally, used the buses in London on more than one occasion. He'd bought first-class tickets for the train but now regretted it. Annie might think he was demonstrating how well off he was, but it was too late to change things.

'We're going in style, my darling, as only the best is good enough for you.'

'I'd have been quite happy in third class, even in the guard's van as long as I'm with you.'

That was the perfect answer. He escorted her to the far end of the platform where the first-class carriage would be stopping shortly, fairly confident this was going to be the best weekend of his life.

They joined a handful of fashionably dressed women, all wearing a hat of some sort as well as gloves. There were also a few businessmen in their pinstripe suits. He was immediately conscious that Annie was the only woman without either hat or gloves – he hoped she hadn't noticed. But he guessed she had as she sat rigid beside him, her usual happy chatter gone. He wasn't sure how to deal with this.

The journey seemed interminable and every attempt he made to talk to her failed miserably. He was sure they weren't the centre of attention – the businessmen had their noses buried in the *Financial Times*, three of the women were friends and chatted exclusively to each other and the others seemed lost in their own thoughts.

When the train steamed slowly into Liverpool Street, Annie was on her feet and waiting by the exit before anyone else had moved. He joined her, standing behind her but not too close.

He had her old-fashioned carpet bag under his left arm and was holding his case on the same side which left him with his right hand ready to hold hers if she'd allow it.

They had to catch the underground so didn't have to leave the station. Annie turned to him as they were about to descend the steps to buy their tickets for the next train.

'I'm not travelling back in first class, Richard, I was humiliated. You should have known how it would be for me. Why didn't you tell me to wear a hat and gloves so I'd look like the other women?'

'It didn't occur to me. I'm a man – I don't see things like that and I'm pretty sure that the other women in the carriage didn't notice either.'

She bit her lip. 'I'm not sure this is a good idea. Look at us – really look at us. You're wearing a bespoke blazer and flannels, handmade shoes and are every inch a wealthy gentleman. I'm wearing a home-made frock, cheap shoes, and haven't even got a hat or gloves on.'

Telling her for a second time that it didn't matter to him wasn't going to help. 'I fell in love with you because you're intelligent, kind, funny and beautiful. I don't care about what you wear on the outside, it's what is on the inside that counts.'

Her smile was tentative but at least she wasn't looking so pinched and unhappy. Then he ruined everything.

'And once we're married your clothes will be tailor-made too. You can have as many pairs of gloves and hats as you want.'

'What you're saying, Richard, is that you don't like the way I look either. Anyway, even if I'm dressed to the nines, as soon as I open my mouth I'll let you down.'

She took her bag from under his arm and backed away from him. 'I'm going to see if I can have my interview today. I'm sorry you've had a wasted journey but I'm not coming with you to Kensington.'

Then she ran off and he watched her go. Running after her

now wasn't going to improve things – better to let her calm down and then go and see her in Colchester.

There was only one thing he could think of that would convince her that she'd be accepted in his world and that was to get his parents to intervene on his behalf. He had two nights free so would head for Hampstead and spend it at home.

14

Annie waited for Richard to come after her, to pick her up, kiss her and tell her that she was being silly, that her fears were groundless, but he didn't come. This proved to her that she was right – he might be in love with her but deep down he knew she wasn't right, wouldn't fit into his world.

She caught the bus to Westminster Bridge and then crossed over the river and headed for the building she'd been told to report to for her initial interview. She didn't need to ask if she'd come to the right place because there was a queue outside of girls and older women all waiting to be interviewed.

Eventually it was her turn. Nobody asked to see her papers and she didn't volunteer the information that her interview was actually the next day. She'd been too miserable to chat to any of the others in the queue and they probably thought her a bit stuck-up. She didn't care. Even if they were interviewed on the same day, it was unlikely they'd end up serving together.

She was sent to a room and told to strip off to her knickers by a WAAF. 'Hurry up, ladies, you've got to have a medical before your interview. If you're not A1 then you can't progress.'

There were six of them and they looked at each other, horrified. Annie was the only one to speak up.

'I'm not taking my clothes off in public. It's not decent and quite unacceptable. Where are the screens we can stand behind? Who is going to examine us once we've removed our outer garments?'

There was a murmur of approval from the other girls. The corporal scowled. 'There's no such thing as privacy if you join up so you'd better get used to it. You go through that door to be examined by the doctor in your knickers and then come back here and get dressed.'

Annie was going to refuse but then shrugged. She turned to the others who were obviously waiting to see what she was going to do before reacting themselves.

'I think if we put our cardigans on over the top of our knickers then we'll be more or less decent. I've got one in my bag.'

Suddenly they were chatting and laughing as if they'd known each other for months, not minutes. Having to face the same ignominious, humiliating medical examination had drawn them together.

'Nobody has asked my name,' one of them whispered, looking around nervously. 'They don't know who we are so how can it go on our records that we're medically fit for duty?'

'Just have your interview paper ready. I'm sure somebody will ask us once we're in the other room.' Annie had hers in her hand. 'I'm not supposed to come until tomorrow, but I couldn't get that day off work. I'm hoping they won't mind.'

They lined up by the door, all clutching their cardigans or coats across their chests, hideously embarrassed by the whole process.

Annie was first and when the door opened she was ready.

She almost reversed and ran away when she saw there were two male doctors, one ancient and the other younger than her. Not a female in sight.

'I think we should all go in together. It's not safe or sensible to be on our own with two men when we're not properly dressed,' she said and the girls followed her in.

The younger medic looked up. 'One at a time, one at a time, if you please.'

'No, we'll come in together unless you find a female to chaperone us,' Annie said bravely.

The old doctor looked around and said something very rude under his breath. 'For God's sake, Reynolds, do your job. These ladies can't be in here with just us. Get a couple of WAAFs in here.' The six of them hovered in the door. 'Come in together, ladies, that idiot might be gone for hours. Absolutely bloody useless. I don't know where they get people like that. There's a war on – I suppose we'll have to make do.'

Annie stepped forward and he listened to her chest, checked down her knickers to see she didn't have anything alive down there and that was all.

She stepped to one side but waited until all the others had been as briefly and professionally examined.

'Excuse me, sir, but nobody has asked us who we are so how do you know who you've examined?' Annie asked.

His sudden bark of laughter made them all jump. 'Good point, young lady, very good point. Utter chaos here today. Do you have your interview papers?'

They all nodded and waved them at him.

'Good show, bring them here and I'll stamp them myself. Before you go for your formal interview, somebody will record that you've been passed fit. All total nonsense – I've no idea if you're fit or not but there you are.'

They retreated, clutching their stamped papers. Annie was no longer embarrassed but trying to hide her laughter.

'Bugger me, he's a funny old sod,' one of the older girls said – Annie thought her name was Eileen. 'They don't know their arse from their elbow in here, but that ain't our problem.'

Annie had never dressed so fast in her life and didn't feel safe until she was decent again. The others were equally speedy. There was no sign of the WAAF who'd been guarding the door in case they tried to escape.

'Shall we go in search of whoever's doing the interviews?' Annie suggested.

'You seem to know what's what,' Eileen said. 'I reckon you'll be an officer in no time.'

Annie laughed. 'I don't think people like us get to be officers but I wouldn't mind being a sergeant.'

The remainder of the somewhat haphazard process was more enjoyable as the six of them remained together. They handed their stamped interview papers over at a long trestle table and one of the WAAFs duly recorded their details.

'You need to go through that door over there and wait until you're called for your interview. You'll be called in turn but I warn you it's going to be a long wait.'

There weren't enough chairs for the hundred or so girls waiting so the six of them found a corner and sat on the floor. She discovered that three of them were from the East End, Eileen, Maureen and Lily – they wanted to join up before the bombs started dropping on their homes. The other two, Jenny and Gladys, were from Essex like her and both wanted to get away from miserable home circumstances.

After two hours, they were all fed up and hungry but they now had chairs to sit on. The rows behind them were filled and another group had nabbed the corner.

'There's a decent caff down the road,' Gladys said, 'if you give us a bob each I'll nip down there and get us something to eat. I know the bloke what owns it and I reckon he'll lend us his mugs so we can have a cuppa as well.'

'You can't carry six mugs of tea and whatever else you're going to buy on your own, Gladys, someone will have to go with you. Why don't you go, Lily? There's at least twenty girls in front of us so you've got time.'

Nobody argued with Annie and she rather liked being in charge. They handed over a shilling each – which seemed rather a lot for a snack – but nobody argued. They were all starving.

'I need the bog,' Maureen said, 'does anyone know where it is?'

Again Annie was able to supply this piece of vital information. 'I heard a lance corporal direct some girls a while ago. It's down the corridor over there. I need to go too, but I'll wait until everyone else has been. Someone needs to keep our place – I've seen several groups of girls eyeing our chairs eagerly already.'

By the time the four of them had visited the WC, Gladys and Lily returned carrying a large tin tray. Every head in the room turned and there were envious eyes fixed on what it contained.

They each had a decent sausage roll, a sticky bun and a mug of tea – excellent value for only a shilling. Gladys and Lily raced off with the empty tray and mugs and had only just returned when their names were called out and they had to go through yet another door to be interviewed by both a male and female RAF officer.

* * *

Emily was looking forward to spending time alone with Grandma. After the boys had gone to the cinema the other weekend it was now her turn for a treat. She'd taken special care with her hair and her outfit. Vanity was a sin – at least she thought it was – but probably a minor one. Emily smiled at her reflection. She was wearing her blue slacks with a white embroidered blouse and had Grandma's cardigan over her arm in case it got cold.

She flinched as a squadron of fighter planes screamed overhead. It was all very well pretending everything was tickety-boo but she was well aware something dreadful was on the way. She didn't often pray, wasn't sure there was anybody listening, but every night she asked that the RAF and the navy would be able to stop Hitler from invading.

'There you are, my dear, I thought we'd catch the bus instead of the train. That way I shall see more of the surrounding area.'

'I've not caught a bus into Colchester so it'll be new for me too. Daddy drove us down when he had the car and that's the only time I've seen Wivenhoe from the road.'

With her annoying gas mask over her shoulder, Emily followed her grandmother from the house. Grandma's mask was hidden inside a pretty velvet box and she wished she'd got something like that to put hers in. The only other thing she was taking was a purse with two shillings in it. Now she was helping out with chores around the house she was getting a regular allowance. She smiled. Even with the bribery of pocket money the boys still didn't want to do housework.

They walked out of the front gate, across the road, and into Station Road where the bus stopped. There were three or four housewives waiting to get on. Saturday was market day and there was probably more chance of getting a few extras for the family in Colchester.

The conductor took Grandma's money, clipped two tickets but they were both for adults. Grandma didn't contradict the bus conductor's error and being thought to be over sixteen made Emily feel very grown-up. Then she thought she'd better point the mistake out.

'I should have had a half-fare, Grandma. Shall I call him back and get him to change it?'

'Oh dear, I did think it was rather a lot. Whatever made him think that you were an adult? You do look older than your age but certainly not sixteen years old.'

Instead of being upset, Emily giggled. 'I expect he's a bit shortsighted. Not many girls my age have short hair, do they?'

The elderly conductor apologised and refunded the money, but he didn't change the ticket. 'No point in wasting paper now, is there? You'll still be able to travel using that one, miss.'

The bus lurched and bounced into Colchester and after passing over the bridge that spanned the river Colne it was faced with East Hill. At one point it would have been quicker to get out and walk as the bus was going so slowly.

Eventually it made it to the top and everybody got off. There was a strong smell of petrol and oil coming from the engine at the back of the bus.

'I hope this poor old thing makes it through the day, Grandma. Otherwise we'll have to get the train home. George said there's only this one bus on the Wivenhoe route now.'

'Well, we don't have to worry about that right now. Is that where you go to school?'

The bus had stopped opposite Greyfriars. 'Yes, I hated it the first few weeks but I've settled in now. School breaks up for the holidays in the middle of July so not long to go. That means I've been there a whole year and will be in the upper fourth next term. Then I'll have six lovely weeks of freedom.'

'You might have your freedom, my dear, but the long holidays were introduced so that children can help with the harvest. I'm sure lots of the local children will be doing that.'

This was very interesting news. 'We arrived at Harbour House at the very end of the holidays last summer so I didn't know that. I go to the Peterson farm most weekends so I hope I'll be able to work in the fields instead of looking after the children.'

'They'll be picking early potatoes soon, I'm sure you'll be able to help with that. Then there'll be pea picking and possibly soft fruit later on in the summer and then apples and pears in the autumn.'

'The farm's mixed, but as far as I know doesn't grow any vegetables apart from potatoes and cabbages. They also grow wheat, barley and oats and have pigs, sheep, a dairy herd and chickens.'

'I grew up on a farm, my dear, so know quite a bit about it. I'd love to walk there with you sometime and have a wander around.'

The crowd of passengers had now rushed off, leaving the two of them alone on the pavement. Emily pointed out the castle as they walked past it, and Grandma was suitably impressed. After that they made their way up the High Street which was now packed full of stalls. Men were standing behind them yelling out what they had for sale – she thought it all very noisy and unnecessary.

'I'd like you to meet Nancy, it won't be so busy in Head Street.'

'I really don't want to go out with that big dog you've been telling me about. If you want to do that then you'll have to go alone.'

'There's a nice teashop opposite Nancy's shop, you could wait there for me. I've got my watch on so we can make a definite time for me to be back.'

'Actually, I'd quite like to talk to Annie. She had her interview last week to join the WAAF and I'm interested in how she got on. I haven't seen Mr Stoneleigh at all – he must be working very long hours again.'

'I hear him moving about in his bedroom sometimes in the night. Everyone must hear his motorbike leaving every morning as it's so noisy, but that's before I go down.'

They dodged through the crowds and went around to the back gate. Emily tried to open it, but it was locked – it was never bolted during the day and she thought this was odd.

'Hello, it's me, Emily, and my grandma, can somebody let us in?'

'Why don't you pop around to the front and ask the girl who works with Nancy to open it for us?'

'Daphne, you mean. All right, I won't be a minute.'

The shop wasn't that big and there were already half a dozen women in there buying bits and pieces for their sewing and knitting. Nancy spotted her at once.

'Daphne will let you in, love.'

'Thank you, Mrs Brooks,' Emily said and backed out.

By the time she rejoined Grandma, the bolt had been drawn back and Daphne let them in. The dog was dancing with excitement.

'Yes, silly boy, I'm going to take you out in a minute,' Emily said as she fussed the big dog.

'I'd like to speak to Annie, if that's convenient, Daphne. Is she working upstairs?'

'Yes, Mrs Roby, but she comes down about now to make a pot of tea. Not that we'll have time to drink it today, we're that rushed off our feet.'

* * *

Annie had been doing her best to appear cheerful, as if the break with Richard didn't mean as much to her as it really did, but it was hard. When she'd got back from London after her interview she'd immediately told Nancy what had happened and her friend had agreed it was probably for the best.

If Richard had come to see her, he hadn't made much of an effort to get in. Nancy had insisted on bolting the back gate so he couldn't arrive unannounced. He hadn't arrived at all as far as Annie knew and there'd been no letters from him either.

This was what was so upsetting. When she'd told him that she wasn't good enough for him, she'd expected him to disagree, to put up a fight for her, somehow show her that she was wrong. Convince her that their love was more than enough to overcome any of the social barriers they might meet.

She'd belatedly realised that he hadn't meant to offend her when he'd said she'd be better dressed once they were married, he'd just been demonstrating how he was going to look after her. She'd overreacted – she was too sensitive about her background. If he'd come to see her then she'd have explained to him that she was prepared to change in order to fit in, learn to speak more like him, if that's what he and his family wanted her to do.

There'd been no opportunity to say this as he'd obviously taken her at her word. The only thing she was glad about was that she hadn't actually gone to bed with him as then it would have been so much worse.

She was on her way downstairs when Daphne scared her half to death by flinging open the door and yelling at her.

'Blimey, sorry, I didn't mean to startle you. Mrs Roby and Emily Roby are downstairs. The girl's come to take the dog out but the lady wants to see you.'

'Ta, I'm coming down now. It'll be good to see both of them.'

Daphne vanished back into the shop and Annie walked into the kitchen. Mrs Roby was busy making the tea as if she belonged there.

'Hello, Mrs Roby, so kind of you to visit. Has Emily taken Boyd out?'

'Yes, I'm not fond of dogs of any size and particularly big boisterous ones like him.'

Annie nipped in with mugs of tea for Daphne and Nancy and then joined her unexpected visitor at the table. The door was propped open, too hot in there otherwise with the range on all the time.

'I'm eager to hear what happened at your interview, Annie. I'd have loved to join the WAAF, do something useful with my life.'

Annie told her about the chaos, the others she'd met and the very brief interview. 'They only asked me my age, my education, why I'd come and what I hoped to end up doing. Then I was dismissed and told I'd hear in a few weeks.'

'What do you want to do?'

'Not work in the NAAFI, stores or doing cleaning, that's for sure. I'll probably end up sewing again, but ideally I'd like to learn how to work in an office, be a telephonist, something like that.' Annie sipped her tea, wondering if she should say anything about Richard.

'Mr Stoneleigh is very unhappy, Annie. It's such a shame, I thought you were ideally suited.'

'We're not though, that's the problem. Chalk and cheese, that's what we are. I'm not good enough for him and he's not been to see me, written or anything, so I guess he agrees.'

'His parents must have persuaded him that you'd made the right decision. But I wanted to see for myself if you were as miserable as he is.'

'I knew they would. I thought he'd choose me, but I was wrong. He's not happy; I'm sure there's more to this than you know. I'm going to take a long time to get over him. Joining the WAAF will help take my mind off things.'

'My dear, I think you should know that I came from a poor family. My father was a farm worker, my mother too, and all of us did what we could to make ends meet. I met the son of the landowner and we fell in love. His family were horrified and he was to be packed off to India.'

'What happened?'

Mrs Roby smiled. 'He refused to go; we eloped and were married. I learned how to fit in and until recently we were happy together.'

'What happened to change things?' It seemed a bit strange talking like this to someone like her.

'He's lost interest in me, changed, isn't the man I married, wants to play soldiers all day, and I refuse to be pushed aside. That's why I'm living in Wivenhoe now.'

Annie mashed the tea leaves, added more boiling water and refilled their mugs. This gave her a few moments to digest what she'd been told. Did it change anything for her and Richard?

15

Richard bitterly regretted his decision to spend the weekend with his parents. He must have been mad to believe they'd support him, want to meet Annie, be delighted that he'd found the woman he wanted to spend the rest of his life with.

The reverse had been true – they hadn't been able to hide their horror at the thought of having someone from the lower classes as their daughter-in-law. They hadn't gone as far as to say that they'd disown him or stop his allowance if he pursued it but had made it abundantly clear that he'd be ostracised from the family and his friends.

He'd only stayed a couple of hours and then roared off, vowing not to return. He'd been as horrified by their reaction as they'd been by his announcement. How could he not have realised that although unfailingly polite to working people they really despised them and thought that they, and everyone else like them, were innately superior by their birth?

He didn't want to go back to Harbour House, had no intention of staying at the flat on his own, so found himself a very modest B&B in Chelmsford and spent the next two days exploring the town. There was a cathedral, two rivers and an important industrial area. He couldn't help thinking that when the bombs started dropping this would be a target.

It was tempting to drink himself into oblivion, but alcohol wasn't something he enjoyed – a glass of claret with his dinner, a pint in the pub with his friends, was about his limit.

He returned to what was now his only home in Wivenhoe on Sunday night, his mind made up. He was being paid a substantial allowance to supplement his somewhat meagre wages as an Admiralty surveyor and he no longer intended to use that. He would be far better paid as an officer in the Royal Navy. He couldn't in all conscience ask Annie to take him back until he was in a position to provide for her in the way that she deserved.

* * *

A week dragged by and he'd not plucked up the courage to visit her, not written and not spoken to anybody about what had happened. Richard hadn't realised heartbreak was a physical thing – that it made a person ill as well as miserable. He tried not to think of his parents, of how close they'd been all his life, but the rift with them had added to his misery.

On the following Friday, he finished work at noon, filled up illegally with petrol at the yard, and headed for the Admiralty. He left the building a sub-lieutenant, had two weeks to get kitted out, learn what would be expected of him before he was sent to whatever ship he would be joining. His only experience with the actual navy had been at Dunkirk but his exploits there had been recorded and the commodore who'd interviewed him had been delighted that Richard had decided to become a naval officer.

Now he could go and see Annie and try and persuade her that it didn't matter who they were, it was how they felt that was important.

* * *

Colchester was quiet when he arrived in Head Street, shops were closed and only the pubs and hotels were busy. He kicked his motorbike onto its stand, outside the back gate, and tried to open it, but it was bolted.

The shop had been closed, the blinds drawn, so there was no point knocking on that door. He rattled the gate in the hope that the dog would hear him and bark and someone would come and investigate. Why wasn't Boyd in the yard?

He couldn't be out for a walk as then the back gate wouldn't be bolted from the inside. Richard had no option but to climb over. He was a tall man, fighting fit, and took two steps back. Taking a run at it would make it easier.

He jumped, grasping the top of the fence with both hands and then let his momentum carry him up. As soon as most of his body was parallel with the top of the fence, he changed his grip and swung his legs over and dropped to the ground on the other side.

He smiled, despite his nervousness, pleased with his athleticism as he'd expected he might end up flat on his face.

The kitchen was empty – well – no humans in there but the dog must have heard or seen him and was throwing himself against the back door and barking loudly. If anybody was in the house they'd come and investigate, all he had to do was wait.

The racket continued but nobody came. Obviously, Nancy, Daphne and Annie were out somewhere. He'd wait. The chair that Dan used was still there, he'd be perfectly comfortable on that until they came back. He was prepared to wait all night if necessary, but he doubted the dog would be left on his own for that long.

He'd been at work by six this morning, ridden to London, had an interview at Admiralty House and then come to Colchester. He'd not eaten for hours but that didn't matter. There was water available in the laundry room which would do for the moment.

He didn't hear the gate open, heard nothing until Annie pushed him off the chair and he sprawled on the ground.

'Bloody hell, that hurt,' he said as he staggered to his feet, rubbing his elbows, which had taken the brunt of the fall.

'Serves you right, Richard Stoneleigh, for not coming to see me sooner than this,' Annie said sternly. She was glaring at him but the joy in her eyes was unmistakeable.

'Darling Annie, I've been miserable without you. Will you please, please agree to marry me? I love you and don't give a f...'

'Don't you dare say that word, Richard, I'll wash your mouth out with soap if you do.'

He grinned and picked her up, holding her in midair, so she was looking down on him for a change. 'I apologise, my love, for my appalling language, for my stupidity, for anything you want me to. Just say you love me too and will marry me, maybe not right away, but sometime in the future.'

'Of course I will, dafty, now put me down so I can kiss you.'

* * *

They remained outside for so long that Nancy sent the dog out. The lead followed. 'Here, you two love birds, take him out for his last walk. I'll get us a bit of supper so don't be too long.'

'Make it a large supper, Nancy, I've not eaten since five o'clock this morning,' Richard called back.

Nancy stepped out of the kitchen. 'Crikey, I was only doing a bit of toast and some tea. I reckon the chip shop will still be open. I'll send Daphne to get some. I'll stick yours in the oven to keep warm.'

* * *

They walked to the nearby large field, no time for the river walk tonight, and let the dog go. Whilst Boyd ran off, he told Annie why he'd stayed away.

'I told you your parents wouldn't be happy. It doesn't bother me now, not after what old Mrs Roby told me.' She smiled up at him. 'I missed you too and have been praying you'd come and see me so we could talk things out.'

He listened and then nodded. 'So that's why you've finally accepted we can make this work. Thank God for Mrs Roby.' He thought now was the time to explain what else had happened.

'So, you're now a naval officer? I wish you'd not done that. I'd be happy living here; I don't need a big house or smart clothes, I just want to be with you, have your babies one day if possible.'

She shuddered and was then sobbing in his arms. The dog bounded up, concerned something was wrong. 'Darling, please don't cry, I've wanted to do something more active than inspecting boats since Dunkirk.'

'I know, I'm proud of you, but am terrified you'll drown, be blown out of the water and I'll never see you again.'

'Then let's get married now, before I go, I've got two weeks.'

She snuffled and he handed her his handkerchief. 'All right, if it can be arranged before you leave then I'll do it.'

He dropped dramatically to one knee, intending to propose in the time-honoured fashion. Unfortunately, Boyd thought it was a game and sent him flying, ruining the romantic moment.

* * *

Annie helped Richard up, half-laughing, half-crying and the dog made matters more complicated by barging into them, wanting to join in the game.

'Then we're officially engaged?' Richard asked.

'Yes, I don't need any ring apart from the gold one when we exchange our vows. I'd much rather get married in church but I don't suppose that's possible.'

'I don't see why not if we can find a vicar prepared to do it at such short notice. There have been two chaps at the yard – not shipyard workers but navy officers – who were being posted away so they married in a hurry.'

'I just started going to St Peter's, the church on North Hill, with Nancy and we could ask him.' She rubbed her face against his jacket, reluctant to step away, well aware that in just two weeks he'd be gone and she might never see him again.

'Then we'll go there in the morning. The Admiralty will let Jonathan know – I just have to get my belongings from Harbour House.'

When they walked home, he had his arm around her waist and she pressed closer, loving the warmth and strength of him.

'Goodness, we've been talking about you and I've not told you that I had my interview and will be getting notice that I've been accepted in a week or two.'

'Can a married woman still be in the WAAF?'

'Yes, you have to leave if you're expecting but can serve alongside everyone else in the same way otherwise. I wasn't sure if I was going to go but now I think I will. Somehow it'll seem easier if we're both in uniform doing our bit for King and country.'

She waited for him to ask her to reconsider, to tell her that if they were married he'd prefer her to remain at home where she was safe. But he didn't.

'Is it something you really want to do? You're not just doing it because of what happened between us?'

'No, I want to be in uniform. I've always intended to join one of the services as soon as I got the compensation I was telling you about. If you really don't want me to then I'll respect your wishes as we'll be married. But I do want to go even more than I did before because then we'll both be wearing blue.'

'Then of course you have my absolute support. I know how hard it is for women to be stuck at home trying to make ends meet, queueing for hours to buy enough food to put on the table, permanently on edge expecting to get that dreaded telegram from the War Office saying their loved one's gone.' He brushed a stray strand of her hair back from her cheek. 'I don't want you to be like that, I want you to be so busy that you don't have time to worry.'

'I love you, I think I always have, but until Mrs Roby told me her story I didn't think it was possible. Are you quite sure you want to exchange me for your parents? I've heard you speak fondly of them several times – your dad sent you that motorbike, didn't he?'

'And very grateful I am to have it. God, did you hear that? My stomach rumbled and it made the dog jump.' Then he kissed her passionately. 'But my parents are no longer part of my life, you're all I want.'

* * *

Over a tasty supper of a large portion of chips and a very small portion of cod they told Nancy and Daphne their good news.

'You've not known each other long but it's obvious you're meant to be together. Dan will be home at the end of the week and he could be your best man if you like, Richard.'

Annie was pretty sure Richard would want Jonathan to have that role but he couldn't really say so. 'He's already asked Jonathan; he told him he was hoping to marry me before he joined his ship when he gave in his notice.'

'Well, how about he walks you down the aisle, Annie? You can't do that on your own.'

'That would be perfect, but don't you think we should ask Dan what he thinks?' Annie said.

'He'll be honoured. What about having the Roby children as page boys and bridesmaid?'

This wedding was becoming something much bigger than she and Richard had planned or wanted. Luckily Richard stepped in.

'Shall we wait until we've spoken to the vicar before we make any plans? If we have to marry at the town hall registry then it'll just be us and a couple of witnesses.'

Nancy raised her eyebrows, which made Annie laugh. 'You won't get away with that, Richard, we're giving you both a proper do wherever you get married.'

Annie had an idea. 'You know, it would be better to be married at St Mary's in Wivenhoe. Then we can have a get-together at the Falcon and invite everyone at Harbour House.'

'Actually, darling, that makes a lot more sense. I'm a resident there and until recently so were you. Neither of us have family we want to invite so having the Robys, Nancy and Dan, plus Molly and her husband, attend the service and the modest reception afterwards would be ideal.'

Daphne was looking a bit forlorn. 'Obviously you're invited too,' Annie said hastily. 'I think if all those we've mentioned can come that's about fourteen guests. Enough to make it special but not so many that it'll be hard to cater for them.'

'Ta ever so, I'd love to come. I'm off to bed now, see you in the morning. Busy day Saturday, need my rest.'

As soon as the girl had gone, the three of them relaxed. It wasn't right to talk about intimate things in front of a girl her age.

Now came the tricky decision about tonight's sleeping arrangements. Whilst Richard was outside using the WC, Nancy told Annie that Richard could share her bed, that as they were officially engaged it was okay with her.

'Thank you, I've not quite made up my mind about that. On the one hand I'd rather wait, on the other we've possibly only got these two weeks to be together.'

Nancy squeezed her hand. 'You've just made your decision, love. Make the most of every minute, anyone could have a bomb dropped on them one day.'

'Cheerful thought, but true. It's a good thing you put a double in my room, I'd not want to share a single with someone as big as him. You go up, Nancy, I'll tidy in here. I need to talk to him first.'

She'd just finished when Richard came in, the dog at his heels, and locked the door behind him. 'Am I in the sitting room, darling? I'll go wherever you want.'

'Nancy said it's fine for us to be together and so am I. We might not get a honeymoon, so we're putting the cart before the horse, so to speak.'

His eyes darkened and he looked at her fiercely, making her hot all over.

Then his expression softened and he put his arms around

her, drawing her close. 'I know you don't want a baby now. But I don't have what we need here, I left them at Harbour House.'

'I don't care if I do fall. I'm not waiting another day to make love with you.'

They tiptoed up the first flight of stairs and then up to her room. She opened the door and stood aside so he could look in.

'A double, how perspicacious of you, my love.'

She giggled. 'I do know what that means, so don't try and impress me with your long words.'

'Damn! I'd better stick to French in future if I want to confuse you.'

Her heart was hammering and it wasn't nerves, it was excitement. She'd been married over three years and had never seen a naked man and she wasn't sure if she should tell him or not.

Suddenly she blurted it out. 'Norm always wore pyjamas, undressed in the bathroom.'

He gently moved her into the room and quietly closed the door. 'Well, my darling, I sleep in the buff and I'm hoping you will too.'

He didn't rip his clothes off but removed his tie and jacket and then stopped.

'Your turn now, darling, let's see who's naked first.'

She should have been embarrassed by his frankness but he was laughing as if it was a game.

She kicked off her shoes, slowly peeled down just one stocking, then smiled at him.

'That's cheating, both stockings, if you please.'

The second one came off even more slowly. She was finding it hard to breathe. Even her toes were tingling.

He then removed both shoes and his socks. There was a hectic flush along his cheek bones. He was finding this as exciting as she was.

She unbuttoned her blouse and removed it. This was too much for him. With something like a groan he was beside her. The remainder of their clothes vanished in a frantic rush.

They fell onto the bed, limbs entwined, and Annie finally understood why intimacy was called making love.

16

Emily was excited to be included in the wedding party. She liked Annie and was happy for her and Mr Stoneleigh. Mummy had offered to have the reception at home so Mrs Bates was busy making delicious things for the party tomorrow and she was helping her.

Mr Stoneleigh had officially moved out and was now living in Colchester but as Friday was the day before the wedding, he was going to spend the night at Harbour House. Daddy had told her that the bride and groom were not supposed to see each other the night before the wedding as it could bring bad luck.

'Emily, can you get the sausage rolls out of the oven, there's a duck,' Mrs Bates called from the kitchen.

'I'm coming, I've just finished drying up,' Emily replied. She was thrilled that everybody considered her sensible enough to use the oven without burning herself. She loved being part of the preparations but was even more excited about attending the wedding as she'd never been to one before.

The sausage rolls were perfect, they smelled wonderful and would be put in the meat safe so Ginger couldn't get to them and would then be warmed up the next day so they could be served hot.

'I'd like to have been a bridesmaid but sadly Annie and Mr Stoneleigh aren't having that sort of wedding.'

'There's a war on, love, it's not the time for anything fancy. No wedding cake, no ham sandwiches, but what we do have will be tasty and appreciated.'

'I don't suppose the bride and groom will mind very much what they eat as they'll be too happy to care.'

'Let's hope so.'

Emily didn't understand why Mrs Bates sounded a bit doubtful but didn't like to ask. Mummy was at one of her meetings so she was looking after Grace. She could see the baby sleeping peacefully under the apple tree in the small back garden and would go out immediately her sister woke up.

The school holidays had started yesterday, otherwise she wouldn't have been able to help out. George and Sammy had gone off somewhere with Neil, the three of them were now best friends, and she rather envied them their freedom. Boys had so much more independence than girls did and she hoped that by the time she was grown up things might have changed and women wouldn't be expected to just do all the boring domestic jobs whilst the men had all the fun.

For the second time that day, the windows rattled as two squadrons of fighters roared overhead. The noise woke the baby who began to cry and wave her little fat legs in the air.

'I'm going to bring the pram in, Mrs Bates, Grace won't get a peaceful sleep with so much activity in the sky.'

'Blooming noisy, but that Hitler would be here already if it wasn't for the RAF.'

Emily was now an expert at backing the pram over the doorstep and then neatly reversing it in the scullery so she could push it into the sitting room. By the time she'd done this, the baby was asleep again.

She carefully pulled over a light knitted blanket as it was cooler in the house and she didn't want Grace to be cold.

By the end of the morning, it was obvious something big was happening – there were people in the street looking up at the sky as the squadrons of fighters flew overhead and then flew back but not in formation, they returned alone or in twos. She was glad they did this as now she couldn't work out how many had been lost.

The boys returned, so happy to have seen Spitfires and Hurricanes in action that she didn't like to remind them why this was happening. It didn't seem right to spoil their fun.

Mr Stoneleigh arrived on his motorbike in time for the evening meal and tonight she and the boys were joining the grown-ups in the dining room. Now was her chance to ask the questions she didn't like to ask either of her parents and didn't think that Mrs Bates would know the answer to.

'Excuse me, Mr Stoneleigh,' she said as he kicked off his outdoor shoes. 'What's happening? Is Hitler invading? Why haven't the air-raid sirens gone off?'

He put his hand on her shoulder and that was reassuring. But what he said next wasn't. 'Hitler's sending his bombers to attack the RAF bases and the merchant convoys and our boys are doing sterling work turning them back. The navy's doing its bit as well. The next few weeks are going to be crucial and dangerous.'

Emily shivered. 'You'll be joining your ship on Monday, won't you? It makes it all seem so much more real actually knowing somebody who's going to be in danger.'

'I don't want you to worry about me, Emily. You just concentrate on keeping safe and helping your family the way you do so brilliantly.'

'I'll try. Will Annie be joining the WAAF soon? Will she be in any danger? If they're bombing the RAF bases, could she be on one of them?'

'Yes, but not for several weeks. The initial training's four weeks and then possibly another four weeks depending on what trade she gets. You don't need to worry about her for ages yet.'

The boys were in the front garden, lying on their backs, watching the planes zooming backwards and forwards, thinking it a lark – still not realising the significance. She wasn't going to be the one to tell them, they'd find out soon enough when the air-raid sirens wailed.

* * *

Richard woke early on his wedding day, surprised that he'd slept as soundly. He stretched and yawned, not sure of the exact time as the blackouts were drawn. The luminous dial of his watch showed him it was not quite six. In five hours, he'd be waiting at the altar for his bride.

His first task this morning was to bathe. For the past ten days, he and Annie had been making the most amazing love, discovering what pleased each other, and it had been a revelation for both of them. However, tonight would be different, they'd be married and they'd both be preparing as if it would be the first time.

His new blue officer's uniform was hanging in the wardrobe. He should have been wearing it from the moment he'd collected it two days ago but had wanted to wait and surprise

Annie today. Even on leave, serving officers and other ranks were supposed to be in uniform.

The clothes he'd come in were already folded and would be stored in the attic here with his other belongings until he was demobbed. Annie was leaving the day after him for her basic training, therefore her clothes would remain with Nancy in her attic until they were needed again. She, like him, had already received her travel warrant and instructions, so next time they met they'd both be in uniform. Different blue but both serving.

Molly would be filling his bath right now; she'd agreed to come in early as she'd be finishing early in order to attend the ceremony. He pulled his silk dressing gown over his pyjama bottoms and with bare feet padded down to the small room, off the scullery, where the large tin bath would be waiting for him.

'Good morning, Mr Stoneleigh, all ready, the water's lovely and hot,' Molly greeted him as he poked his head into the kitchen to say good morning.

'Thanks, I'm going to shave first in the cloakroom.'

'There'll be a lovely cooked breakfast ready when you come out. No need to dress first, it's far too early for anyone else to be up.'

He wasn't sure he wanted anything substantial but as she'd gone to so much trouble he just smiled and thanked her.

'Going to be fine again, let's hope we don't get an air raid. I feel it's imminent, don't you?'

'Don't jinx things, Mr Stoneleigh, nothing bad should happen on someone's wedding day.'

* * *

Half an hour later, he was tucking into egg, bacon, field mushrooms and fried bread with gusto. Molly had pointed out he probably wouldn't be able to eat much at the reception as he'd be circulating with his new wife, talking to the guests.

At ten forty-five he was walking to the church with Jonathan.

'That uniform suits you, Richard, goes well with your extraordinary russet hair.'

'I admit I do feel very smart. I'm glad we added the doctor and his wife to the guest list; I like them both.'

'Elizabeth wasn't having thirteen, unlucky, so it made sense to include them.'

The church doors were open and the elderly vicar was waiting to greet them.

'Good morning, gentlemen, lovely day for a wedding. Your guests are here, as they should be, if you care to make your way to the altar. I'll bring your bride when she arrives.'

Richard shook hands with the cleric and walked down the aisle. St Mary's wasn't a big church but could hold around 150 so only the front pews had occupants.

They had divided themselves equally, the Robys on one side and the others on the other. As neither Annie nor him had family present that made sense.

There was no music, no organist available, so Annie would walk down the aisle with Dan without accompaniment.

'Are you nervous?' Jonathan asked.

'Surprisingly not. I've never been more sure I'm doing the right thing with the right woman. I just wish we had longer for our honeymoon, two nights is hardly enough.'

'I have the ring, in case you were worried,' Jonathan said.

'I wasn't, in fact I'd totally forgotten about it. Good thing you hadn't.'

Then Annie was there, not wearing a white bridal gown, but

a stunning floral dress, flowers in her hair and carrying a bouquet of roses.

He caught his breath, couldn't believe this wonderful, beautiful woman was actually marrying him. The vicar progressed slowly down the aisle; the small congregation were on their feet. Dan was walking proudly beside Annie and she was holding his arm.

Her smile said more than words ever could. He wanted to stride forward and snatch her up.

Dan gravely handed over his charge and Richard took her hand, shocked it was trembling.

'I love you, my darling, and you look absolutely stunning.'

'I've never seen you look more handsome. I'm so proud to be marrying you.'

The service started and the vicar asked the congregation if anyone had any objection to speak up, or something like that.

'We have – this cannot be allowed. My son cannot marry that woman. She will ruin his life.' The strident voice of Richard's mother rang out in the church.

Then his father spoke too. 'This Annie Thomas is illegitimate, was married before, can't have children and this travesty of a wedding cannot be continued.'

Annie snatched her hand away, and before Richard could stop her ran out of the church. For a moment, he was too shocked to react.

Jonathan shook his shoulder. 'Go after her, I'll get rid of those two. Bring her back and we can continue.'

It didn't matter if Annie returned. Their wedding day was ruined.

* * *

Annie didn't run out of the main gate of the church but took the steps that brought her out at the end of West Street. She fled down to the station and arrived just as the bus was about to pull away.

All she could think was that she was glad she wasn't holding her bouquet of roses. Her frock was pretty, but no one would suspect it was her wedding dress. She always had two silver coins tied in a handkerchief and slipped into a pocket – just in case.

This was the first time she'd ever had to untie the knot and remove one of the shillings. She paid her fare and took a seat on the left of the bus, the side where she wouldn't be seen if anybody came out of the church looking for her.

How could she be travelling on a bus away from the man she loved, from a wedding she'd been looking forward to? Less than fifteen minutes ago she'd been about to exchange her vows with Richard.

She wasn't exactly sure why she'd run off. If she'd not done so then maybe Richard would still have wanted to marry her. He knew her and had accepted it, but now everybody else was aware of her shameful birth then he might well reconsider.

How had his parents discovered they were getting married today? She didn't understand where they'd got this personal information from as they hadn't announced their wedding and as far as she knew only the guests were aware it was taking place.

By the time the bus was halfway to Colchester, Annie was sorry she'd abandoned Richard at the altar and caused him even more embarrassment. She didn't have a key to Nancy's house, the back gate was locked from the inside, as they'd all left through the front door of the shop.

Nancy had hoped Auntie Ethel would be prepared to run it

All Change at Harbour House

for her today but her Uncle Stan was having one of his poorly days and couldn't be left alone. Therefore, the shop was closed for the day.

Only now did tears trickle down Annie's cheeks. Nancy had given up a day's takings to be at her wedding, Dan had walked her down the aisle and Mrs Roby was putting on the reception and now it was all for nothing.

Then the bus was flagged down in Greenstead Road for others to get on and without thinking she flew down the bus and jumped off. Maybe she'd be lucky and a bus going in the opposite direction would come past and she'd be able to get back to Wivenhoe before the vicar and the guests had dispersed.

Her best shoes were not the most comfortable as they weren't meant to be worn to take long walks. She was limping, had blisters on both her heels after walking only a hundred yards or so.

A car was approaching from behind her but she wasn't sure she had the courage to ask for a lift from a stranger. There was no need for her to make that decision as it pulled up beside her.

'You look as if you could do with a lift, young lady. I'm going to Wivenhoe Shipyard.'

The driver was a man in his thirties wearing spectacles and an old-fashioned tweed suit.

'Thank you, you're an absolute godsend. I need to be at the church as soon as possible. I'm late for a wedding.'

He didn't ask any further questions, probably assumed she was a guest who'd missed the bus, but he put his foot down and they travelled far faster than was safe. He screeched to a halt outside the church.

'Hope you're not too late, young lady. Good luck.'

'Thank you very much.'

She was out of the car in a flash and as she ran up the path to the main doors she could hear voices inside. She wasn't exactly sure how long she'd been gone but a lot less than an hour.

The vicar, the children and their parents, Molly and her husband, the doctor and his wife, and old Mrs Roby were there but not Richard, Nancy or Dan. Thankfully Mr and Mrs Stoneleigh were no longer there either.

'My dear girl, thank goodness you've come back,' Mrs Roby senior said and rushed up to embrace her. 'What a dreadful shock for you. My son and the doctor evicted Mr Stoneleigh's parents. They'll not be back to cause any more trouble.'

'Where are the others?' Annie asked.

The vicar came up to her. 'I can wait for your bridegroom's return, Mrs Thomas, as long as he's here before one o'clock. I have another wedding at one thirty.'

Annie collapsed onto the front pew. She closed her eyes and sent up a sincere prayer to the Almighty, apologising for her behaviour and asking him to send Richard back in time for the marriage to go ahead.

She wasn't exactly sure how long she'd been communing with God when she heard the distinct sound of a motorbike.

'Is she here, has she come back? Thank God for that.' It was him and she turned to face him, not knowing how she could apologise for putting him through this.

People didn't run in church, but Richard did. Her feet moved of their own volition, and she rushed to meet him.

'I'm so sorry, I don't know why I ran away. It was such an awful shock. I thought it was God's way of telling me I shouldn't be marrying you.'

'No, my darling, it was my vile parents. God has brought us

back together in time to get married and put this unfortunate event aside.'

'We can't go ahead until all the guests are back, it wouldn't be fair.'

The vicar, overhearing her remark, smiled and nodded. 'The children went in search of them, I'm sure they'll return imminently.'

The old man was right and a few minutes later the children, looking flushed and excited, ran in, closely followed by Dan and Nancy.

Richard kept his arm around her and moved her back to the place they'd been standing between the choir stalls before the horrible interruption.

The remainder of the service was a blur to Annie. She repeated the responses when asked to and held out her hand for the wedding band to be pressed over her ring finger.

'Congratulations, you are now man and wife,' the vicar said and the guests sitting on the front pews jumped to their feet, cheered and clapped. Most unseemly in a church, but today it seemed even the vicar thought it appropriate as he joined in the applause.

Richard kissed her. 'I think, Mrs Stoneleigh, that we'll never forget our wedding day.'

'I think, Mr Stoneleigh, that you might be right. Despite everything that happened I couldn't be happier.'

'And neither could I. Now shall we get off to Harbour House and enjoy the splendid spread that Molly has got ready for us?'

17

Emily watched the bride and groom leave the church hand in hand then realised Annie had forgotten her bouquet. She grabbed it and ran after the happy couple but she wasn't sure how Mr Stoneleigh and Annie could be happy after what had happened.

'Mrs Stoneleigh, you've left this behind,' she yelled and everyone stopped and stared at her. Shouting wasn't done in a churchyard.

Annie laughed. 'Thank you, Emily, I really want to keep those flowers to remember today.'

The guests laughed and Emily hoped this would mean her parents would forget about her shouting by the time the reception was over.

She looked around, expecting the other pedestrians and villagers to be pointing and talking behind their hands after the upset in the church. It wasn't usual to have an actual motorbike in with the tombstones.

Mr Stoneleigh ignored his bike and continued to walk with his new wife so Dan wheeled it to Harbour House. Mrs Bates had hurried home first and Nancy was helping her mother put the spread out on the lovely white tablecloth on the dining-room table especially for today. Food couldn't be left out as Ginger would eat it.

The house shook as more fighters flew out to sea. George and Sammy rushed into the garden, sausage rolls forgotten, to watch. They were hoping to see a dogfight overhead, have a plane crash near Wivenhoe so they could collect souvenirs. If their parents knew what they were planning they'd be kept indoors until the war was over.

The room was full of laughing, chatting guests and not one of them was talking about the fact that the wedding had almost been cancelled. Emily ran back and forth fetching and carrying plates, glasses and cups of tea all afternoon.

Dan made a short speech, then Mr Stoneleigh said a few words and the party was over. Annie came into the kitchen to speak to Emily before she left on the back of the motorbike.

'Thank you for helping, love. I've got something for you at Nancy's – you can collect it next time you visit.'

'That's very kind of you, Mrs Stoneleigh. You and Mr Stoneleigh look so happy. I'm sure you're going to have a wonderful marriage.'

'I know we are, love. I've got to go; we're going to London for a couple of nights for our honeymoon.' As Mrs Bates left immediately after the bride and groom, Emily volunteered to finish the washing up and put everything away.

She and Grandma worked happily together. 'I love helping in the house, Grandma,' she said as she dried another plate.

'I bet you won't say that in thirty years' time, my dear. I can assure you the novelty soon wears off.'

'Don't you have somebody to do your washing up?'

'I have someone come in weekdays but like this household I

have to do everything at the weekend.' She smiled and handed over another plate. 'I didn't come from a home like this, I was like Annie. Like she'll have to do, I had to learn how to behave.'

'Grandpa must have really loved you, like Mr Stoneleigh loves Annie, to have gone against his family.'

'He did, I'm sure he still does, but I don't like rattling around in that big house on my own whilst he spends most of his time organising the home guard and going on trips with them.'

'I'm sure that he misses you dreadfully, but we all hope you stay here for a long time; we love having a grandma living with us.'

* * *

Now Annie had gone, it meant if they were going to have a proper Sunday lunch either Mummy or Grandma had to cook it.

This Sunday it was Grandma's turn and when Emily asked politely if she could stay behind and help, not go to church, her parents agreed.

'You're going to make a wonderful wife when you grow up,' Mummy said. 'When you're old enough, when the war's over, I'm sure that we can find someone suitable for you.'

Emily was going to say that she didn't want to marry anybody before she'd been to university and had a career of her own. She didn't need to as Daddy gave Mummy one of his terrifying looks.

'Don't look so horrified, sweetheart, when you grow up you'll be able to choose your own path. If you want to go to university or want to get married that's entirely up to you.'

'I don't know what I want, but I do know I want to make my own decisions about everything. If women can drive buses, fly aeroplanes, become doctors then we can certainly organise who we marry when the time comes.'

A year ago, her mummy would have been upset, angry even at being corrected. Today things were different, she was different, and she laughed.

'You're right, darling girl, to reprimand me. I chose my own husband against my parents' wishes so I can hardly expect you to do something that I refused to do.'

George scowled at Emily as he followed their parents out of the front door. 'It's not fair that you get to stay at home and miss the boring church service.'

Daddy overheard him. 'If you want to stay and do housework, peel potatoes, wash up then I'm sure Emily will be happy to relinquish her place and come to church instead of you.'

'Boys don't do things like that. Sammy and I want to watch the dogfights. We're hoping to see a plane shot down; we've not seen anyone bail out yet either.'

For a horrible moment, Emily thought Daddy was going to smack her brother. From George's expression he thought so too. His eyes widened and he flinched.

Daddy leaned down so his face was close to George's. He spoke so quietly she couldn't hear what he said but she did hear George gulp and his shoulders slumped.

The church party left and Grandma hugged her. 'Don't worry, my dear, my son would never raise his hand to any of you, whatever you did. Mind you, I was sorely tempted to smack his legs myself. I don't think your brother will talk so casually again about our brave pilots being shot down, do you?'

* * *

Richard decided to risk leaving his precious motorbike at Colchester station. Knowing she was going to be on a motorbike from Wivenhoe to Colchester, Annie had put a warm coat and headscarf in one of the panniers.

'I feel we might be tempting fate, my darling,' he said as she was putting on her coat and tying the scarf over her glorious dark brown hair. The bright floral scarf made her stunning dark blue eyes even more beautiful. 'Are you sure you want to go to London and stay in my friend's flat?'

'After what happened in the church, I have to admit that I'm feeling a bit superstitious about trying to repeat that visit.'

'I agree. Where do you want to go instead?'

'I don't care where we stay as long as it's not at Nancy's. I hope we're going to spend every minute in bed so why not a hotel in Chelmsford? There must be a nice one there.'

'I spent two nights there, not in a hotel but in a bed and breakfast. However, I ate lunch at a rather splendid hotel called Saracens. I'm sure there are other places. After all, Chelmsford is the county town of Essex, isn't it?'

'Well, I do know that it's a city and Colchester isn't, they have a cathedral and we don't. Apart from that I've no idea as I've never been there.'

'Then we'll try Saracens first, if they can't accommodate us then I'm sure they can recommend somewhere else. As you say, my darling, we won't want anything but room service.'

* * *

Fortunately, the best suite in the place was available and Richard immediately took it. They were conducted upstairs with due ceremony, a lot of bowing and scraping by the concierge who'd conducted them there himself.

The man unlocked the door and opened it with a flourish. 'Sir, madam, these are our best rooms. I know that you will be very comfortable here. Congratulations on your wedding.'

Richard looked around and nodded. 'Splendid, this will do perfectly. Please send up a bottle of your best champagne, well chilled, at eight o'clock along with whatever your chef thinks appropriate for the occasion.'

'Yes, sir, eight o'clock. If you ring down to reception when you require breakfast tomorrow it will be brought up to you.'

The concierge handed Richard the key, bowed and backed out. Richard was smiling as he picked Annie up and carried her over the doorstep.

'This isn't our own home but it's tradition to carry your wife over the doorstep after the wedding.'

'Why are you laughing? What did that man say? I didn't hear anything funny.'

He kissed her and then put her down. 'It wasn't what he said, it was his behaviour. I can assure you that if you're treated like royalty then the bill will be fit for a king too.'

She didn't laugh as he'd hoped but looked stricken. 'We could have stayed at that B&B; I really don't want you to pay so much just for a couple of nights.'

'It doesn't matter what it costs, this is our honeymoon, my darling, and for forty-eight hours we shall forget about the war, about my despicable parents, and my forthcoming deployment. We shall just enjoy each other's company.'

Now she giggled. 'I was hoping for a bit more than your company, Richard. We've got three hours before the champagne comes – let's make the most of it.'

* * *

Annie was taking a long, luxurious bath with far more than the regulation five inches of water when the expected knock came on the door. Luckily, Richard had had the sense to pull on his underpants before opening it.

He stood aside whilst two waiters laid the table by the window as if they were dining downstairs. There were candles, flowers in a vase, and whatever was under the silver covers smelled wonderful.

Neither of the men said a word, they didn't look in his direction, in fact he might as well have been invisible, and set out their dinner, put the champagne in its bucket on the table and vanished before he could give them a tip.

Richard was tempted to join Annie in the bath but then this delicious dinner would be ruined and no doubt the floor would be awash. Instead, he remained outside the door and called softly to her. 'Dinner's on the table, darling. I'm just going to open the champagne.'

They devoured every morsel and it was as good, better even, than either of them had expected. Although neither of them were big drinkers, they finished the bottle whilst they ate.

'Shall we return to bed, my love? I don't think I can do more than sleep, but I'll do my best.'

'Sleep is exactly what I want to do. Do we have to put all this outside the door?'

He grinned. 'Leave it to me.' He picked up the entire table and she held the door open for him. He put it in the corridor and then added the empty champagne bottle in its bucket.

They were both laughing when they fell into bed where they remained. They weren't making love the entire time, that wouldn't have been possible. They talked, planned and got to know each other better.

* * *

Now it was Monday morning and reality hit home hard, especially for Richard. He propped himself on one elbow and gazed down at his sleeping wife, the woman of his heart, his reason for staying alive. If a ship was torpedoed then officers had more chance of surviving than those poor sods working in the engine room below decks. They'd go down with the ship.

Would he ever see her again? He didn't need to memorise her face as it was already etched in his mind. Dan could have drowned when his barge had sunk but he'd managed to swim, in rough seas, to shore and miraculously survived. Think positively, don't dwell on the worst thing that could happen.

Richard's ship was a destroyer, the HMS *Brazen*. They would be escorting convoys and protecting them from submarines. They were equipped with depth charges and sonar and were an essential part of the navy's battle against the U-boats. Leaving Annie was hard but it was his duty to fight to protect Britain from the German invasion.

He'd been roused a few times when squadrons of fighters left Hornchurch, only a few miles from Chelmsford, and again whenever a solo fighter returned to refuel and rearm. The Luftwaffe were bombing the RAF bases as well as attacking the convoys of merchant ships that were trying to bring much-needed supplies into Britain. If they succeeded, then the invasion might well begin.

'Darling Richard, please don't look so sad. Let's not reflect on anything but us for these last few hours of our honeymoon.'

She reached up and pulled him down. He forgot the war, the Germans and was lost in the wonder of making passionate love to the woman he adored. Whatever happened, they had these incredible memories to hold on to. He prayed there would be more wonderful things in the future to share.

* * *

Annie didn't want to think about Richard leaving. She wasn't stupid, knew he might well not return. She believed that a naval officer had more chance of living to see the end of the war than the brave young men flying back and forth overhead.

He had to collect his bike and the rest of his kit from Colchester before he set out on the short ride to Harwich where his ship was waiting.

The wind whipped her tears from her eyes as they travelled from Colchester station to Head Street but at least Richard wouldn't realise she'd been crying but just think it was because she'd been on the back of his motorbike.

They glided to a halt outside the back gate. In the few weeks since he'd had his motorbike he'd become an expert and she no longer worried about him having an accident when he was on it.

'I'll leave it out here, darling, I'm sure nobody will steal it today.'

What he meant was that he wasn't going to be inside long enough for anyone to do that, but tactfully didn't say this.

For some reason the dog was subdued – did he sense how sad they both were? Annie leaned down and stroked his head and he licked her hand and leaned against her.

Nancy and Daphne would be working in the shop and Dan would have left ages ago. He walked down to the Hythe where his barge was moored.

Annie was glad they were alone as she was dreading saying goodbye to Richard. She didn't want to cry, to cling to him, but had a horrible feeling that was exactly what she was going to do.

'I could do with a cuppa before I leave, darling. If you put the kettle on, I'll collect my gear from upstairs.'

She nodded, unable to answer, her throat thick with tears.

The kettle was always left full and simmering on the range and it only took moments to bring it to the full boil and tip it into the waiting teapot. He didn't want a cup of tea, neither of them did, but it had given her time to try and compose herself.

He gave her five minutes before coming into the kitchen with his massive blue cotton kitbag over his shoulder. He'd had to go up to London twice to get fitted for his uniform and she was surprised they'd managed to get it done in just over a week. Thinking about something mundane was better than thinking about what was about to happen.

'Don't worry about the tea, I really need to get going. I'm supposed to report to my captain at four o'clock and that will be pushing it.'

'I'll make tea for Nancy and Daphne now it's boiled. I won't come out with you. Please, dearest Richard, just go. I love you. I know you can't send me a letter until I'm settled somewhere after my training, but I'll write to you.'

His eyes were glittering, his voice choked. 'I can't promise that I'll receive anything as obviously when we're at sea we don't get mail. But please write, I'll read them when we return to port.' He cleared his throat and then pulled her almost roughly into his arms. 'God, this is so hard. You're my world, I love you, Annie Stoneleigh, and I promise I'll do everything in my power to come back safe to you at the end of this bloody war.'

He kissed her hard, his cheeks as wet as hers, and then grabbed his bag and was gone. She remained stationary until she heard the distinctive roar of his motorbike. Moments later, she collapsed on the nearest chair and sobbed.

Boyd pressed against her and when this didn't stop the tears he tried to climb onto her lap. It was difficult to cry when a huge hairy dog was licking your face enthusiastically.

'Go away, silly animal, I bet you've laddered my only pair of stockings.'

She hugged him briefly and then pushed him off. Women all over Britain had been saying goodbye to their men since the war started last September – if they all sat in a chair sobbing all day, nothing would get done.

She washed her face at the sink in the scullery and the cold water calmed her a little. The dog was still glued to her side, somehow knowing his presence was making things a bit easier for her.

'I gave you a few minutes, Annie love, before coming in. Your man will come back to you – like my Dan, I think he's going to stay safe,' Nancy said.

They hugged and Annie was finally able to speak without gulping. 'We were both crying, isn't that ridiculous? I didn't ask him how he was going to get his huge bag onto his motorbike but he must have managed it as he was gone only minutes after leaving me.'

'He wasn't leaving you; he was just going to Harwich to join his ship. Now, we'll have a cup of tea together. Daphne can manage the shop as we're never busy on a Monday morning.'

* * *

Several days passed before Annie was able to smile again. One morning she was sitting at the kitchen table when Boyd put his huge head in Annie's lap and Nancy smiled at her dog.

'You should have seen him when I thought Dan was dead, he followed me to bed and didn't leave me until Dan appeared and sent him packing. Don't understand how his family could have abandoned him the way they did.'

'He must eat a lot so that's probably why,' Annie said. 'By the way, I've not seen Tabby today – is he asleep upstairs?'

Nancy nodded. 'He spends the night hunting and as you know he brings two or three nice plump rabbits from the fields every week. I think he's actually bringing them back for his best mate, Boyd.'

'I think good people attract goodness to them so that's why both your dog and your cat are so extraordinary.'

'I wouldn't be without either of them.' Nancy nodded at the untouched mug of tea in front of Annie. 'Are you going to drink that?'

'It smells funny, I really don't fancy it. It's making me feel sick.'

Nancy didn't question this but quickly removed the tea. 'I'll take this one in to Daphne, I'll be back in a minute.'

Annie tipped the remainder of the hot water from the kettle into a mug and drank that instead. She must have eaten something to upset her stomach as she'd never turned down a cup of tea in her life before.

* * *

Richard reported to HMS *Badger*, the shoreside headquarters of 1st Destroyer flotilla where the vice admiral was stationed to control his ships. Richard was told by the leading seaman manning the desk that he had two hours before his transport arrived to collect him. He'd hoped that his ship would have been docked at the naval port but she was obviously at sea waiting to sail. He wasn't given any explanation, but he was logged in as having arrived in good time so it didn't really matter when he got aboard HMS *Brazen*.

'I'll leave my kit here. Keep an eye on it,' he said to the rating who nodded and saluted. He returned the gesture.

Richard had read the Officers' Handbook from cover to cover and hoped that he remembered all the salient points. One of them being that you should always return a salute from a rating, always answer any questions politely, and when issuing orders make sure they are followed to the letter.

He'd been told at Admiralty House that he'd be promoted to lieutenant as soon as he was familiar with life aboard a naval ship. He'd never been on a destroyer; in fact he'd not been on any naval ship.

When he'd studied for his navigational qualifications and taken his first mate's certificate he'd been a civilian. Therefore, everything had been done on a merchant ship and had been completed whilst he'd been studying for his naval architect's degree at Oxford University. Although he'd been officially attached to the Admiralty since he qualified, his only contact with naval officers had been at Brightlingsea.

Captaining a tug at Dunkirk didn't really qualify in his opinion, but it had given him his sea legs, so to speak. Despite having grown up in leafy Hampstead he'd spent as many weeks of his school summer breaks as he could in Hastings where he'd learned to sail as well as fish.

Harwich was new to him. He intended to spend half the time he had before the small boat arrived to ferry him out to HMS *Brazen* to getting a feel for it. He decided to use his motorbike, not walk, as that would mean ratings wouldn't have to salute and he wouldn't have to return the gesture.

Harwich had always been a busy port, had a fishing fleet as

well as receiving and sending an abundance of cargo ships across the North Sea. Ships had been docking there with passengers and goods for hundreds of years, but everything was different now.

The port was militarised, concrete pillboxes with machine guns poking out of the slits, navy-blue uniforms predominated but there were almost as many khaki-clad men. He didn't bother to look up when the RAF fighters deafened him, and scarcely noticed when the ground shook from the explosions out to sea.

What he was interested in was the 1st Destroyer flotilla, part of the Home Fleet, and seeing the ship he was going to be berthed on. He smiled grimly. He'd be an officer on this ship for the remainder of the war – or until it was sunk. These ships were on escort duty in home waters, but that could all change. It was quite possible they'd be reassigned and sent out to join a fleet in foreign waters and then he'd never get home.

Richard kicked his bike into life and cruised around the port, impressed with what he saw. There were few civilians along the waterside, but that was only to be expected. He wasn't interested in the civilian part of this town as he wouldn't be visiting any of the pubs or shops if he was lucky enough to get any shore leave.

The pocket binoculars he'd managed to find in a pawnshop in London, on one of the two trips he'd made to organise his uniform, were ideal for looking out to sea. With the engine running, still astride the motorbike, he peered through them and nodded.

He ran through what he knew about HMS *Brazen*. She was a comparatively new B-class destroyer, her top speed was 35 knots and she had only recently been assigned to Harwich. He couldn't wait to get aboard. Her role was to sink U-boats and shoot down enemy aircraft.

After finding a safe place to leave his motorbike, Richard still had half an hour before he had to report to the dock. He decided to write a letter to Annie even though he knew she wouldn't receive it. He'd address it to Head Street and hopefully Nancy would forward it when she knew where Annie was based.

He wasn't fighting this war for just King and country, he didn't think any man was, they were doing it for their own loved ones. None of them wanted the Nazis marching down British streets where their wives, mothers, daughters and children were living.

He blinked away tears. Was he ever going to see his beloved Annie again? Leaving her this morning, so soon after they'd been married, was the hardest thing he'd ever done.

18

Emily and the boys were going to help with the potato picking at the Peterson farm this week. Daddy had said George and Sammy were old enough to be trusted as long as they stayed with her.

'We have to be there by half past eight, you two, so if you're not ready in five minutes I'm going without you,' Emily said as she packed the last of their greaseproof paper-wrapped sandwiches into a basket.

Mrs Bates nodded approvingly. 'It's blooming hard work picking spuds but if the three of you work as one team it won't be so bad. You should get ten shillings each for the week.'

'That's a lot of money, especially for the boys. Jimmy explained how it works – we'll get a section of the field between us and have to pick potatoes, put them in the buckets and tip them in the trailer. We don't finish until four o'clock. I'm not sure the boys will be able to keep it up for a whole day.'

'We jolly well can,' George said from behind her. 'Lots of the village boys and girls are going to be there and we're not going to let Harbour House down by giving up halfway through a day.'

'Good for you, love,' Mrs Bates said. 'You're lucky, it's been fine and dry this past week and it won't be too bad. It's nasty picking potatoes when it's wet so let's hope it doesn't rain until the crop's in.'

With their buckets clanking noisily, Emily set out with her brothers and wasn't surprised to find they weren't the only children and women walking towards the farm.

She didn't know anyone and if her friends at the girls' grammar school knew she was going potato picking they'd be horrified. It wasn't as if her family needed the extra money, but when Jimmy Peterson had suggested she and the boys participated, she'd immediately agreed.

Once they got to the farm, they piled onto a trailer attached to a tractor to be transported to the field. She was surprised that there were little children, far too small to be picking potatoes, accompanying their mothers. She thought these little ones would have a good time roaming about the fields getting muddy whilst their mothers were busy but might well get in the way or get bored.

Only as the tractor pulled out of the farmyard did she notice the four girls who'd bullied her when she'd briefly attended the local school were also on the trailer. Her knuckles were white on the handles of her bucket. Pete Bryant, Sammy's older brother, had scared them off, but she'd have to deal with them on her own today. Mind you, it was almost a year ago and she hoped they might well have forgotten and not be bothered about her now.

* * *

One of the land girls was driving the tractor but the farmer, Mr Peterson, was waiting to greet them. He allocated a section of field to each group – the women had a section to do on their own, but the children shared one. They had to stand at the beginning of their bit and the three of them would work together. They had to get to the end of their row before the tractor was ready to plough up the next one.

A section was quite wide, so the fact that those horrible girls had the next but one along shouldn't matter – at least she hoped it wouldn't because they'd definitely recognised her and hadn't looked pleased that she was there.

The pickers started at alternate ends of the field as the tractor would travel down in one direction and back in the other. This meant they were standing more or less alone as the next row would be started at the far end of the field.

At precisely half past eight, the tractor started. It rumbled down the first row of plants. Theirs was the third one in so they'd a little while before it reached them.

This gave Emily time to watch how the experienced potato pickers worked. They straddled the row, plonked their buckets in front of them and bent from the waist to pick them up. As soon as they'd filled the bucket, they hurried to the nearest trailer to tip them in.

It looked simple enough and Emily thought that it would be easiest for the boys who were closer to the ground and didn't have so far to bend. The idea was that the potato pickers finished their row and were ready at the opposite end to begin the hard work all over again.

* * *

When they eventually stopped for a break at ten thirty she was exhausted, covered in mud, and wishing she'd never agreed to come. The boys were so tired they didn't even have the energy to complain. They flopped on the grass next to her.

Her precious food basket that she'd hidden at the end of the field under her coat was intact and she removed the Thermos flask and the old tin mugs and half-filled each one. 'Here you are, boys, a nice hot drink will perk you up.'

They gulped it down and did look a little bit better.

'I'm not keen on this potato picking, Emily. I don't think I'm going to come tomorrow. We'll only get a shilling a day each and it's just not worth it,' George said.

'I think we get two shillings; the women get more as they have a bigger section to do.'

'Two shillings a day is still not worth it,' George insisted.

'I don't disagree. We have to finish today as we can't walk out and leave our section half done. But one day is more than enough.' She prodded George who was nearest to her. 'This was your idea. I didn't want to do it.'

'Worst idea I've ever had,' he said with a grin.

She handed over half a sandwich and this was eaten along with the mud on their hands.

'No one looks happy,' Sammy said. 'I reckon that maybe if you did this every day by the end of the week it won't seem so bad.'

'At the end of the week I'd be dead,' George said. 'I think I might well expire before the end of today.'

The fifteen-minute break was too short and with considerable reluctance the three of them returned to their position. Emily looked around and wasn't sure if the fact that everybody looked really tired was a good thing or not. Even the children who'd been so full of beans when they'd arrived two hours ago were now whining and hanging around their mothers asking to go home.

By lunchtime, her back was hurting so much she'd been forced to drop to her knees to pick and she noticed that a lot of those on the field were doing the same. She also saw that at least two sections had been abandoned – she thought they'd been occupied by children.

The three of them devoured the remainder of the picnic, drank all the tea and the bottle of water, and then stretched out on the warm grass.

'Don't go to sleep, boys, you'll never get up again and we only get half an hour.'

'You can wake us up, Emily. I can't keep my eyes open. I'd rather be a soldier than a potato picker,' George said as a dozen or more Spitfires headed out to sea.

Even their favourite fighter plane wasn't enough to keep them awake. Emily had a horrible feeling she might have to pick the entire row on her own. Nine years old was really too young to be working like this. The fact that in Victorian times children had worked down the mines, gone up chimneys even, didn't make it right.

* * *

Somehow the three of them got to the end of the day but the tractor had finished ploughing and they still had a whole row to pick. The women had completed their allocated sections, collected their miserable children and clambered onto the trailer. The land girl had driven off with them.

Fortunately, they weren't the only ones left behind. 'George, Sammy, we can't go home until this last row is picked so we'd better get on with it.'

'No,' George said firmly. 'We're going. You can pick the blooming potatoes if you want, we've done our day's work. It's after four o'clock – we won't get paid for picking these.'

'I can't do the entire row on my own, I'll be here until six o'clock,' Emily said, hearing the whine in her voice and hating it.

'Then leave them, come home with us,' George said.

'No, I'll work for another hour, then I'll come. You go home and tell Mummy I'll be along later.'

The boys abandoned their buckets and headed for the hedge. If they went through that it would be much nearer the lane than walking back to the farm. She was too dispirited to call back and the thought of carrying three buckets and the basket the mile and a half home was a depressing one.

* * *

Annie sipped the hot water, puzzled about her reaction to her favourite drink. Nancy returned and sat down at the table with her. She had a strange look on her face.

'Have you missed one of your monthlies, by any chance?'

'I'm a few days late, but that's all,' Annie said.

'I think you're expecting. You told me you're as regular as clockwork, like me, and always come on the dot. Not wanting tea, along with being late is good enough for me.'

'I was married for three years and didn't fall; it doesn't seem possible that I'm pregnant.'

'I'm expecting too. I'm two weeks late, can't stand the smell of anything fried and have been sick the last two mornings. Imagine that – both of us having babies.'

Annie couldn't take it in. From being unhappy, a flicker of joy ran through her.

She did a quick mental calculation. 'I reckon we'll both be having babies sometime in March and that's a good time, the babies will have all summer to get strong.'

Nancy's eyes were shining; they were grinning at each other as if they'd won the football pools. 'I'd like a girl, but as long as it's healthy, I don't really mind.'

'A girl would be nice, but like you I don't care. Isn't this exciting?'

'I've not said anything to Dan. By the time he's home I'll have missed my next one so I'll tell him then.'

'I'm not saying anything to Richard until I'm absolutely sure. I think he said they do get an occasional shore leave, about every six weeks or so. He won't get any letters until then anyway.'

* * *

Nancy had to return to the shop as she didn't like to leave Daphne alone for too long. The girl hadn't really settled in and Annie knew it wouldn't be long before she and Nancy were living in this big house alone. She couldn't stop smiling. Next spring there'd be two babies as well as four adults, a cat and a dog.

When she settled down at the treadle sewing machine a bit later to get on with her sewing, her heart was singing. This was something she could do right the way through the pregnancy and then continue when the baby was born.

This evening she'd put all the forms she'd been sent about becoming a WAAF, along with her travel warrant in an envelope and post it back to London. If things went well, and she knew they didn't always, then in around eight months she'd be a mother and would never be alone again.

When she returned to the kitchen at lunchtime there was a spam sandwich with piccalilli waiting for her along with a mug of hot water. Daphne was in charge and Nancy had taken the dog for his midday walk. The shop, like all the others, closed for lunch every day and their half-day was Wednesday. The girl didn't appear to have made herself any lunch and was hovering nervously by the back door. Something was up.

'Thank you, Daphne, you don't need to look after me, I could have made my own sandwich.'

'I prefer being in the kitchen, I'm not keen on dealing with people all the time.' The girl hesitated then continued. 'Actually, I've found a nice little job at the Red Lion, cooking and that, not waiting on the tables.'

'Will you be living in?'

Daphne shook her head. 'No, I have to be there at seven for breakfast and then finish after lunch. I can stop at home which suits me much better. My mum's lonely without me, she's not got anyone else. My dad died when I was a toddler.'

This was the longest speech the girl had ever made to Annie. 'Have you told Nancy that you're leaving? I'm sure she'll understand.'

'Will you tell her for me? I start my new job tomorrow. I'm all packed and I'm going now – tell her ta for everything and I'll call in for what I'm owed next week.'

By the time Nancy got back, Daphne had already left. Annie explained what had happened and the news didn't come as a surprise.

'I'm a bit upset she didn't tell me to my face, but then she's not much more than a child really, just fifteen. Do you know her mum, Lily Turner? She lives somewhere in West Street – one of those wooden cottages near the station, I think. Lily's my dad's cousin, or something like that.'

'I don't. Even though I lived in Wivenhoe for almost four years I didn't mix, didn't even join the WI. I'd probably know her by sight if she went to church as that's something I always did.'

Nancy hung the dog's lead on the nail by the door and then joined her at the table. 'Lily was sixteen when she was wed and only seventeen when Daphne arrived. She looks younger; I'm surprised she hasn't found herself another husband.'

'Not many men about now, I suppose,' Annie said. 'I've been thinking, now Daphne's gone we could get the sewing machine moved into her room which would give you and Dan the sitting room back. Also, it would be easier to fit somebody's frock if we've got a separate place to do it. More private.'

'I've also been thinking. Will you help me in the shop? It's not really busy enough to employ somebody full time but if you're willing to come down when I need help that would be really good.'

'I'd be happy to. It doesn't seem fair that I'll have a nursery and you and Dan won't. It would be better if the sewing machine was with me.'

Nancy couldn't decide whether having the heavy machine moved up a flight of stairs was worth the convenience of having a room to use as a nursery.

'Let's leave things as they are – we've got months before either of us need a nursery – Dan and Richard have to be home at the same time to move things around. No point in paying someone when we've got two strong men of our own.'

* * *

That evening, Annie wrote the letter to the WAAF explaining why she wouldn't be joining up. The windows rattled for a third time that day. The losses in the RAF were dreadful and she was glad that she didn't have a wireless as then she'd have to listen to the news.

The War Office printed the names of those that had died, were missing presumed dead, or POWs after a plane or a ship went down. Sometimes folk had to wait weeks to find out. Richard's ship was called HMS *Brazen*, a destroyer based at Harwich; at least this meant he didn't have far to come when he did get time off. She prayed she'd never hear that name mentioned on the news or see it in the newspaper.

She was just sticking on the stamp when Nancy called up the stairs. 'We've got the house to ourselves now. When Dan's not here you should be in the sitting room with me so we can make plans.'

This was exactly what Annie had been hoping. Much better than sitting upstairs brooding about what might or might not happen.

Nancy had already made them both a cocoa and Annie sniffed it nervously.

'I can drink this; it doesn't make me feel sick at all. Isn't that strange?'

'I've heard that some women eat coal when they're expecting, that's even stranger.'

Annie took the armchair and Nancy curled up on the sofa. 'We'll both need a layette, something to put the baby in when it arrives, and a pram of some sort. Not that you can get one of those for love nor money at the moment,' Nancy said.

'Mrs Roby has got a lovely pushchair for when Grace is older. I'm sure she'd let us have the pram and we could share it. We don't have to go out at the same time, do we?'

'Even if we do, we can put one at each end, like twins. I can't knit very well,' Nancy said. 'What about you?'

Annie shook her head. 'I can sew anything, like you, but I don't knit. Does your mum?'

'She's a dab hand at it. We'll get her to make matinee coats, booties, bonnets and mittens for both the babies. In fact, Annie, I'm sure she'll be happy to be a nanna to both of them.'

'We can use a drawer for the first few weeks. With a blanket at the bottom it'll be snug and warm for them. I'm sure your dad can make you a crib,' Annie said. 'I don't have anybody to ask so I'll just have to hope Richard's a competent carpenter.'

Thoughtfully she rubbed her tummy. She'd never expected to ever be married again, to have a baby, but couldn't be happier that she was. It wasn't what she'd expected to be doing, had hoped to be in the WAAF, but she wouldn't want things to be any different.

19

Emily grudgingly picked up her bucket and returned to the row of potatoes left in her section. On the far side of the field a handful of pickers remained, some old, some young, but all determined to finish what they'd started.

'Here, posh girl, you'll be here another two hours getting all them spuds in the trailer,' a well-remembered voice yelled from the other end of the field. 'You'll not get done on your own, we reckon.'

With a resigned sigh, Emily turned to answer. To her astonishment, the three girls who'd bullied her last year were now at the end of her row picking up the potatoes for her.

She wasn't sure what to say, didn't feel comfortable yelling her thanks down the field, so set to with as much energy as she had left and worked towards them. Were they just helping in order to make her relax before attacking her?

Head down, she filled and emptied her bucket, all the time moving closer to the three older girls, wondering what was going to happen when they met. She was older, stronger, and more confident than she'd been a year ago and thought that maybe she could talk them out of hurting her. Perhaps if she gave them the two shillings tied in her hanky for emergencies they'd be satisfied and leave her alone.

They were twenty yards away when she stopped and stood up, feeling really foolish. These girls weren't going to hurt her, they were helping her. They could have come over to her easily enough without lifting half a row of potatoes for her.

'This is so kind of you, I really appreciate it. I know I could have left them but that didn't seem fair to Mr Peterson,' she called to them.

The taller one – she didn't know any of their names – straightened and waved. She dropped her bucket and walked up to Emily.

'Least we could do after what we did when you came to school last year. You never told on us and you could have done.'

'That's all forgotten. I'll let Mr Peterson know you helped me.' She rubbed her aching back. 'Field work's too hard for me. I think country folk are much tougher and fitter than people from cities.'

'You get off home, Emily Roby, we'll finish this row.'

The tall girl was smiling at her and Emily realised the three of them were actually nice girls, all of them looked pretty despite being in shorts and Wellington boots.

'If you're sure, then I'll do that. My brothers went through the hedge but I'm not sure I'm prepared to do that as I've got to carry the basket and three buckets.'

'You wriggle through, we'll throw them things over to you. I'm Renee, she's Maud and that's Jean.' Renee pointed at the other two as she introduced them. 'Where'd you get that smashing haircut? We're going to spend our first week's wages getting ours done the same.'

Emily was thrilled they'd asked her this. 'I don't know the

name of the hairdresser, but it's halfway up Queen Street on the right. I didn't pay a penny as I gave her my hair, if you don't have anything apart from a cut it only costs one and sixpence anyway.'

'I ain't got the curls you've got so I reckon I'll need a perm as well,' Renee said.

'I'm afraid I've no idea how much that would cost but I do know the lotion they put on your head smells absolutely horrid.'

The three girls laughed. 'There's a social at the old boys' school next week and we want to look our best. You ought to come along, you'd get all the best boys wanting to dance with you.'

'I'd love to come but I'm not allowed to go out on my own. I hope you have a lovely time. Thank you so much.'

The four of them plodded across to the hedge and her new friends carried the buckets for Emily.

'There, that's where they went through,' Maud said and pointed to a gap right at the bottom of the thick hawthorn hedge.

Emily bent down to examine it. 'Golly, I hope I can get through that, I'm a lot bigger than my brothers.'

'I don't reckon you're any fatter,' Renee said. 'Any road up, we'll hold the branches open for you so you can wriggle through.' She waggled the buckets. 'We'll throw everything over to you once you're the other side. You'll not get the buckets through that gap. I'll shove the basket through after you.'

'That makes sense, thank you, you've thought of everything, Renee.'

Ten minutes later, somewhat dishevelled and covered in greenery, Emily was on the other side of the thick edge.

All Change at Harbour House

'You stand right close to the hedge, Emily, then we'll throw your buckets over and push the basket through the gap,' Renee yelled.

Emily stepped away from the gap, then pressed her back into the prickly branches and held her breath.

The first bucket sailed over her head and landed with a clank, the second and third followed. She waited for the basket to arrive at her feet, but it didn't.

'What about my basket, Renee?'

Nobody answered. She dropped to her knees and peered through the gap in the hedge and saw the three girls, with her basket, walking away, laughing.

Keeping the basket was fair enough really, they deserved compensation for helping her out. Explaining this to Mrs Bates might be difficult though, as Emily was quite sure their housekeeper wouldn't agree that losing a precious basket was any sort of fair exchange.

The buckets were somewhat dented after their aerial travels but they hadn't been in the best condition in the first place. She fitted the three of them together and was about to head home when with a sickening jolt she realised that not only did those girls have her basket, they also had the incredibly expensive and precious Thermos flask.

She couldn't let them keep it. With the buckets banging painfully against her side she ran flat out to the farm. The only way she was going to get back what had been stolen was to ask Mr Peterson to intervene. She didn't want to do this but had no choice.

* * *

She arrived in the farmyard and saw Jimmy doing something technical with one of the tractors and he immediately hurried over.

'What's up, Emily?'

After explaining, he nodded. 'Don't you fret, I'll sort this out. You go home, Emily, leave those buckets here and I'll bring them and your basket and flask down later.'

Emily was close to tears. She'd been taken in completely, felt really foolish and gullible. 'Thank you. This is all my fault. I don't know why I thought they'd magically changed into nice girls.'

'That's because you're a good person, want to think the best of everyone. That's why people take advantage of you.'

'Another thing, Jimmy, my brothers and I won't be coming tomorrow. It was just too hard for us.'

He grinned. 'I had a bet with my dad – he said you wouldn't come at all and if you did you wouldn't last more than a couple of hours. You stopped all day and I'll get half a crown because of that.'

'Then in that case, I think it's perfectly fair that you recover my stolen property. I'd better go home before they send out a search party. I'll see you later with my things.'

Emily couldn't stop smiling all the way home. Jimmy had turned what could have been an absolute disaster into what Daddy would call an amusing incident. She wasn't exactly sure how long it would take him to get her things back, but she'd have time to wash and change before he arrived.

Hopefully the items would turn up without her having to explain how silly she'd been to believe those three girls were genuinely friendly when she'd known people don't change that much.

It would be supper time soon and she was absolutely

ravenous. She slipped through the back door, hooked off her boots and headed straight for the washroom. She was horrified to find her hair and face were liberally coated with mud.

Grandma must have heard her come in and knocked on the door. 'We were beginning to worry you weren't coming home in time to eat. I'll be dishing up in ten minutes, my dear.'

'I'll be ready, Grandma, I've just got to change.'

* * *

Annie was now anxiously checking each morning that she hadn't started her period. Each day that passed made it more certain she was expecting. So far, she'd felt a bit nauseous but not been sick like poor Nancy was every morning.

For the past three days she'd been opening the shop and taking care of the few early-morning customers, restocking where necessary, and keeping an eye on things until her friend felt well enough to take over.

Usually, Nancy came in around ten o'clock and it was the same this morning.

'I'm here, Annie, I've managed to keep down a piece of toast and a cup of tea. Poor Boyd's got his legs crossed, he's that desperate to go out.'

'I'll take him now; I'll go down to the river and make sure he has a really good run then if we're busy and I don't get time later we won't feel so guilty.'

It was hard to ignore the war nowadays as there was the constant roar of fighters, both Hurricanes and Spitfires, heading out to sea to fight the German planes. These were constantly bombing the convoys of merchant ships, as well as the RAF bases, and she tried not to think about how dangerous it must be for Richard right now.

'Right, dog, let's go. I'll take you down to the river so you can have a good run.'

The dog whined and wagged his tail, seeming to understand what Annie said although she knew this was impossible. Dogs spoke dog, not English. Idly she wondered if cats understood dogs or did they have their own language too?

She was smiling as she left the yard. It was possible to walk down to the river without going out onto North Hill and she detoured to the large field close by so Boyd could answer his call of nature immediately.

The river at this end wasn't tidal like it was the other side of Colchester, it also wasn't really salty either and had freshwater fish in it rather than edible fish. This didn't stop boys and men from fishing in it as any food was welcome. Annie had decided she'd rather do without than eat the muddy-tasting offerings from the river this side of Colchester.

When she reached the riverbank she unclipped his lead and Boyd raced off. He never went out of earshot and if she wanted him, and whistled, he'd come back like a bullet.

She'd heard boys messing about amongst the reeds but hadn't taken any notice. What better place to be on a warm July day than up to your knees in river water trying to catch the occasional fish?

Then the laughing became shouting, then screaming for help. She ran towards the boys, not sure what she could do as she couldn't swim. If one of them had fallen into deep water then she'd have to find a log, or something that floated, and throw it to him.

As she approached, two boys, one about the same age as George and Sammy and the other considerably older, burst through the reeds.

'Quick, quick, missus, our Geoff's fallen in. You need to save him.'

'I can't swim either, but we can throw something for him to hold onto. Find a log, a big branch and bring it to me.'

Having something to do calmed the two of them and they vanished into the coppice nearby. She got to the riverbank and saw a small boy floundering about, screaming for help.

'Don't struggle, turn on your back and spread your arms and legs out then lie quietly. Everybody can float, even if they can't swim,' she called out, hoping she sounded as if she knew what she was talking about.

Then something huge and furry cannoned into her knees, almost sending her headfirst to join the child in the river. Boyd landed, sending a cascade of water over her. The dog then swam strongly to the little boy.

'Geoff, grab hold of the dog's collar. He'll bring you safely to me.'

She held her breath, in the frenzy of splashing and shouting she couldn't see if Geoff was even able to grab hold of the dog. She'd heard that the third time you went under then you didn't come back and she didn't know how many times the child had done this already.

The screaming stopped and her breath whistled through her teeth. The boy wasn't holding onto the collar, he'd buried his hands into the dog's fur, but that seemed to be enough to keep him afloat. Boyd was swimming strongly towards her.

'Good dog, good dog, keep swimming. You're almost back.'

The water was no more than knee-high but it dropped suddenly and she wasn't sure if she'd be out of her depth if she took another step.

Thank God the river wasn't wide, she didn't think the dog could have swum any further towing a small boy.

She leaned out, grabbed the child and pulled him onto the bank. He was coughing and sputtering but obviously unharmed. Boyd scrambled up the bank, shook himself vigorously, and barked a few times.

'Well done, you clever boy, but you can be quiet now, Geoff's safe and well.'

'Cor, that's a smashing dog you've got there, missus, I thought I was a goner until he came to fetch me,' Geoff said as he attempted to squeeze the water from his shorts.

His brother ran up, laughing and crying. 'Blimey, I never knew you could swim, Geoff, blooming miracle, that's what it is,' the younger one said as he dropped to his knees and hugged the little boy.

The third one, darker and a lot older than the other two, was staring at Boyd. 'That ain't your dog, that's mine. My dad said he'd run away.'

'I'm sorry, he isn't your dog. He belongs to my friend, Mrs Brooks, his name's Boyd.' She snapped her fingers the way she'd seen Dan do and instantly the animal went to her side and sat down. As she was already soaked to the waist, it didn't really matter that he was equally wet.

All three boys were staring at her. 'I suggest that you take Geoff home and get him changed. I'm going to do the same. You need to take more care when you're playing by the river in future as this could have had fatal consequences.'

The bigger boy scowled and made a move towards her. Instantly Boyd's hackles were up and a low threatening growl rumbled from his throat.

Annie clipped the lead on and turned her back on the children. If the dog had belonged to the family, then he'd not be happy going back there. Nancy had been sure the dog had come from a good home, had been well trained and loved, which meant this boy certainly couldn't be his previous owner.

'That ain't your dog, Ernie, it blooming hates you. Let's do as the nice lady says before my brother catches his death of cold.'

Geoff, who appeared to be fully recovered from his unexpected dip, joined in. 'You just want him for yourself, thought you could bully that nice lady into giving him to you.'

'He looks like our lost dog, but he obviously ain't.'

20

Emily had been disappointed that Jimmy had called to return her basket and buckets when she was upstairs playing Monopoly with the boys and her parents hadn't thought it necessary to call her down. She'd only known he'd been because the items were in the kitchen when she went down to make the three of them a snack. Potato picking had been hungry work.

Later, when she was getting ready for bed, she wondered why Jimmy hadn't asked to see her. On the pretence of needing to use the WC she went, after noisily pulling the WC chain, in search of Grandma and found her making cocoa in the kitchen.

'I thought you'd retired, my dear. Are you unwell?'

This was how the family, at least the adults, referred to her monthlies. 'No, not this week, Grandma. Did you see who kindly returned my buckets and basket which I left behind in the field?'

'A young man from the farm dropped them in. He said he'd call by with your wages when they're made up.'

'That would have been Jimmy Peterson.'

'He said he's going to a social in the village on Saturday afternoon so would be happy to bring them on the way. You must make sure to see him yourself next time and thank him personally.'

'I will. Do you know what's involved at a social? Is it just for grown-ups?'

'I love them and no, it's a family thing. The adults can play cards, dance, chat and drink tea and eat biscuits. There are silly party games for the children, although the adults often join in too. Such fun. I've not attended one for years. If your parents agree, would you and the boys like to accompany me?'

'Yes, please. I'll tell the boys, if they're not asleep yet.'

She didn't need to wait for permission from her mummy and daddy, they'd say yes. Those horrible girls had mentioned a social, so they'd not been lying about everything. She didn't want to see them but with Grandma and her brothers there they'd not be able to annoy her.

'Boys, I've got the most terrific news for you,' she said as she knocked on the door.

It took some time to explain to them exactly what a social was but by the time she'd done so they were as excited as she was to be attending.

'Why haven't we been to one of these before?' George asked.

'Because Grandma wasn't living here with us, and our parents don't go to things like that. There have probably been several since we moved here last year. It's a shame that we missed them all,' Emily said.

'I've been to something like that, a bit of a knees-up we used to call it, but it was held in the back room of the Bell and Whistle and everyone got drunk. We did play a few games before it all kicked off,' Sammy told her gleefully.

'Good heavens, it won't be like that here. They don't have alcohol and only tea and biscuits are served.'

George looked at her and shook his head. 'There are loads of pubs in Wivenhoe, are you saying that no one at the social will sneak off for a drink or two during the evening?'

Emily laughed. 'That's a good point. I expect you're right and the Greyhound and the Park Hotel, being the nearest, will do a roaring trade. I just hope that they do the party games first as I expect Grandma won't want us to remain if things get a bit rambunctious.'

The boys laughed, knowing how much she loved to be able to use the long words that she discovered from her reading.

'Jimmy's going to drop off our paltry earnings on the way to the social on Saturday. I don't actually know if we have to share the two shillings or if we get two shillings each. But as I did far more than you two did, whatever we get I think it would be fairer for me to have half and then you split the rest between you.'

Emily waited for them to disagree, to argue, but they exchanged a glance and nodded.

'That's what we'd thought. I ache all over and I certainly won't be a farmer when I grow up,' George said firmly.

'We're going to be fighter pilots, aren't we?' Sammy pointed to the drawing of a Spitfire and a Hurricane that she'd done for them a few months ago.

'The war will be over long before you're old enough to join the RAF, thank goodness. I don't think any of us want to get up early. Goodnight, boys, we'll find out more about this exciting event tomorrow.'

* * *

Emily daringly decided to wear her new blue cotton slacks for the social. If she was going to join in the games then a skirt might not be suitable.

Her parents seemed subdued, Daddy rarely laughed and Mummy was distracted. Thank goodness for Grandma, without her there things at Harbour House would be a bit miserable. She thought it was because the war was going badly. Certainly, the fighter planes flew overhead all day and occasionally at night too. The constant bangs of explosions from Harwich sometimes shook the house.

Mr Stoneleigh was on a destroyer based there and she prayed he wouldn't be blown up by German bombers or the ship sunk by U-boats. If she was concerned about him, it must be absolutely awful for Annie. She smoothed non-existent creases from her new slacks, mentally thanking Annie and Nancy for making them for her. They were a birthday present, rather early as she wouldn't be twelve until September.

Satisfied she was ready, Emily ran down to join the boys who were in the garden turning cartwheels. Then she remembered Jimmy was supposed to bring their wages but she didn't think he'd called in yet.

'Grandma, did Jimmy drop off our money?'

'No, my dear, not yet. Being a farmer's son, I expect he sometimes has emergency jobs to do.'

'It doesn't matter, we don't need the few shillings. We're lucky, aren't we, Grandma?'

'We certainly are. Shall we go before the boys get covered in mud?'

'I'll just say goodbye to Mummy, then I'll catch you up.'

Her mother was reading a book, her sister playing with her toes on a rug on the floor. Daddy, of course, was at work. He was rarely home nowadays. This must be why her mummy was so quiet.

'Mummy, we're going to the social now. I'll stay and keep you company, take Grace for a walk in the pram if you want me to.'

Her mother looked up and smiled. 'No, darling girl, you go and enjoy yourself. You've been looking forward to it.'

'All right, thank you, Mummy. Jimmy from the farm was supposed to be calling with our money but he hasn't come. Ignore a knock on the back door if you hear one as it will be him.'

Mummy suddenly smiled and looked like her old self. 'I won't need to, darling, he's just walking up the front path.'

Emily's heart unexpectedly thudded. She didn't know why this news frightened her. She said goodbye and tried to walk calmly to join the others in the front garden. Why had Jimmy come to the front door?

He looked very smart in his long grey trousers and navy-blue pullover. He was talking politely to Grandma and the boys were standing next to him listening to his every word. She wished they did that for her when she spoke to them.

'I'm sorry if I've kept you all waiting,' Emily said nervously. 'Shall we go now?'

As soon as she'd spoken, she realised she should have said good afternoon to Jimmy and thanked him for calling in.

'You look a picture, Emily. I've not seen a girl in slacks before,' Jimmy said.

'I thought I'd be better in these if I'm going to play silly party games.' She smiled at him and he turned a bit pink, which she thought was odd. 'A frock would be better if I was intending to dance, but I'm not.'

'Neither are we, we want to play musical chairs and pass the parcel – are those the sort of things they do, Jimmy?'

They were now stepping out of the front gate onto the narrow pavement and Emily saw there was a steady flow of eager partygoers walking just ahead of them.

'They did last time, also bumps, and the hokey pokey, that sort of thing.'

It took the short walk for him to explain what a hokey pokey entailed. This convinced Emily that her choice of outfit was the best one for the occasion. She couldn't wait to do this strange dance and hoped that Jimmy would teach her the words and actions before they had to do it.

* * *

Annie heard nothing from the War Office, which she thought was probably good news – if she'd broken some rules by cancelling her application then she'd have received something from them by now.

She was now two weeks late and Nancy had just missed her second monthly. Dan was due home today so Annie had volunteered to run the shop which meant he could be told the news and they could celebrate in private.

Boyd's rescue of the little boy and the older boy's attempt to take the dog from her had made a good story, but neither she nor Nancy had thought any more about it. However, she now took the dog for a walk in Abbey Fields and not down to the river as she didn't want to meet the older boy again.

Being a Saturday, market day, the shop was busy and by eleven o'clock she was desperate for the WC. Being pregnant had played havoc with her waterworks. If Nancy didn't come in soon she'd have to lock the shop for a bit.

'Sorry, Annie, I'm here now. Dan's thrilled to bits about my news. He's up in the attic looking to see what he can use to make a crib. I didn't tell him about you obviously. You'll want to tell Richard before anyone else knows.'

'I'll be back in a minute,' Annie said as she flew out of the shop, through the kitchen and into the yard. Boyd was happily gnawing on a large marrow bone – a gift from the butcher – and thumped his tail on the ground as she ran past him.

She was just adjusting her clothing when Boyd started to bark, then this changed to growling. She froze for a second. There were at least two people in the yard. Dan must've forgotten to lock the gate when he came in earlier.

After taking a deep breath, she flung the door open so violently it hit one of the intruders and sent him sprawling on the concrete. Boyd took this as a sign that he could attack the other one – she recognised him as the boy who'd insisted the dog belonged to him.

The boy yelled in agony as Boyd sank his teeth into his leg. 'Get that bleeding dog off me. My dad will remind him of his manners when I get him home.'

'Boyd isn't your dog, you're trespassing, I'll call him off if you get out of here right now.'

'Leave this to me, Annie, you get inside. I'll send these buggers packing.' Dan must've heard the racket from upstairs.

She watched from the safety of the open doorway as he commanded the dog to release the boy and then grabbed each of the ruffians by the scruff of their necks and threw them out of the yard. He then slammed the gate shut and put the bolts across.

'What the hell was all that about?' Dan asked. Annie explained about the incident at the river. 'A dog that can rescue people from the water like Boyd did must be worth a lot of money. How did they know where to find him?'

Annie shook her head. 'I've no idea. I think he must have followed me when I came home after the incident. I'm afraid I wasn't thinking about anything but getting back and changing out of my soaked frock.'

'I'm not happy about you two being here on your own even with the dog to protect you.'

'There's not much you can do about that, Dan, and I think that Boyd's not going to let anybody take him away.'

'Maybe so, but I'm going to report this incident to the police.'

She was going to protest but it was really none of her business. The dog belonged to Nancy, this was Nancy and Dan's home, she was just a tenant. She was quite sure that if Richard knew he'd be just as concerned and probably insist that she find somewhere else to live. Involving the police, in her experience, never ended well.

'Why don't we find another dog to keep Boyd company? There must be other families who can't keep their animals, and Tabby catches enough rabbits in a week to feed two dogs easily,' Annie suggested. The idea of having a dog of her own appealed.

'Now, that sounds like an excellent idea. I'm going to go to the police station now and after I report the incident I'll ask if they know of anyone who is looking for a new home for a large dog.'

'Let's hope if we find one that Boyd and Tabby accept him – it has to be a him or we'll have puppies every year.'

'Would you tell Nancy where I've gone and why? I'm that excited about being a dad and having you living here means I don't have to worry when I'm at sea.'

* * *

Annie helped out all morning in the shop and the two of them took it in turns to dash off to the WC. It was a relief to lock the door at one o'clock and have an hour's break before starting again.

Saturday afternoon was always quieter than the morning because the market stalls would be packed away and folk would have returned home. That said, it would still be quite busy until around five when Nancy closed the shop.

Dan was at the range heating up the soup that Annie had made the previous day. 'I've got some lovely fresh bread to go with it, ladies, so sit yourselves down and I'll dish up.'

'How did you get on with the police?' Annie asked immediately.

'They know the boys and will go round to their house and give them a talking to. They'll be warned that if they come anywhere near this house or either of you or the dog they'll be arrested.'

'That seems fair enough,' Nancy said. 'What about getting another dog? Do you still think we need to do that?'

'I do and Constable Smithers thinks he knows a family who'll be happy for us to take their family pet. The husband's a stoker in the navy and overseas somewhere. The dog's called Rusty and was his. Now the wife's working at the munitions factory down at the Hythe and doesn't have time to take him out.'

'Rusty? Does that mean he's got a red coat?' Annie asked eagerly. 'As it was my idea, this dog will be Richard's and mine, so I'll be responsible for his upkeep and when we move to our own house after the war he'll come with us.'

'Fair enough,' Dan said. 'All I know is that he's a big friendly mutt and with enough exercise and attention should settle in well.'

Nancy tucked into her soup. 'This is even better than the last lot, Annie. Why don't you and Dan go and see the dog when we've finished lunch?'

'No need to do that, love,' Dan said. 'Constable Smithers is going to fetch him for us.' He winked. 'I think he's got an interest in that family, if you know what I mean.'

Nancy grinned. 'I reckon that there'll be a lot of unwanted babies in families for the men to deal with when they come home from the war.'

All the talk about babies made Annie wish she could tell Richard the good news. Soon she'd be able to as she'd have missed a second monthly. Tonight she'd stay in her own room, let Dan and Nancy have the sitting room, and she'd write the letter ready to post next week. They couldn't start changing the rooms round until Richard knew so Dan hadn't been asked to move anything.

Nancy was fine during the day, only sick first thing. As long as Annie avoided tea, she was all right, but having to go to the WC every five minutes was a nuisance.

'I'm going to open the shop. I'll send Dan for you if it gets busy,' Nancy said.

'I'll get on with the two summer frocks for the lady from over the road, she's coming for them on Wednesday.'

Dan pulled a face. 'Then I'll clear the table and wash up for you fine ladies, shall I?'

'Someone needs to let the policeman in with this dog, love, and it had best be you. If you don't think Rusty will fit in with our two then we won't take him.'

Annie frowned; she really wanted her own dog for when she was living alone in her own house one day. This dog was going to be hers, not theirs, but whilst she was living here she supposed it was up to them to make the decision.

* * *

Annie had just finished hand hemming the first dress when Dan called her. 'The dog's here. I'm pretty sure you're going to love him.'

She'd had time to think over the past two hours and was worried that maybe she shouldn't be taking on a dog without talking to her husband. Then she smiled. He wasn't going to be around much for the next couple of years at least, therefore it was up to her.

It had also occurred to her that in a few months both she and Nancy would be hugely pregnant and walking two big dogs might not be possible for either of them. They'd manage, they had to, that's what folk did in a war.

Dan was outside talking to someone, presumably the constable, but she couldn't see any sign of either dog through the kitchen window.

She stepped out and her mouth dropped open. Flopped down beside Boyd was a dog with short curly russet fur the exact shade of Richard's hair.

'Oh, he's lovely. Rusty, come here and see me,' she said and the dog bounced over to her, his orange eyes shining and his long pink tongue hanging out.

She dropped to her knees and hugged him. He tried to wriggle onto her lap as if he was a small terrier, not a dog almost as large as Boyd.

'Silly fellow, you're too big to sit on me. Let me give you a hug instead.'

He didn't object and within a few minutes a bond was made.

'Right, Dan, I can see Rusty's going to be happy here. You'll not regret taking him, he's a good dog, just needs too much exercise and attention for his owner who's working long shifts at Paxman's.'

The constable left and Annie stood up. 'I'm going to take him for a walk, will you come with Boyd?'

'Right, give us a minute. I'll let my Nancy know we're going out. You go through the gate and take both of them then I'll lock the gate and come out the front.'

Annie clipped on the leads and was delighted they didn't pull and were getting on well. Rusty already had a place in her heart.

21

Emily followed the boys and her grandma into the hall and wasn't sure if she was entirely comfortable having Jimmy walking beside her as if they were together. One thing she was quite certain of was that her parents would be horrified if they thought Jimmy was taking an interest in her. He was almost an adult and she wasn't even twelve until September.

'Crikey, it's heaving in there. Thank God they've got the windows open or we'd suffocate,' Jimmy said as they stopped at the table outside the double doors where people were queueing to drop in their entrance fee.

'It looks and sounds as if there must be more than a hundred people in here. I really don't like crowds, I'm not sure I want to stay after all,' Emily said.

'Neither do I, shall we go for a walk instead? Or we could catch the bus into Colchester and have our tea and biscuits there.'

Emily opened her mouth to say no thank you but found herself saying exactly the opposite. 'Yes, that sounds spiffing.'

There was no chance to change her mind as he put his hand

in the small of her back and sort of ushered her out. She looked over her shoulder, hoping to see Grandma, but she couldn't. She really shouldn't go but didn't know how to say no as Jimmy was a boy she admired and wanted to please.

'There's a bus goes past the Park Hotel in five minutes. We should be able to catch that one easily.'

'I'm not sure I should just leave like this, Jimmy.'

'No one will even notice that you've gone.'

Before she could think of something to say, of a way to not go without seeming like a baby, they were at the bus stop and an ancient, dilapidated vehicle was rattling to a halt beside them.

They took the first empty seats and the conductor wobbled his way to them. He didn't ask if they wanted half-fare or adult and Jimmy didn't say that she wasn't even twelve years old yet. He paid for the tickets and this made her even more nervous.

Her heart was thudding painfully, her mouth was dry and she wished she'd not agreed to come but was safely in the hall enjoying the social.

'I should have got a half for you, Emily, but I'd already handed over the pennies before I realised. You look a lot older but I know that you're not,' Jimmy said, his expression serious. 'I don't have any friends my age and I can talk to you like a little sister.'

A rush of relief made her smile. He was making it clear he wasn't taking advantage of her, was just a friend.

'It's not that that's making me worried, I don't know what I'm doing here. I should have told my grandmother – she'll be frantic. I'm going to be in such awful trouble when I get home.'

'Then we'll get off at the next stop and walk back. I shouldn't think we'll have been missed by then. It's my fault, because I can do what I like now, I'd forgotten that you can't.'

'Thank you, I'd much rather do that. I'd like to go to Colchester with you another time, maybe we could go to the cinema together, but not today. I need to have my parents' permission.'

'I'll hold you to that. Quick, the bus is stopping. I don't think I'll ask for my money back.'

Emily giggled, now enjoying the excursion. 'I'll pay for my fare. I'm hoping there will be enough in my wage packet to cover it.'

The conductor, who was as old as the bus, didn't seem to think there was anything odd about the two of them jumping off after one stop when they'd paid to go all the way to Colchester.

'We'd better hurry, I don't want to be missing for more than half an hour,' Emily said, and Jimmy nodded.

'Here, I should have given you this when I turned up at your house earlier. Because you and your brothers were working the same section the money's all in one envelope.' He winked at her and handed it over.

They were walking briskly along the pavement and he'd made no attempt to hold her hand or do anything silly like that. She did like him, but wasn't ready to even think about having a boyfriend. She'd heard older girls talking about their boyfriends and didn't like the sound of that sort of thing at all.

Emily glanced down and her eyes widened. 'Gosh, I didn't expect to get six shillings. The boys have agreed to have half between them and I'll have the other half. I'll pay for your entrance to the social as you bought my bus ticket.' She waggled the envelope which clinked satisfactorily. 'I'm rich now so can afford it.'

'Okay, that seems fair to me.'

He'd adjusted his longer stride to suit her but they were still covering the ground at a satisfactory pace. They were already at the Park Hotel and should be at the hall in minutes.

'There are still people going in, so nobody should have noticed that we didn't. I don't know what I'm going to say to my grandmother as she's bound to have noticed that neither of us are in there.'

'Just tell her the truth, you didn't want to go in at first because of the crowd so we went for a short walk until you felt ready.'

'I won't mention the bus ride. Thank you for being such a good sport. Do you think those horrible girls will be there? I didn't ask you what happened when you went to find them.'

For a second he looked fierce, really grown-up, and then he grinned and was Jimmy again. 'I just asked for your basket and flask back and told them to push off. I also told them they wouldn't be paid and weren't welcome on the farm again.'

'Goodness, that seems a bit harsh.'

'I could have reported them for theft. I suggested if they objected to having their wages docked that I'd do that instead. They didn't argue.'

'Then I don't suppose they'll come to the social. At least I hope they don't, I'm not exactly frightened of them but am embarrassed that they tricked me so easily.'

'They won't be here; I told them I never want to see them again and they knew that I was coming.'

Emily wasn't sure if she was impressed or dismayed by his treatment of those three girls. She couldn't help remembering how Sammy's horrible brother, Pete, had protected her from the very same girls and look how he'd turned out.

She glanced sideways at the boy – no, he was a young man now – striding along beside her and wondered if he was going to turn out not to be the person she thought he was. She was also puzzled as to why he was with her at all when there were so many other girls his age he could be walking with.

He seemed to sense her disquiet as he let her go in alone and she realised she couldn't pay for him if he wasn't with her. She dropped her shilling into the saucer and stepped into the crowded room.

There wasn't live music but there was a boy in short trousers about her age putting records on and he seemed to know what he was doing. The music was lively, made her tap her feet, and she forgot she was afraid of crowds and threaded her way through the happy partygoers to her brothers and grandmother.

'Goodness, my dear, where on earth have you been? I was really worried you'd been taken poorly and gone home.'

Emily quickly explained and Grandma nodded sympathetically. 'I'd forgotten that you and the boys have never been to something like this. Are you all right now to be in here?'

'I am, thank you, I just needed to calm down a bit. Wasn't Jimmy kind to keep me company? I think I might have run home if he hadn't been there.'

'He's a charming young man. I see he's joined his own friends now. He's already got a gaggle of young ladies hanging round him – I doubt he'll be sitting out any dances today.'

Emily didn't need to look round to know that Jimmy had deliberately joined his peers to make things easier for her. Her brothers had joined a group of boys their own age, boys they played football with at weekends sometimes. Neil wasn't there and she thought that a bit odd. Perhaps Jimmy hadn't wanted his young brother there watching him.

'Grandma, I see there's a piano at the far end of the hall. Do you think somebody might be going to play? I'd really love to hear that.'

'Yes, Mrs Cousins told me they usually have a singsong at

some point. I don't suppose they've got a record with the hokey pokey on it so someone will have to play for that.'

The afternoon flew by and Emily played all the silly games, danced the hokey pokey and joined in the singsong at the end. From the corner of her eye she'd seen Jimmy doing the same and was pleased that he was enjoying himself too.

As they were leaving, he drifted up behind her in a casual sort of way. 'When do you think you'll be allowed to go to the pictures with me?'

She didn't look round as she answered. 'Not until my birthday in September, and I'm not even sure they'll agree then.'

'Then I'll make sure my mum asks you to look after the little ones. Then I can walk you home.'

George bumped into her and when she looked round Jimmy had gone.

'That was super-duper, Emily, I've had such amazing fun. They'll be holding another one before we go back to school. I can't wait.'

'Neither can I. I've decided that I'd like to learn to play the piano. I wonder if Daddy will be able to get hold of one for me to learn on. By the way, boys, I've got three shillings to split between you. That's one and sixpence – what are you going to spend your wages on?'

Later, as she was settling down to sleep, she thought about her almost trip to Colchester. Maybe in future she'd not be so friendly with Jimmy. Sometimes he looked at her a bit like Pete had and that made her uncomfortable and scared. Jimmy was a nice boy, but too old to be a friend.

* * *

Richard settled in well, liked his fellow officers, admired and respected the captain and found dealing with those under him less difficult than he'd feared. Working as an Admiralty surveyor, having to issue orders on a regular basis to the foreman, other workmen in the yard, for the past three years had given him a much-needed air of authority.

The flotilla was escorting a convoy of merchant ships, guarding them from U-boats and overhead attacks from the dive bombers. The ship had sunk one U-boat on this patrol so far but not brought down any of the Luftwaffe who were constantly attacking.

The escort met the incoming convoy in the mid-Atlantic and handed over their charges to be escorted by another flotilla of destroyers, sloops and corvettes for the remainder of the journey. Richard was confident he'd acquitted himself well so far. Today he was the officer overseeing the gunners – although his actual role on the ship was navigating, the captain wanted him to broaden his experience. His intention was that all his officers would be able to function in any capacity in the event of an attack and loss of life.

They were still several days from port, shepherding the slow-moving convoy of merchant ships, when his keen hearing picked up the thunder of dive bombers approaching at full speed through the low clouds. For the second time he was facing almost certain death. He sent up a fervent prayer that he'd survive this encounter, that the men on the guns would be successful this time. That by some miracle the ship wouldn't be hit and he'd see his beloved Annie again.

He yelled for any sailor able, those not actually firing the machine guns, to take cover and they threw themselves onto the deck. His eyes widened as he saw two black bombs released from beneath the approaching bomber. In the first few seconds they didn't look big enough to do any harm but grew in size as they dropped towards the ship. The ship would be sunk if the bombs found their target. The noise from these incoming monsters made his hair stand on end; they screamed towards them, bringing certain death to anything they hit.

Richard remained at his post, watching, expecting to die, wanting to be in a position to help anyone who might be injured by the incoming impact.

The bombs hit the ocean on the port side, sending a deluge of mud and icy water over the deck. The gunners continued in their posts, steadfast and brave. Two died but the others continued to fire and this time succeeded in bringing the Stuka down. A cheer of triumph echoed across the ship despite the dire circumstances.

He fulfilled his duty as the officer in charge, had the bodies removed to the mortuary and the three injured taken to the sick bay. Unfortunately, they were now five guns short, which could be disastrous if they were attacked again.

He'd been soaked to the skin and his teeth were chattering by the time he was able to go below decks to his cabin and strip off his sodden uniform.

The captain shook his hand when he eventually returned to the wardroom.

'Well done, Stoneleigh, I was impressed by your behaviour today. I'm going to recommend you be promoted to acting lieutenant immediately.'

'Thank you, sir, I was just doing my duty as was everybody else on this ship.' Richard saluted and his captain did the same. 'I'll continue to do my best to serve whilst I'm under your command.'

The two gunners were given a maritime burial and Richard found this sad. Their loved ones wouldn't have a grave to visit, but a warship couldn't keep corpses. They had to be disposed of rapidly. Luckily the three injured men would make a full recovery eventually and would be shipped off to hospital to do so when they docked at Harwich.

After dinner, the officers gathered in the wardroom and the mood was surprisingly jolly considering everything that had happened. Richard realised he'd have to get used to crewmates being injured and killed and life then continuing as usual.

He got into conversation with his roommate, Sub-lieutenant Harry Jenkins. 'The captain said that we'll be docked at the naval yard in Harwich for two weeks of repairs. Do we remain on board or get time ashore?'

'Not everybody wants to go ashore; there's not much going on in Harwich. If they've got family locally then they'll apply for leave – do you have anyone you want to see?'

'I was married two days before I joined the ship. My new wife won't be at home as she joined the WAAF and will be away doing her preliminary training. I'm more interested in receiving any mail that might have arrived whilst we've been away.'

Harry slapped him on the back. 'That calls for a round of drinks – your shout, Richard. Yes, to answer your question, letters will be brought on board as soon as we're docked.'

Richard wasn't a heavy drinker, had only had two half pints before he made his excuses and retired to his bunk. He shared his cabin with Harry and he'd become a good friend in the short time that they'd been together. He sent up a quick prayer of thanks to whoever might be listening and added a request that they not be attacked by the Luftwaffe or a U-boat on the remainder of their patrol.

22

Annie picked up Rusty's lead and the dog bounced around her.

'No, quietly.'

She shortened her grip on the leather and gave it a sharp tug. The dog immediately sat down and looked up at her. Her actions were instinctive as she knew very little about dogs as the only one she'd had any interaction with was Boyd.

'Good boy, let's go for a walk.'

Dan followed her to the gate, nodding approvingly. 'You let him know you're in charge, exactly the right thing to do.'

She heard Dan push the bolt across the gate behind them and, keeping the new dog close to her side, Boyd walking beside him, she walked around to the front.

When she went out with Boyd, she never went down North Hill but Dan must be intending to do so. Maybe seeing how Rusty behaved in public was a good idea, but she wasn't so sure. If the animal misbehaved, was frightened by the traffic or other pedestrians, Dan might say she couldn't keep him.

Annie came to a startling decision. She was going to use her compensation money to buy or lease a house in Colchester, then she wouldn't be beholden to anyone but her own husband. She loved Nancy, would have remained where she was if Dan wasn't in the picture, but finding a home for her and Richard, Rusty, and the baby was now a priority.

Dan emerged from the shop door, his dog walking to heel, and she dropped in beside him. 'They seem to get along really well, Dan, and he's not pulling at all.'

'So far so good. I want to see how they behave on a busy pavement. Why don't you take both leads? You'll be the one walking them, won't you?'

'No, I don't think it's sensible for me to do that here with all the other people and the traffic. I would never take them this way to the fields, and I don't understand why you're insisting that we do so.'

He looked a bit startled that she'd disagreed with him. Nancy wasn't a doormat by any means but since Dan had almost drowned just before they'd married she tended to do whatever he suggested when he was home.

'Then we'll cut through to the back path, not go this way. To be honest, I didn't really think this through. As I was coming out of the front it just seemed to make sense for you to join me rather than the other way round.'

They took the narrow alley between two houses which came out onto the one Annie used every day. Dan held out Boyd's lead and she took it with a smile.

'Right, you two, let's see how you behave.' Both dogs looked up at her and wagged their tails. She could have had one on each side but thought it made sense to have them walking together, after all, that was the whole point of going out.

This meant there was no room for Dan to walk alongside so he had to be behind them which made conversation difficult.

Today she headed just for the nearest field, the one where

they took Boyd to when there wasn't sufficient time to go all the way to the river, or to Abbey Fields. She was pretty sure she'd not manage the longer walk without needing the loo.

'I'm going to let them off the lead, do exactly what I do normally when I just have Boyd,' she said.

'Go ahead, from what I've seen so far Rusty won't leave Boyd's side.'

* * *

Half an hour later they returned to the house. The dogs had galloped around the field chasing each other but had come back as soon as they were called.

On the return, Dan took both dogs and Annie walked behind him. Rusty kept looking over his shoulder, dropping back and whining until she was forced to take him.

'I've only known him a short while but he seems to have become attached to me, and I to him, if I'm honest. It's a good thing that I'm going to be the one doing the dog walking as I don't think he'd go with Nancy unless I went with her.'

She couldn't tell Dan that as the months went by it was going to be hard for either of them to take the dogs out.

'I expect he'll adjust to both of you. Anyway, he's obviously a good match so he can stay.'

'I intended to keep him whatever you thought about it, Dan. I think it might be best if I look for somewhere of our own. I'll still work for Nancy, I'll come every day, and I won't move unless I find something close.'

Dan shook his head. 'You mustn't do that; I'd worry if Nancy's on her own at night. Please, Annie, reconsider.'

'It's not my own place, I've never had a home of my own,

and it's something I've always dreamed of. I won't move until I've found the right place and that could take months.'

He was obviously upset. She wished she hadn't said anything to him but waited until she and Nancy were alone. What he said made sense, especially as she was expecting too.

'Obviously, it's not a decision I'll make without consulting Richard. It'll be his home too when the war's over.'

'It's not my place to tell you what to do, I'm sorry for trying to do that. Nancy will have my guts for garters if you tell her I tried bossing you about.' He grinned sheepishly and she smiled.

'I won't mention it. It's hard having Richard on a destroyer, thinking every time I hear an explosion or see a dogfight that maybe it's his ship that's being attacked. Looking for a permanent home will give me something else to think about, but it doesn't mean I'll actually be moving, certainly not until after Nancy has the baby.'

He laughed. 'I'd forgotten that you're a woman of substance now, you could afford to buy somewhere and then rent it out. You'd make more from your money than you will by just leaving it in the bank.'

They'd both forgotten that the back gate was bolted so they couldn't get in. Dan handed her Boyd's lead and vanished around the corner. She didn't have long to wait before he was on the other side unbolting it.

* * *

Annie wrote to Richard, telling him she was almost certain she was expecting a baby, that she'd not be joining the WAAFs and that they'd now got their own dog. In the letter she mentioned that Nancy was also expecting. She asked him what he thought about buying a home of their own at some point. He was going to get a bit of a shock when he opened this letter and she hoped he'd be as delighted as she was by the changes in their lives.

The letter would be posted tomorrow and it was just possible he'd read it the following day – but unlikely. She knew his ship returned to Harwich to refuel, rearm and restock food and water, but wasn't sure how often this happened. When it did the accumulated mail would also be transferred to the ship, even if those sailing on it couldn't come ashore.

With any luck he'd get her letter soon and reply immediately. Although she'd intended to keep the news of her pregnancy to herself until she'd missed a second monthly, she was certain she was pregnant.

Nancy hadn't booked a midwife yet as they'd decided they'd do it together. It made sense for the nurse to visit both of them at the same time and it would probably be cheaper too. Annie was smiling as she considered what her baby might look like. Would he or she have glorious red hair like Richard or be dark haired like her? She had dark blue eyes, he had green, maybe their baby would have a combination of their colouring. One thing was certain, the baby would be exactly what they wanted.

Before getting into bed, she checked her dog was quiet and, pleased that there was no whining or scratching coming from the kitchen, she settled down for the night. If there wasn't a war on, if Richard wasn't in the navy, then everything right now would be perfect.

* * *

Emily waited for the promised message from the farm to invite her to look after the children but after three days of hearing nothing she intended to go there without an actual invite. Then things changed at home and this made her even more determined to spend time away.

Emily was in the back garden playing with the baby, who was on a rug on the grass. As there were buildings between the garden and the railway cutting, the steam, smuts and smoke weren't as big a problem as they were in the front. Because she was so close to the kitchen, she heard every word of the conversation that changed everything.

'I'm sorry, Mrs Roby, but I'll not be working here after tomorrow.'

'Goodness me, this is a terrible shock. I don't know how we'll manage without you,' Mummy said. 'Aren't you happy here?'

'I love it, but my boys are getting out of hand what with me being away so much and them on holiday,' Mrs Bates said. 'Since my sister shared her inheritance with us, I don't really need to work full time. I'm going to concentrate on the WI and WVS and volunteer to be a fire watcher as well.'

'I understand but am so sorry to see you go. We really appreciate everything you've done for us this past year. I expect my mother-in-law and I will manage somehow.'

Emily heard Mrs Bates laugh. 'Crikey, I'm not leaving you entirely in the lurch, Mrs Roby. I've found someone to take my job if you want her. Her name's Lily Turner; her Daphne was working for my Nancy at the shop in Colchester up until last week.'

'If she's a young woman then won't she be expected to do war work?'

'That's the thing, Mrs Roby, she's got poor vision, wouldn't be any good doing munitions and that, but she's a dab hand at cooking and domestic things.'

'Then she sounds perfect. Of course, I need to meet her before offering her the position.'

'She knows that. I suggested she come round after lunch.'

'Yes, that will be ideal. Do you think she could start right away so you can show her everything she needs to know?'

'We thought that would be a good idea too. Another thing you should be aware of, Mrs Roby, Lily was married at sixteen, had her Daphne at seventeen, and her blooming hubby pushed off when Daphne was a toddler. Not been seen since.'

'How unfortunate, that means the poor woman's tied to that man and can't do anything about it.'

Mrs Bates snorted – at least that's what it sounded like. 'He's been gone thirteen years; I don't think anyone would think twice about her setting up home with another bloke.'

The two of them moved away and Emily could no longer hear what they were saying. She'd met Daphne and liked her but hadn't known the girl had left her job at Nancy's. She remembered that Daphne had told her that her mother worked at the canning factory and hated it.

The baby was looking sleepy and Mummy didn't like Grace to fall asleep on the ground. Emily stood before bending down and picking her up. 'Into the pram, little sister, and I'll take you for a walk. I'll just tell our mummy that we're going out.'

Mrs Bates was busy getting things ready for tonight's meal – there were plated egg salads and strawberries and evaporated milk waiting for their lunch.

'Please could you tell my mother that I'm taking Grace for a walk whilst she sleeps? I'll be back in an hour.'

'I'll do that, love. You're a good girl to help out the way you do.'

Sometimes her grandma came when Emily went out with the pram but she was out somewhere today. She didn't know where and as nobody had told her it might be better not to ask questions.

* * *

She decided to call in at the farm. She was sure that she wouldn't see Jimmy, he'd be busy, and she really wanted to speak to Mrs Peterson. Helping at home, taking care of Grace, was enjoyable but she preferred to be in charge of the Peterson children. Spending so much time at home was becoming a bit tedious. She was already doing a lot, and helping at the farm was for some reason more interesting than doing it at Harbour House.

The boys only had to tidy their room, bring their dirty laundry down, and then they were free to roam about the village and just come back for meals. Since they'd got friendly with Neil they spent more time on the Peterson farm than she did. Being a girl wasn't nearly as much fun.

Grace was asleep before she reached the bumpy lane that led to the farm. Emily pushed the pram into the yard and was immediately greeted by the oldest girl who was delighted to see her.

'Have you come to play with me?' Jenny yelled when she saw her. 'Mum didn't say you were coming.'

Jenny was seven now but still babyish for her age as she sucked her thumb.

'I've just come for a visit. I'm looking after my sister this morning but I'd love to come another time. Where are Gwen and Neil?' Gwen was five and Neil was now nine and he was almost certainly playing with George and Sammy somewhere. Her brothers roamed about the village on their own too.

'My sister's in our bedroom in disgrace. She scribbled all over the wall and Mum smacked her and sent her upstairs.'

'Oh dear, then I certainly won't be seeing her. I'm taking Grace for a walk and I'd love you to come with me but we have to ask your mother first.'

Mrs Peterson saw her out of the kitchen window and instead of beckoning her to come in she joined them in the farmyard.

'Let me look at the little one, my word, she looks just like you now her hair's growing.'

'Thank you, Mrs Peterson, it would be lovely for her to look like me. She did look a bit strange with no hair.'

'I expect Jenny's told you about Gwen. Naughty little girl, I should have put her over my knee but she got away with a couple of smacks on the back of the leg because she apologised.'

'Yes, she did tell me. I'm just taking the baby for a stroll through the fields. I have to be back for lunch so I won't be long, but I wondered if Jenny could come with me?'

'Yes, love, that's a good idea. I'm glad you called in as I want to ask you a big favour. Could you possibly look after the girls from breakfast until late on Friday? My mum's poorly and I've got to go and see her and I can't take the children.'

'Yes, I'm sure that will be fine. How late is late, Mrs Peterson?'

'I'll be catching the train from Chelmsford that gets into Wivenhoe around nine. My Jimmy will walk you home so don't worry about that.'

'What about meals? I'm proficient in the kitchen but don't think I could manage to cook for so many. However, I'm certain I could heat up whatever you've prepared and serve it. I could also make sandwiches and so on.'

'Bless you, I was going to ask the land girls to do that but they're so busy on the farm right now it would be a great help if you did it. I'll make soup and a nice ham salad for tea, then there'll be rabbit and chicken pie with potatoes and vegetables for lunch followed by a nice fruit crumble for afters with cream.'

'I can heat up all that. I'm sure Jenny and Gwen can help me lay the table and do the washing up.'

'You don't have to wash up, love, that can keep until I get back. You're an absolute treasure. You can be sure I'll pack up a lovely parcel for you to take home as I know you won't take any money.'

'I'll be here in good time on Friday, Mrs Peterson. I won't let you down.'

Emily had tried to sound confident but the thought of being in charge of not only the children but also the catering filled her with dread. Mrs P wouldn't have asked her if Emily hadn't been showing off, pretending to be a grown-up when she really wasn't.

* * *

Emily was still worried about what she'd promised to do when she returned home. Grace was sleeping soundly and not due for a feed for another half an hour at least so the pram was left under the apple tree in the back garden.

'Mummy, Mrs Peterson has asked me to spend the day at the farm on Friday as she has to visit her mother in Chelmsford as she's unwell. I said I could do it – I hope that's all right.'

'Yes, of course you can. I know you love to go up there, although I don't quite understand the attraction as you have to do more there than you do here.'

'I like the extra responsibility, Mummy, and I do get a bit bored on my own. Will Grandma be back for supper? The house seems different without her here.'

'No, she's away overnight. I'm hoping she'll be back tomorrow sometime.'

George had waited politely before speaking but it was obvious he was bursting to tell them something. 'You'll never guess, Emily, Mummy, but we've been out on a boat. It was jolly good fun.'

If he'd expected Mummy to be as excited as he was then he was sadly disappointed. 'You did what? You know very well that you're not to go anywhere near the river and you both gave us your word that you wouldn't. Neither of you can swim and the river at high tide is a dangerous place.'

George swallowed and Sammy seemed to shrink in his chair.

'I'm very disappointed in both of you. You can't be trusted so in future you'll remain in the front garden and not go out of sight. Is that quite clear?' There wasn't a sound at the table and Emily held her breath too.

'Well, I'm waiting for your answer, boys?' Sammy nodded and then George did the same.

'Good, when you've finished your lunch, go to your room. I don't want to see you downstairs until teatime. I can promise you that your father isn't going to be impressed when I tell him.'

The remainder of the meal was eaten in silence and it was a relief when Grace started to cry. Mummy dropped a napkin on her plate and went to collect her.

'What were you thinking? You know the rules – if you broke them why did you think it sensible to tell us about it?' Emily said, shaking her head. She hated it when her brothers were in trouble.

'It was such good fun we just wanted to share it. It's not fair really because she didn't give us a chance to explain. I should have said that we went across to Fingringhoe on the ferry, not in just any old boat.'

'Goodness me, that's even worse. How long were you in Fingringhoe?'

'Not long, Dr Cousins said we could go with him and we walked up to the Whalebone pub and had a lemonade and then came back with him.'

'That's not nearly as bad but you were still told not to go near the river. You should have come in and asked permission and I'm sure you'd have got it. Now you've got to accept your punishment. When they hear the full story, if you haven't made a fuss, then I'm sure you'll only be kept at home for a day.'

23

Emily's worry about Friday hadn't gone and the fact that her grandma was still away made things worse. Daddy was so busy at work she didn't like to bother him with questions. Mummy now had to deal with a new housekeeper and didn't have Grandma to help as she had for the past few weeks since Annie had left.

Mrs Turner wore thick glasses but this didn't seem to stop her doing her job. She was friendly and smiled a lot. Emily thought she rather liked her.

The boys hadn't been let off their punishment as she'd expected and were still confined to the house. Neither of them was talking to her because she'd said they would be allowed out today. It wasn't her fault. They needed to grow up a bit and accept responsibility for their actions.

Until she was walking safely down Hamilton Road, Emily was still hoping that she might be prevented from going to the farm. Being at home at the moment was depressing but she'd rather not be going to the farm today. What if she burned the lunch, lost one of the girls? All sorts of dreadful things could happen. It was different being there with Mrs P around.

Both Jenny and Gwen were waiting for her in the yard and squealed with excitement and hugged her.

'Good morning, girls, we're going to have fun today.' She hoped she sounded confident. She was half an hour early and the fact that the little girls were waiting on their own by the gate was concerning.

'Has your mum left for the station already?'

'Yes, she went just a few minutes ago. Dad, Neil, and Jimmy said they'd be back for breakfast at eight o'clock. The land girls will come with them I expect,' Jenny said as they headed for the kitchen.

Emily's stomach clenched. She hadn't expected to have to cook breakfast for eight people as soon as she arrived. She knew how to cook eggs, make fried bacon and fried bread so that's what she'd do.

She'd expected the huge central kitchen table to be laid, but it wasn't. Mrs Peterson must have left early and not had time to do it. She hoped that didn't mean her mother was worse. Her heart was thumping painfully, she felt sick, but had no choice. She'd agreed to help and had to get on with it somehow.

'Right, you two lay the table. I'm sure you know how to do that. I'll get started on the breakfast.'

Ten minutes after she'd arrived, the table was done, more or less, the huge kettle was hissing gently on the range and the teapot standing ready. The bread was cut and the girls said they knew how to toast it on the end of the forks in front of the open range.

'I don't want you to get in my way whilst I'm cooking, girls, so could you please get butter, milk and marmalade or jam from the pantry and put that on the table too. I also need enough big plates for everyone. I think we won't bother with side plates this morning.'

She'd found two huge frying pans and the bacon was beginning to sizzle in one of them and the fried bread would join it when it was done. There'd been a bowl of cracked eggs – there always were at the farm as they didn't have to be given to the Ministry of Agriculture to be handed out according to the rations.

The crisp bacon and fried bread went into a roasting tin and into the slow oven. Mrs Peterson hadn't asked her if she was familiar with a range so it was a good thing they had that at home as well as the modern gas cooker.

She moved to one side and two girls stood next to her holding a piece of bread on the end of their long toasting forks.

'Don't get any closer, you two, and I'll turn the bread over when it's done on the first side as I don't want you to burn your fingers,' Emily told them sternly.

'Those eggs look lovely, Emily,' Jenny said, 'and I'm ever so hungry.'

'So am I, I didn't have time for any breakfast before I came up here. It's a good thing I arrived early or nobody would have got any.'

'Mum said we could make do with cornflakes and toast and make it ourselves,' Jenny said.

Gwen handed her fork to her sister. 'It's too blooming hot standing here, I'm not doing it any more. I'm going to wait outside for Dad and the others to come.'

The little girl vanished. 'I can do both, Emily. Mum doesn't let her do it because she loses interest before it's ready. Mum says she's more trouble than she's worth in the kitchen department.'

Emily thought this a bit harsh as Gwen was still very little but didn't say so. 'Thank you, you're doing a wonderful job for me. I think I just heard a tractor pull up outside so I'm going to start dishing up.'

The toast was a bit singed but perfectly edible and lovely and hot. Mr Peterson was astonished that he'd come home to a proper breakfast and so were the land girls. Jimmy gave her a special smile which made her feel very proud.

'Sit down, love, and eat yours before it gets cold,' Mr Peterson said and patted the chair next to him.

'I thought you might want more toast.'

'We can make it ourselves if we do, love, you've done more than enough.'

* * *

Half an hour later the table was empty, as were the plates, and Emily was left with an enormous pile of washing up to do. Only then did she realise why Mrs Peterson had said they could have a cold breakfast – she'd used the plates they needed for lunch so she had to do the washing up after all.

Gwen and Jenny had disappeared but she could see them playing hopscotch in the yard so she wasn't worried about their safety. She was supposed to be here really to look after the girls, but it looked like she was going to be tied to the kitchen all day.

She cleared the table and stacked everything neatly in the scullery. They'd be back for lunch and it had to be served exactly at twelve thirty as they only had half an hour to eat. It would be much simpler if they had the salad midday but that was for tea.

This had already been plated up on smaller plates which were stacked on metal rings in the larder. All she had to do was put them on the table along with a pile of bread and butter.

There were two pies ready on the slate shelf and they just needed putting into the hot oven to heat through at midday. The potatoes and carrots had been scraped and the beans were topped and tailed. All she had to do was cook them nearer the time.

Pleased there wasn't as much to do as she'd feared on the cooking front, Emily carefully carried the big kettle into the scullery and filled the enamel washing-up bowl with hot water. Half an hour later, the washing up was done. She decided to leave the plates and other things to drain and go and see how the girls were getting on. Last time she'd looked they'd been watching the sky, obviously as enthralled by the spectacle in the sky as her brothers were.

Twice during the washing up the house had shaken as fighters screamed overhead. The boys would be on their backs on the front lawn at Harbour House watching the dogfights, but knowing men were trying to kill each other upset her. She couldn't see how it was heroic or praiseworthy.

Then the most horrific noise made Emily grip the edge of the sink. Something huge was screaming towards the house. Then the plane flew past, smoke trailing behind it and she heard the whoomph as it crashed somewhere close by.

Her first thought was to comfort the girls. She looked out of the window but they were no longer playing where they'd been a few minutes before. She flew to the back door and rushed out, calling them. After a frantic search, she was sure they'd left the farmyard. Her main task was to keep them safe and she'd failed to do that.

* * *

Richard's prayers were answered as the Luftwaffe left them alone for the remainder of the return journey to England. They steamed into Harwich with the crew in good spirits because the captain had given everybody five days' leave as only a skeleton crew would be needed on board during the two weeks of repairs. Some were going to head into London, others were going to see their families. Richard thought he might as well return to Colchester, sleeping in the marital bed would make Annie seem closer.

Nobody would be leaving on the first day back, everything had to be squared away, the ship left immaculate, and no leave would start until that had been completed. However, that evening letters from home were brought into the wardroom for the officers and handed out by the postal clerk.

He recognised Annie's writing on the front of his envelope and was pleased she'd written to him. He didn't want to read it in public so headed for the deck. It was warm, but then it should be as it was the beginning of August.

He propped himself against the bulkhead and carefully opened the letter. His yell of excitement sent a dozen perching seagulls screaming into the sky. They also attracted the attention of Chief Petty Officer Ryland.

'Anything wrong, sir?'

'No, Chief, nothing could be more right. My wife hasn't joined the WAAF because she's expecting a baby.'

'Good for you, sir, a nipper's always nice to go home to.'

He scarcely slept that last night aboard and was the first to leave the ship. He'd spoken to his captain and got permission to begin his leave at six o'clock. If his trusty motorbike had been stolen, he thought he could have flown home, he was so happy.

* * *

Richard covered the distance from Harwich dangerously fast. Only as he was approaching Colchester did it occur to him that nobody would be up yet. He sincerely hoped the back gate wasn't locked as he really didn't want to have to clamber over that again.

He throttled back through the town, there were people about but not many and he didn't want to wake up anyone enjoying their last half hour of sleep. He pushed his motorbike around to the back of the shop and tried the back gate, delighted it opened beneath his hand.

He pushed his bike through and just had time to kick it onto its stand when not one, but two huge hairy dogs hurtled towards him. He'd forgotten that Annie had told him they were now the owners of a dog.

'Sit.' He faced both dogs and pointed to the ground and to his surprise they skidded to a halt and sat at his feet, eyes shining and long plumy tails wagging furiously.

'Well, Boyd, I see you've got a friend.'

Richard stroked the dog he knew first and then turned his attention to the second one, presumably now belonging to him and Annie. 'Now, you're an amazingly handsome fellow, aren't you? We're a matching pair, don't you think?'

There was an old blanket next to a large bowl full of water and two evil-smelling bones close by. The dogs obviously slept outside which was why the gate could be left open. He tried the back door but as expected it was locked.

'Well, I might as well make myself useful and take both of you for a good long walk.' As soon as he mentioned that word, the dogs rushed to the gate. The leads were hooked on a nail outside the wash-house door and he grabbed them.

'Stand still, you two, we're not going anywhere until I've got you secure.'

He met no one on the path down to the river, not even other dog walkers. He released his canine companions and they raced into the long grass and he could just see their tails waving as they romped about.

There was no need for him to call them back, he could see them and he was sure if Boyd returned when he whistled then the other dog would come too. Before he could do that they both jumped into the river.

He ran to the bank and saw them swim to the other side and scramble out. He picked up a piece of wood and threw it into the water. This time the red dog jumped in first – Richard thought the animal must have retriever in his blood, he certainly had red setter to be that extraordinary colour.

For the next twenty minutes he tossed the wood, and the dogs took it in turns to fetch it and drop it at his feet. He was almost as wet as they were but didn't mind. A sailor was often wet, and this water was warm, not like the Atlantic.

'Right, boys, time to go home. I think the ladies will probably be up by now.'

He stood well back as they both shook from the tips of their noses to the end of their tails, sending showers of water in all directions. They trotted along beside him and he was proud to be in charge of such a handsome pair. He'd had labradors at home when he was a boy and was fond of dogs.

They had to pass the rear of the local bakery, a few doors down from Nancy's shop, and the smell of baking bread made his mouth water. He hadn't eaten since dinner last night.

The dogs stopped by the gate and barked. Immediately a man called out from the other side. 'Morning, Annie, have you come for your order? Come in and get it, the gate's open.'

'I'm Richard, Annie's husband, I've got two very wet dogs so won't come in.'

The gate opened and a man, middle aged, in a white apron smiled at him. 'Good to meet you, your Annie will be beside herself when she sees you. Them two been in the river, then?'

'They certainly have. I might as well have joined them as they got me almost as wet as they are. I know Boyd, what's his friend called?'

'That's Rusty, he belongs to your missus.' He nodded at Richard's hair and chuckled. 'Small wonder she wanted him – I ain't never seen a dog that colour nor a man neither.'

Richard smiled and nodded, not sure how to answer, and was relieved when a large, freshly baked loaf and a paper bag of buns were handed to him.

'Do I pay you now?' He was about to dip into his trouser pocket but the man shook his head.

'No, Annie or Nancy settle up on a Saturday. You got much leave?'

'Five days – we had a bit of bother on the last patrol and the ship's in for repair.'

'Good for you. I reckon you lot on them boats deserve a blooming medal. Dan's due back tomorrow. He don't have any more than a couple of nights usually.'

'That's good to hear, we get on well. Thank you, I'll get this back to the kitchen and hopefully the back door's open now.'

'Here, don't forget the treats for the dogs. I always keep a bit of something back for them.'

Richard wasn't going to feed them in the street; they could wait until they were in the yard and then when they were sitting politely, he'd give it to them. He put the large lump of baked dough in his pocket.

He could hear someone retching in the WC and guessed that Nancy was up. Annie had told him Nancy was suffering from morning sickness. He didn't call out but headed for the kitchen.

He shut the door behind him in case the dogs wanted to come in and make everything wet and muddy. Then he put the bread and buns on the kitchen table and after removing his shoes he held them in one hand and headed for the stairs.

The house was quiet, Annie must still be asleep. The shop didn't open until nine and it was only just after seven so she wouldn't have to get up for another hour. He pushed open their bedroom door and, sure enough, his beloved girl was beneath the sheet and breathing quietly.

Not wanting to wake her, he stripped off to his underpants – fortunately they weren't damp like the rest of his uniform – and slid into bed beside her.

'Goodness me, Sub-lieutenant Stoneleigh, you've taken your time getting here.'

Annie rolled into his arms. She was naked and his heart pounded.

'You're overdressed, husband, don't you think?'

Richard hadn't expected to be able to make love to her, had thought that her being in the early weeks of pregnancy might make this inadvisable. Things inevitably moved on too far and too fast to consider that.

24

Emily could think of only one place the girls might have gone and that was to see where the plane had crashed. She ran to the gate and saw a spiral of smoke coming from what she and her brothers called the blackberry field – the one where the big bull lived when he wasn't busy in the barn with the cows.

She'd heard him bellowing just a few moments ago and was glad the magnificent beast hadn't been in the field when the plane crashed. She ran towards the smoke and saw the two girls standing on the gate, gazing down.

They were staring at the burning plane, wide-eyed and open-mouthed, not realising they were watching the poor pilot being burned to death. It was a German plane – Emily could see the swastika on the side. But that didn't make any difference. This young man had been killed by another young man and they were strangers to each other.

She hated war, if women were in charge there wouldn't be any. They'd sit around a table with a cup of tea and sort things out.

'Jenny, Gwen, get down off that gate immediately. How dare you leave the farmyard when you know that's absolutely forbidden?' Emily didn't mention why they were there as they were far too young to understand what they were actually looking at with such interest. She wasn't going to be the one to explain it to them.

The girls tumbled off the gate and ran to her side. They took one look at her face and knew they were in big trouble. Emily thought she'd scare them a bit more.

'Your mother would give you both a sound spanking for disobeying. As I'm in charge I could do the same.'

'We're sorry, Emily, we just wanted to see a plane close up,' Jenny said.

'I haven't decided on your punishment. I'm very, very angry with both of you.'

They slunk along behind her as she strode ahead, trying to look like an angry adult and not a terrified almost-twelve-year-old.

Jimmy was just leaping from a tractor as they arrived in the yard. 'Dad sent me to see if you were all right. We thought that bloody plane was coming down on the house. Where the hell have you been?'

The girls hid behind Emily. She didn't like this new version of Jimmy but thought he was trying to be an angry adult too, not a youth of fourteen.

'I'm dealing with it, thank you, Jimmy. Please tell Mr Peterson that everything's absolutely fine and lunch will be served in forty-five minutes.'

'Those two know better than to leave the yard. You need a damn good hiding, both of you.'

Emily turned and pushed the girls towards the back door.

'Off you go, straight to your room and stay there until I give you permission to come down.'

The terrified girls didn't need telling twice and were inside and banging the back door before their big brother could react.

'It's none of your business, Emily. You're not family. I'm their big brother.'

'I'm well aware of that, Jimmy, but your mother left me in charge of the girls so it's up to me how they're punished. I don't believe in physical punishment so they'll just stay in their bedroom. I think that's sufficient.'

She was about to turn her back on him and was surprised that her legs still moved, that he hadn't seen that she was shaking. Then she blurted out what she was really feeling.

'The pilot was still alive and your sisters were watching him die. They didn't realise what they were seeing. Please don't make this worse for any of us.'

She swallowed, tried to stop the tears, a grown-up wouldn't cry but everything was just so horrible.

'Emily, don't cry. I'm sorry you had to see that. I'm sorry I shouted at you. You did the right thing. I'll stop here with you, you're not in any fit state to serve lunch for eight of us.'

She'd now found her handkerchief and wiped her eyes and blew her nose, feeling very childish. 'I'll never forget what I saw. It's just not right, Jimmy, that young men are dying so horribly. I don't care if he is a German – nobody deserves that.'

'Try not to think about it. Let's go inside and make you a nice cup of tea. As it's an emergency I could put a bit of brandy in it.'

The very thought of drinking alcohol at her age was enough to stop the tears. 'You'll do no such thing. I hope that was a joke. I was going to say I don't need your help but actually I'd be really grateful. I do feel a bit shaky and sick.'

'I'll tell Dad that everything's fine and come straight back. Get the kettle on, Emily, love, I'm parched.'

* * *

Having to threaten the little girls with physical punishment was also upsetting. If her parents knew just how much responsibility she'd had to assume today they'd never let her come here again. Maybe they were right. She was trying to do things that just weren't right for someone her age. She might be very mature, but she wasn't old enough to deal with this sort of situation.

Then she giggled, started to laugh and ended up gulping back her sobs. Jimmy had spoken to her as if she was his wife and he her husband coming back from work. They were both playing at being grown-ups and it had been fun initially. After what had happened today, she was going to be a sister to her brothers, join in with their games, not spend all her time doing responsible things and pretending to be an adult.

Jimmy didn't come back and she was glad of that. The less she saw of him the better as he made her feel like someone much more grown-up than she actually was. She didn't want to be his girlfriend, to be called love, she wanted to be a girl with nothing on her mind but playing, studying and enjoying herself with her friends and siblings.

In the end, she had to call the girls down from their bedroom to help her. She didn't mention what they'd done and they didn't mention what she'd said which suited them all.

The table was laid, there were jugs of water, mugs of tea and a plate of thickly sliced bread. She'd whipped the lovely yellow cream from their own dairy cows and it was now really thick.

The vegetables were cooked, drained and ready to be plated.

The pies had been cut into slices but were still in their tins, the gravy was bubbling in a saucepan and the rhubarb crumble was almost ready in the oven for dessert.

'Emily, do we have to go back upstairs before our dad and brother come?' Jenny asked nervously.

'No, I don't think Jimmy'll have said anything to your dad about what you did. I think you gave us all a scare, but I've put it aside and don't want to talk about it again. I certainly don't think your mother needs to know.'

'Does that mean we can play after we've had lunch?'

'It certainly does, and not only that, I'll play with you. I've done more than enough today and we'll just stack everything in the scullery. I'm afraid I can't stay after six o'clock as I said I would, but Jimmy can look after you. He's certainly the right age to do it.'

They didn't argue and Jenny helped her sister onto the chair with two cushions before scrambling up beside her. She didn't use cushions but knelt on the seat and then sat back on her heels. Emily thought it looked rather uncomfortable but Jenny was obviously happy sitting like that.

When she heard the first tractor crunch into the yard she started dishing up. It looked perfect. She thought she wouldn't be able to eat but her stomach rumbled and she was looking forward to the rabbit and chicken pie.

Half an hour later, the adults were ready to return to work. She followed them into the yard. 'Excuse me, Mr Peterson, I'm afraid I have to leave at six o'clock. I'm sure Jimmy can look after the girls until Mrs Peterson returns.' She swallowed the lump in her throat. 'I'm really upset by what I saw and just want to go home.'

He nodded. 'I need him on the farm, but I'll get one of the

girls to keep an eye on them. You run along now, love, you're a good girl to help us out.'

Emily bit her lip and nodded. 'Thank you, that's exactly what I want to do. I'm sorry to let you down.'

'Don't you fret, love, what you saw was horrible. I'll send someone down with a few things tomorrow to say thank you.' He smiled and patted her shoulder. 'Your mum and dad must be that proud of you. I hope my two turn out to be like you.'

She felt mean abandoning the girls after she'd said she'd play with them. She'd run all the way home, and wasn't sure she'd ever go there again knowing what was in the field behind the house.

If she went in to collect her gas mask she'd have to see the children and she couldn't face that.

Emily hurried away from the farm where she'd spent many happy hours over the past year, sad that she might not visit again. She didn't understand any of it and she didn't understand why she suddenly felt like this.

Everything was such a muddle. She thought maybe she was a pacifist, no longer believed in a God that allowed this kind of dreadful thing to carry on in his name and didn't want to be thought of as a grown-up, given responsibilities she wasn't ready for.

She touched her hair. It had grown a couple of inches since she'd had it cut and she wouldn't have it short again until she was a real grown-up – maybe when she was fifteen or sixteen.

If she played with her dolls again, raked around the village with the other children, did jigsaw puzzles and used her skipping rope then maybe she'd be able to forget what she'd seen today.

* * *

All Change at Harbour House

Annie left her husband – how she loved saying that word – asleep an hour later and dressed quickly and left him to it. He'd told her after they'd made love that he and the other men had worked four hours on, four hours off continuously and they were all seriously sleep deprived. He'd laughed this off, saying that the RAF weren't getting any sleep at all, so he was better off than them.

When he woke up there'd be plenty of time to talk about the future, discuss their plans, but all that mattered at the moment was that he was here, safe and well, and would be at her side for the next five days.

After doing her stint in the shop, she checked upstairs to see if he was awake but he was still dead to the world. She returned to the kitchen just as Molly came in.

Now she was no longer working at Harbour House, she'd been coming every other day and Annie was beginning to feel in the way.

'I'll make us a brew, shall I, Annie?' Molly said cheerily and Annie smiled.

'Ta, Molly, but no tea for me, just hot water. Being pregnant has made me go right off it.'

Molly almost dropped the kettle. 'My Nancy didn't say you were expecting too. Congratulations. I expect she said I'd knit you some matinee jackets, and I'd be happy to. I've got more time on my hands than I need, I'm not used to being idle.'

'Yes, she did. I hope you don't mind; it will be really kind of you. Do you regret giving up your housekeeping job?'

'No, it was the right thing to do. I've brought the boys with me today and they've gone for a walk round and then we're going to the pictures later.'

'How's Lily getting on in your job?' Annie asked.

'She's fitted in a treat. Mrs Roby told me how pleased she is with my replacement at the last WI meeting. My boys are minding their Ps and Qs now and my Bert and I are moving to a nice house halfway up the High Street. It's a five-year lease with an option to buy at any time. Who'd have thought it? We're going up in the world, that's for sure.'

'That's lovely news, Molly, I'm so happy for you. Richard and I are going to look for a house of our own whilst he's here. It's going to be a bit crowded with two families and two large dogs. I'll carry on working here but won't be under Nancy's and Dan's feet all the time.'

'Are you sure, Annie love? If you think it's a bit of a squash here, you should have tried living in a two-up two-down in Alma Street the way I have these past twenty years.'

Annie ignored the first part of this suggestion. 'Another thing, Molly, you'll be able to help Nancy in the shop in the mornings, at least once your boys are back at school.'

Molly half-smiled but didn't comment. She changed the subject completely.

'I've come to tell my Nancy the news from Harbour House. I'll tell you first, I'll have plenty of time to tell her later. The old Mrs Roby went home, not sure where that is, and was gone for three days and came back with old Mr Roby in tow. From what Lily said he's a nice old gentleman but a bit confused sometimes, if you know what I mean.'

'I know exactly. If he's not well then I'm surprised she brought him back. Why wouldn't they rather be in their own home and get somebody in to help out? I'm sure they come from somewhere grand, the whole family's ever so posh.'

She heard movement upstairs and was on her fleet in a flash. 'That's Richard moving about. I don't want to miss a moment of him being here. I'll take him that mug of tea, ta, and leave you to go in and help Nancy.'

* * *

Annie sat with Richard in the sitting room whilst he drank his tea and she kept her distance as even the smell of tea made her heave. He agreed with her that finding their first home together was a priority during his leave.

'I'm not entirely comfortable with you using your precious nest egg, my darling, but I'll make it up to you. I didn't have time to tell you earlier that I'm now an acting lieutenant and will be getting more money than before.'

'It's not my money any more, everything I have is yours as far as I'm concerned. We need somewhere this side of town so I can take Rusty to Abbey Fields or down to the river. I also need to be able to walk here easily, for it not to be too far to push a pram with the baby when it comes.'

'Then if you're ready, if you're feeling up to it, shall we walk down to the solicitors at the other end of Head Street and see if they can recommend an estate agent? I think that's a good place to start our search.'

Annie couldn't believe their luck when the ancient clerk who sat behind the front desk, like something out of a Dickens's novel, told them they'd got two suitable properties both available and both well furnished.

'I take it, sir, that you and Mrs Stoneleigh would like to see them right away?' He didn't wait for their answer but sent a boy to fetch the keys. 'The first is a bigger property, three large bedrooms and a boxroom, indoor plumbing and WC but has no front garden and only a yard at the back.'

He handed over the keys to that one which was one street back from where they were living now.

'The second property might be better. It has three bedrooms, a bathroom upstairs, a modern kitchen and a pretty front garden and a decent-sized back. The previous owners are going to live in Canada. They are leaving at the weekend and are desperate to find somebody to take over their house for the next few years. They've got chickens and two pets.' He paused and Annie thought that whatever they were going to have to look after wasn't a cat or a dog.

'Go on, Mr Moffatt, tell us the worst,' Richard said after winking at her.

'Parrots – I'm afraid they live mostly in the house. I also understand that they have the ability to speak and not much of it polite.'

'Good heavens! I'm perfectly happy to have parrots as companions especially if they talk. However, they need to get on with our dog and be safe with children.'

'I don't know about either of those things, Mrs Stoneleigh, you'll have to ask the owners of the property.'

* * *

They returned home to collect Rusty as they needed to be sure that he and the parrots would get on. They did and the dog flopped down on the floor beneath their perch and they dropped nuts on him and told him he was a scurvy sailor and that it was time for a tot of rum.

'Look at that,' Mrs Cunningham said, 'Polly and Percy have taken to your big dog just like that. I do hope you're going to agree to move in here. I'd take my birds with me but Archie won't hear of it.'

Mr Cunningham was out somewhere sorting out last-minute details of their emigration to Canada.

'You look around the place on your own, you don't want me breathing down your neck. My Archie might be a bit of a curmudgeon but he's a generous man and he has done this place up lovely for me. I'll be sorry to leave it.'

The house was everything Annie had ever dreamed of. 'Imagine me having an actual bathroom, Richard. The bedrooms are more than big enough even if we have more children later.'

'It's immaculate, and the furniture's good quality. We need our own bedlinen, towels and so on but apart from that it's fully equipped.'

The main bedroom was at the rear of the property and Richard walked to the window. Annie joined him and he put his arm around her waist, holding her close.

'A dozen chickens in that coop at least, a decent vegetable plot, and more than enough room for the dog and a baby to play together,' she said happily.

'I noticed there were nappies on the washing line next door so there must be a young family there. Do we need to look at the other place?'

She shook her head. 'No, my darling Richard, we've found our perfect home. I never imagined six months ago that my life would be so wonderful.'

He gazed down at her, his eyes blazing with love. 'I love you so much, my darling Annie, and I'm the luckiest man alive.'

Fighters screamed overhead and she stepped into his arms, not caring they might be seen. 'It doesn't seem right somehow to be so happy with all this going on.'

'I know, darling, but we have to be happy when we can. We've got a house, a baby on the way and a large dog. Everything any couple could wish for. Whatever happens in the future is the future, let's enjoy the present.'

* * *

MORE FROM FENELLA J. MILLER

The latest instalment in another emotional wartime saga series from Fenella J. Miller, *Army Girls: Operation Winter Wedding* is available to order now here:

https://mybook.to/ArmyGirlsWinterWedding

BIBLIOGRAPHY

A to Z Atlas Guide to London, 1939 reproduction
Wartime Britain by Juliet Gardiner
One Child's War by Victoria Massey
Sea-change by Paul Thompson
How We Lived Then by Norman Longmate
The Home Front by Marion Yass
The Battle of the East Coast by J. P. Foynes
The Story of Wivenhoe by Nicholas Butler
River Colne Shipbuilders by John Collins and James Dodds
The Wartime Scrapbook by Robert Opie
Oxford Dictionary of Slang by John Ayto
The Royal Navy Officer's Pocket Book 1944
Citizen Sailors by Glyn Prysor
Lost Voices of the Royal Navy by Max Arthur

ABOUT THE AUTHOR

Fenella J. Miller is the bestselling writer of over eighteen historical sagas. She also has a passion for Regency romantic adventures and has published over fifty to great acclaim. Her father was a Yorkshireman and her mother the daughter of a Rajah. She lives in a small village in Essex with her British Shorthair cat.

Sign up to Fenella J. Miller's mailing list for news, competitions and updates on future books.

Visit Fenella's website: www.fenellajmiller.co.uk

Follow Fenella on social media here:

facebook.com/fenella.miller
x.com/fenellawriter

ALSO BY FENELLA J. MILLER

Goodwill House Series

The War Girls of Goodwill House

New Recruits at Goodwill House

Duty Calls at Goodwill House

The Land Girls of Goodwill House

A Wartime Reunion at Goodwill House

Wedding Bells at Goodwill House

A Christmas Baby at Goodwill House

The Army Girls Series

Army Girls Reporting For Duty

Army Girls: Heartbreak and Hope

Army Girls: Behind the Guns

Army Girls: Operation Winter Wedding

The Pilot's Girl Series

The Pilot's Girl

A Wedding for the Pilot's Girl

A Dilemma for the Pilot's Girl

A Second Chance for the Pilot's Girl

The Nightingale Family Series

A Pocketful of Pennies

A Capful of Courage

A Basket Full of Babies

A Home Full of Hope

At Pemberley Series

Return to Pemberley

Trouble at Pemberley

Scandal at Pemberley

Danger at Pemberley

Harbour House Series

Wartime Arrivals at Harbour House

Stormy Waters at Harbour House

All Change at Harbour House

The Duke's Alliance Series

A Suitable Bride

A Dangerous Husband

An Unconventional Bride

An Accommodating Husband

A Rebellious Bride

The Duke's Bride

Standalone Novels

The Land Girl's Secret

The Pilot's Story

Sixpence Stories

Introducing Sixpence Stories!

Discover page-turning historical novels from your favourite authors, meet new friends and be transported back in time.

Join our book club
Facebook group

https://bit.ly/SixpenceGroup

Sign up to our newsletter

https://bit.ly/SixpenceNews

Boldwood

Boldwood Books is an award-winning fiction publishing company seeking out the best stories from around the world.

Find out more at www.boldwoodbooks.com

Join our reader community for brilliant books, competitions and offers!

Follow us
@BoldwoodBooks
@TheBoldBookClub

Sign up to our weekly deals newsletter

https://bit.ly/BoldwoodBNewsletter

Printed in Dunstable, United Kingdom